"You've hit the nub of it. I *must* marry a fortune."

Penelope rose and wandered away. "How great an heiress do you require?"

"Lady Julia was very rich. As rich as you, I would imagine."

"Indeed?"

"But there are very few heiresses with that deep of pockets." He smiled wryly. "I believe I can live with a lady who has a lesser legacy."

"I see." Penelope sounded as if she were choking. "I am glad to hear it, since there are not any other heiresses as well heeled as I."

"Indeed. And that is why you must help me, Penn." Matthew strode up to her and clasped up her hands. "Help me to win one of those ladies. Do not let Aunt Clare destroy my chances."

"Wh-why would she wish to do that?" Penelope gazed up at him with wide, curious eyes.

A thrill passed through Matthew. Penn's eyes had grown greener over the years. And her hair had darkened to burnished brown. Her petite frame was fuller and rounder. He tightened his clasp upon her hand. "She wants me to marry for true love."

"I see." Penelope licked her lips. "Is there something wrong with that?"

"I must marry an heiress. There is no doubt about that. Else the family will be in debtor's prison." Matthew couldn't seem to take his gaze from her lips. Sweetly curved, he realized. And of the freshest rose. Faith, how would it be to kiss those lips?

"C-couldn't you marry for true love *and* money?" Penelope whispered.

BOOK YOUR PLACE ON OUR WEBSITE AND MAKE THE READING CONNECTION!

We've created a customized website just for our very special readers, where you can get the inside scoop on everything that's going on with Zebra, Pinnacle and Kensington books.

When you come online, you'll have the exciting opportunity to:

- View covers of upcoming books

- Read sample chapters

- Learn about our future publishing schedule (listed by publication month *and author*)

- Find out when your favorite authors will be visiting a city near you

- Search for and order backlist books from our online catalog

- Check out author bios and background information

- Send e-mail to your favorite authors

- Meet the Kensington staff online

- Join us in weekly chats with authors, readers and other guests

- Get writing guidelines

- AND MUCH MORE!

Visit our website at
http://www.zebrabooks.com

THE MISSING BRIDES

Cindy Holbrook

ZEBRA BOOKS
Kensington Publishing Corp.
http://www.zebrabooks.com

ZEBRA BOOKS are published by

Kensington Publishing Corp.
850 Third Avenue
New York, NY 10022

All Kensington titles, imprints and distributed lines are available at special quantity discounts for bulk purchases for sales promotion, premiums, fund-raising, educational or institutional use.

Special book excerpts or customized printings can also be created to fit specific needs. For details, write or phone the office of the Kensington Special Sales Manager: Kensington Publishing Corp., 850 Third Avenue, New York, NY 10022. Attn. Special Sales Department. Phone: 1-800-221-2647.

Zebra and the Z logo Reg. U.S. Pat. & TM Off.

First Printing: August 2001
10 9 8 7 6 5 4 3 2 1

Printed in the United States of America

Prologue

Dear Aunt Clare,

I regret that I will not be able to attend you at present. I am leaving town this day. I thank you for your kind offer to help me find my true love and perfect mate.

However, we have held this discussion before. I do not require your assistance in procuring a wife. I hope I do not appear surly, but I will obtain my own mate without your services. Indeed, I am taking steps in that direction even as I write this letter.

Since my requirements in a wife are far different from yours, I ask that you refrain from any interference.

Your servant,
Matthew Severs

PS: I hold you in the deepest affection, Aunt Clare, but I warn you, I will not tolerate any of your ruses or schemes employed in regard to me. I know it will be difficult for you, but you must abstain.

One

The ornamental clock upon the mantel marked the passing minutes relentlessly. The five occupants of the room sat silent, morosely so. The sound of rain without might have been soothing, except for the excessive crash of lightning and the roll of thunder that accompanied it.

"I hate to say this, brother." Andrew Severs shook his head, pale gray eyes focused wryly on the person standing before him. With his flaxen hair and fair complexion, Andrew Severs looked a regretful angel heralding sad tidings. "But it is as plain as a pikestaff. Your brides are missing."

"Confound it!" Matthew Severs, the Earl of Raleigh, spun from his position at the fireplace. He cast the clock one last condemning glare. With his dark blue eyes blazing beneath black slashing brows, he, however, did not look like an angel. Rather, he looked to belong in the opposite camp. "She did it. I know she did it. I vow I shall kill her."

"Now dear, you mustn't jump to conclusions." Lady Florence, as fair in coloring as that of her youngest son, placidly drew a thread through a tambour frame. She worked upon yet another chair covering. "They are but seven hours late."

"Perhaps they are detained by the weather." Monica, having just reached the sincere age of fifteen, nodded.

Her guinea-gold curls bobbed. "It is quite monstrous out."

"Matthew could be so lucky." Andrew laughed. He looked to Matthew. "What do you think the old girl did with them?"

"Surely it couldn't be Aunt Clare's fault." Christine, exactly one year younger than her sister and dark as her eldest brother, frowned with due consideration. "You never told her your *plan.*"

"That is true, Matthew." Lady Florence picked through her threads and pulled up a deep amber strand. "You only informed her that you would be out of town. How could she know you were hosting a house party here with the express purpose of finding a bride?"

"The entire *ton* should know by now, I make no doubt." Matthew grimaced. "You cannot expect the ladies not to have gossiped. I did not invite them here without informing their fathers of my intent. I refuse to fly under a false flag, even if it did mean tipping Aunt Clare off."

Monica shook her head. "I still think you must be wrong, Matthew. We haven't seen or heard from anyone. If Aunt Clare has abducted your ladies, wouldn't we receive word from their parents?"

"Indeed." Lady Florence nodded. "It would be bad *ton* for them not to inform us that they would not be attending. We have worked an entire week to ready ourselves for them. I have spent the last groat for wax candles. As for the menu, I fear we will have to sell the Berline carriage and suffice with only the one small barouche remaining, if we are to offer them anything reasonable at table. . . ."

Christine giggled. "I don't think Aunt Clare had anything to do with it. I think the ladies are merely snubbing Matthew."

Matthew smiled. "Imp."

She pulled a face. "You can be a rum customer at times, you know?"

"Christine, do not use such disgraceful language!" Lady Florence clucked.

"Ha! That ain't Matthew's problem." Andrew sighed. "It's the opposite. He's too infernally polite. It is honor and propriety with him at all times. He'd have himself a bride already if he hadn't have been so kind to Aunt Clare. And what kind of gratitude does he receive back? Aunt Clare steals away his ladies."

"Indeed." Matthew clenched his teeth. "Where in blazes would she have taken them?"

Andrew sprang up. "Well. Let us not tarry. Let us go and hunt for them."

"In this torrent?" Lady Florence blinked. "I do not think that would be wise."

"No, it would not be." Matthew crossed over to the cabinet and picked up the brandy decanter. "She would only have us chasing all over Christendom to find them. I know her games now. We need only wait. She will show us her hand sooner or later."

"I think you are being beastly about Aunt Clare," Monica said. "I have never met her, but she sounds like a dear old lady."

Matthew snorted and poured himself a full bumper. "That 'dear old lady' can be diabolical. Positively diabolical."

"Hello!" Andrew, his eyes sparkling, rubbed his hands together. "Who wants to lay bets upon where Aunt Clare has stashed Matthew's brides?"

"I do!" Monica jumped up.

"Me, too!" Christine squealed.

"You may count me, too." Lady Florence promptly laid aside her needlework.

"B'gads!" Matthew rolled his eyes and downed his brandy. "We are all to pieces. Just with what do you intend to bet?"

His beloved family fell silent as he glared at them.

"I know!" Monica cried. "We shall write each other vouchers."

"That will do." Lady Florence nodded. "I will accept them."

Matthew rolled his eyes toward the heavens. "You would be the only one in the entire *ton* then to accept a voucher from a Severs."

"Of course, dear. I have complete faith in all of you."

"We can pay each other when Matthew has married one of his heiresses." Andrew nodded. "Of course, he has to discover *where* Aunt Clare secreted them first! Now. Let me hear your bets! Where do you think Matthew's brides are?"

Gracious, it was a fine mess. Penelope's head swam as she stood in the center of the great hall of Lancer Manor. She now possessed an entire houseful of lords and ladies, as well as the accompanying requirement of mountains of trunks and band boxes. Footmen of four different liveries swarmed about her like so many drenched and droning bees. Her own servants blended in, lifting and dropping the baggage in confusion.

"I tell you, Penelope, I want them sent packing! Do you hear me?" Jacob Lancer roared his decree from the safe distance of the other end of the hall. He glared at her and shook his finger.

"Yes, Papa." Penelope bit her lip. He was acting as if it were her fault. Indeed, as if she would be so totty-headed as to invite a bevy of complete strangers into their house. She looked to a footman just then entering the hall. In truth, he had very little room in which to maneuver in from out of the rain. And even less space for the baggage he carried. "Are you the last one then?"

"Yes, mum." A large report of thunder crashed,

shaking the rafters of the great hall. The footman jumped and dropped his trunk. "Gore!"

"Confound it, it looks like a posting house in here!" Jacob Lancer rapped his cane upon the floor from a safe distance away. "I'll not be a damn posting house for Severs. By God, I shall not!"

"Yes, Papa." Penelope signaled to her butler, Finch, to close the door against the rain. "Remember your gout. It is not good to become so excited."

"I am not excited!" Jacob's face turned purple. "I'm bloody . . ."

A crash of lightning drowned him out. In his irascible state, it could only be a good thing.

"Yes, Father. Why not go and rest beside the fire for now? But no port, mind you." Penelope lowered her voice as her butler came close. "Finch, have our footmen take these footmen and find them quarters. Once they have changed into dry clothing, inform them to go to the kitchen for a tankard of ale." She shrugged helplessly. "By that time I might ascertain where I have put their masters and mistresses. I placed them in their rooms in such a pell-mell fashion that I'm not certain just who is who and who is where."

"Yes, Miss Penelope." Finch nodded and then circulated through the servants, clearly giving them orders.

"I'll not have it, Penelope. Toss the earl's party out on their ear. It is their own fault if they are lost." Jacob rapped his cane all the harder upon the stone floor. "Lost. Ha! Severs probably did this just to embarrass me. That or the brass-faced jackanapes hopes to cheat me as his father did before him!"

"I do not think those are his intentions, Papa." Penelope flushed. She was grateful to see the servants departing. When father was in a tirade, the less public, the better. "He—we've not heard from him in five years. I do not know how it happened, but it appears all these people have been given faulty directions.

Someone is clearly playing a hoax on Matthew . . . I mean, Lord Severs."

"Hogwash! It is Severs himself behind this. The villain!" Jacob hit his cane down with vehemence. Directly upon his gout-ridden toe. "Ooouch!"

"Finch, you did send Joseph with a message to Lord Severs, informing him that we have accidentally acquired his house party?" Penelope took the advantage to ask as her father hopped about and cursed.

"I did, Miss Penelope. Quite over an hour ago." Finch frowned. "I do fear for his success. You know the state of these roads when inclement weather sets upon us."

"I do." Penelope blanched. "Pray, Finch. And then pray again. I do not know how we will survive elsewise."

"Yes, Miss Penelope. I quite agree." Finch paled to an equal degree.

"The devil take it." Jacob wheezed one last curse. He glared at Penelope. "I'll not have you disobedient, daughter. I want them out of my house this instant."

"Very well, Papa. I will go and do that immediately." Penelope cast her butler a speaking glance. She knew she was about to commit an unconscionable act, but sending strangers back out into the torrent and onto roads infamous for their danger in such a storm would be more so. "Why not let Finch assist you to the fireside in your own room? It will be such a brouhaha down here while I . . . er, send them packing."

Finch's eyes widened in alarm.

Penelope drew in her breath. "I think perhaps one glass of port might not be that harmful for you, if you wish it. Indeed, it might prove a soothing draught, under these conditions."

"One measly glass won't do it!" Jacob looked cagey.

"Finch might permit you two if you are still unsettled."

"Very well. Fetch me a bottle, Finch, and come with

me." Jacob spun and stumped off without his butler's assistance.

"Forgive me, Finch." Penelope bit her lip.

"No, Miss Penelope." Finch actually smiled. He bowed. "You are a trump, if I may take leave to say so myself. Don't you worry over the master. He hasn't been castaway for nigh onto a sennight. It always mellows his disposition, it does."

Fortunately, Finch did not wait for her response, but sprinted away before Penelope could succumb to her guilt and call him back. Worse, Finch was right. Doctor Hobson may declare abstinence of port good for Jacob's health, but it did little good for his spirits. As for now, it would give her the time needed to settle the pressing question of what was to be done with her entourage of noble guests.

Penelope sighed, enjoying the moment as the great hall fell silent. Except for the roar of the rain, that was. She ran her hands upon the skirts of her green baize apron and then flushed as she pulled her hand away with a glutinous mass of lye soap. She had scheduled a day to make soap and had worn her oldest dress now grayed to a steely blue. Over it was the spotted, frayed apron. In point of fact, the apron was so old and worn as to be deemed by the maids as a spare to be used only in dire circumstances. She looked frightful. Here she stood, streaks of yellow lye running to her hem, her brown hair pulled back into a serviceable ponytail and, worse yet, her sleeves rolled up almost to her elbows. The voluminous apron only showed her lack of stature, making her feel a little squab of a female. Why, oh why, did it have to be today of all days? She'd felt a perfect drudge in front of those fashionable and elegant ladies with their equally fashionable and elegant parents.

Penelope shook her head. Gracious, what was she thinking? As if she could have awakened and said to herself, *Oh, yes. My house will be overrun by total strangers.*

Lords and ladies will travel fifteen miles out of their way to visit me rather than Matthew Severs. I must be sure to don my best finery in order that I will not feel so very inconsequential.

No, there was no way for her to have known that such a strange occurrence would transpire. Indeed, it surely must be the strangest thing to have ever happened to her.

A knock sounded at the door, a small tattoo beneath the larger rumble of rain.

"Not another one." Penelope stiffened her spine. If she must face one more beautiful girl she was sure she would scream. That had been the most obvious trait of all of her uninvited house guests. The girls were all lovely.

Prepared to bite back her scream, Penelope walked to the door and opened it.

It wasn't she who screamed. The figure upon her doorstep was not one to cause her to do so, to be sure. She was the sweetest-looking older lady, with a halo of the loveliest silver hair.

No, indeed it wasn't Penelope who screamed. Or the dear little lady, either. The clamor that arose was distinctly feline in nature.

"Gracious!" Penelope danced back as a scourge of howling and spitting cats, drenched and completely displeased about it, darted into the great hall.

"Kitties, kitties! No!" The little lady sighed and looked at Penelope with great, apologetic blue eyes. "Dear me, I am so sorry. They have quite lost their manners, I fear. To enter your house without permission is most impolite of them. They are generally not so discourteous, you know? But they do hate the rain."

"I understand." Penelope wasn't quite attentive. Her gaze was rather mesmerized by a battle-scarred marmalade cat who resided within the lady's arms. Its look was rather cantankerous. Indeed, it reminded her of her father in some fashion.

"Brr. Meow!"

"Yes, Sir Percy, I am going to ask." The little lady nodded. "Excuse me, but could we please enter?"

Penelope jumped back and waved her hand. "Forgive me. Please, do enter."

"Thank you." The little lady stepped forward. She gazed about, her smile benign. The clutter and disorder in the hall did not seem to surprise or affect her. "Why, what a lovely home you have, my dear."

"Thank you." Penelope attempted to ignore the cats as they climbed over trunk and box. "Have you . . . are you lost?"

"Oh, no, dearest, I do not think so." She set the large marmalade cat down. "This is the Lancer estate, is it not?"

"Why yes, it is," Penelope said. "Then you meant to come here?"

"Most definitely. I am so pleased that my directions were correct."

Penelope laughed. "Then you are the first person today who actually meant to come here."

The little lady beamed. "Famous. Then the others have arrived safely? Only imagine if I had sent them to the wrong estate."

Penelope's mouth fell open as the most impossible suspicion entered her mind. "It was you. . . ."

"I do so hope you are Penelope. You are, are you not?"

"Yes, I am. But . . ." Penelope halted. Now she had fresh questions. It took her a moment to decide which to ask first. "Very well. How do you know who I am? And who are you?"

"I am Clare Wrexton. And this is Sir Percy. He has been just recently knighted. Not by the Queen, of course, but by my newly acquired nephew, Garth Stanwood. Sir Percy will still answer to Percy, being of a democratic bent, you see. And I would prefer you call me Aunt Clare. Everyone does, you know."

"Do they?" Penelope frowned in an attempt to regain control of the conversation. "Did you . . . were you the one who . . ."

Aunt Clare nodded—rather eagerly, in fact. "Yes, I am the one who sent Matthew's brides here."

"Brides!" Penelope hoped her complexion had not paled, even if her insides had.

"I said that incorrectly. They are not exactly brides. It has not gone that far yet, thank heaven. It is always such a coil when it does. However, he is determined that one of them will be his bride by the end of these next two weeks."

"Indeed." Penelope swallowed hard.

"Oh, yes." Aunt Clare dug into her reticule. "Permit me to take a tally."

"What?"

"Here it is." Aunt Clare drew out a crumpled, wadded paper and smoothed it. "I learned this from my niece. Always make a list, my dear. Now, there should be four of them." The little lady lifted the list close to her nose. "Lady Estelle Hastings, Miss Cecily Morris, Lady Sherrice Norton and Lady Violet Stapleton."

"Yes." Penelope found herself clenching her teeth. It was a stellar list. "They have all arrived."

"How delightful. It is so nice when one's plans transpire as one hopes." She sighed. "Penelope, dearest, we have our work cut out if we are to save dear Matthew from making the dreadful mistake of marrying the wrong woman."

"Ah . . . we? Wh-why we?" Penelope disliked the wail to her voice. "Why me?"

"Because you are his friend," Aunt Clare said calmly. Then the worse possible *knowing* look entered that lady's vague blue eyes. "And you love him."

"No!" Penelope said quickly, very quickly. "I do not!"

"Oh." Aunt Clare blinked and frowned. "Then I must have been mistaken."

"How . . . who told you?" Penelope flushed to her very toes. That a total stranger could have known her secret—her past secret, that is—was mortifying. She actually shivered from the chilling thought.

"Well, dear," now it was Aunt Clare's turn to blush, "I fear I jumped to a conclusion. Matthew had told me you were friends when you were young and I could not imagine any young girl not falling in love with him."

"Oh, yes," Penelope breathed. Then she started and straightened. She owed this peculiar stranger nothing. Still, she could not bring herself to boldly lie. "I will admit that I did have *tendre,* a very slight one, for Matthew, when we were young. But that was long ago." She didn't add *before their families feuded and Matthew dropped her from his social register.*

"I see." Aunt Clare beamed. "Then I was not wrong. You do care for Matthew and that is what I am seeking. You are just the dear, sweet girl to help me save him. You must tell me more about him than I know, you see. You must tell me how he was when he was young." She reached out and clasped Penelope's arm.

She then shrieked loudly.

Thunder rumbled ominously.

Cats yowled.

A chill raced down Penelope's spine. It was the look upon the lady's face which did the trick. A look of astonished fear. "What? What is the matter?"

"Gracious." Aunt Clare lifted her hand from Penelope. She held it out as if it had been bitten. "I— oh dear. I just had . . . well, I just had a . . . *foreboding.*"

"Foreboding?" Penelope asked cautiously.

"Yes. Something very threatening and dangerous is going to happen to you."

"I beg your pardon?"

"But do not fear." Aunt Clare squared her shoulders. "I will not permit anything to happen to you. I promise. I will watch over you."

"Thank you . . . I think." Penelope shook off her own presentiment with determination. Clearly "Aunt Clare" was a rather erratic lady. She would overlook the "foreboding" issue. She had enough on her plate for the present. "But . . . what about Matthew?"

Aunt Clare blinked. "Oh, I have no foreboding about him. As I said, I have never experienced one before. It is quite an unusual undertaking, my dear."

"I mean . . ." Penelope flushed. "Why do you think . . . ?"

A pounding at the door rudely interrupted them.

"Oh my!" Aunt Clare jumped. The cats howled. The thunder rolled *again*.

Penelope contained herself this time. It was simply all too Gothic. She'd not tolerate one more alarm.

That was just before the door crashed open!

Two

Matthew Severs, the Earl of Raleigh, stood within the door's frame. Lightning shot across the sky behind him, silhouetting his formidable size, casting a shadow over a score of glossy marble tiles in the entry hall, its length almost reaching the foot of the stairs. He wore a tiered cape which dripped water. His hair was slicked from the downpour. For him to have arrived here so swiftly and successfully, he would have had to come by horse. Which would explain the displeasure that rolled from him faster than did the current of water streaming from the many tiers of his overcoat to leave a puddle about his high-polished Hessians.

Penelope's heart stopped as she studied him. She assured herself it was due to his abrupt entrance. Certainly it was not due to the fact that she gazed upon the man for whom she had suffered a schoolgirl's first *tendre* and tears more than five years ago.

"Matthew, my dear boy." Aunt Clare, her face flushing with relief, dashed up to him. Four cats followed her. They were the brave-hearted ones. Penelope herself remained a judicious distance from the man. His anger appeared to be mounting. Aunt Clare hugged him. "Thank heaven you came."

"Of course I came." His words were clipped, his

gaze dark blue ice. "That was the purpose of your conniving scheme, was it not?"

"Conniving?" Penelope winced. Apparently Matthew was aware that Aunt Clare had been behind the misdirection of his prospective brides and was not pleased about it, but "conniving scheme" was rather harsh.

"Something frightful has happened." Aunt Clare clutched his arm. "I have had a *foreboding* about Penelope here. She is in danger."

"What?" Matthew finally glanced up to look at Penelope.

Penelope forced a calm smile. "Hello, Matthew."

"Hello, Penelope." Something passed through his eyes. He looked back to Aunt Clare promptly as if Penelope were not worthy of one second's notice. "You may cease trying, Aunt Clare. I will not be gulled. Penelope isn't in danger. You are merely saying that."

"No, dear, I am not." Aunt Clare's eyes widened in consternation. "I did not plan this whatsoever, I promise you. I have never had a foreboding in my life. It is quite the most unsettling thing, I assure you."

"Do cease. I will not be bamboozled. I . . ." Matthew halted. He considered for a moment. He shook his head, his smile grim. "I see your ruse. You must be dicked in the nob, Aunt Clare. I have no intention of marrying Penelope."

Penelope gasped in astonishment. If there ever was an understatement, that certainly must be one. What would Aunt Clare's foreboding have to do with marriage to her, pray tell? Then fire shot through Penelope as the words sank deeper. She picked up her skirts and stalked toward him. "That is fortunate, Matthew Severs, since I would never marry you!"

"Children . . ." Aunt Clare exclaimed.

"Do you hear me?" Penelope's purpose was to stare the insufferable man down, eye to eye. Unfortunately, the orange marmalade cat darted into her path at the most inopportune moment. Trying to avoid the battle-scarred feline, Penelope stumbled. Rather than looking Matthew in the eye, she found herself looking him in the chest as she tripped into it. He promptly placed steadying arms about her. Penelope tingled at his touch. She gave him a good glare for that. "I will never marry you!"

"Good." Matthew glared back. Penelope had forgotten how stunningly blue his eyes were. "For I am not going to marry you."

"Thank heaven." Aunt Clare drew in a deep breath. "I am glad the issue is settled. It is so very good to have people say exactly what they think. It is so much better for one's constitution. No one has to ponder long over the matter, or try to be delicate and diplomatic. In truth, I would not wish for either of you to suffer insult, but I do not intend for you to choose Penelope for your wife, Matthew."

"What?" Matthew's head shot up. Penelope gurgled slightly as his arms tightened about her. "You honestly do not?"

Aunt Clare flushed red. "I said it was the truth, dear. I did not mean to create such a tempest. I came here for Penelope's advice. She is your friend. I thought she might be able to study your ladies and advise me about them."

Matthew's face darkened. "She *was* my friend."

"Tsk. Do not confuse me, dear. Either you two are friends or you are not. There is no such thing as 'was' with friends."

"Then what about your foreboding?" Matthew frowned. "You didn't say that to engender my protective nature toward Penelope?"

"Oh no, dear." Aunt Clare visibly shivered. "I assure you, such a feeling is not something you wish to sham. It is true, Matthew. I have had a foreboding about poor Penelope."

"Ooof!" Matthew shored Penelope up against his length even more firmly. There wasn't even a quarter of an inch between them now. He was frightfully wet and it was seeping onto her. Penelope grew hotter by the moment. Both in temperature and temper.

"Aunt Clare, do not try my patience." He growled. "Just what kind of danger did you think you saw Penelope in?"

"Why, I am not quite sure." Aunt Clare blinked. "Which is quite tormenting. I merely touched her and I—I suddenly felt this *foreboding.*"

"Aunt Clare, please . . ." Penelope wheezed. If they didn't change the subject soon, Aunt Clare's foreboding would come true because Matthew would have squeezed her to death. "Let us not talk about it."

"Oh, dear. Forgive me." Aunt Clare's gaze showed abject apology. "I do not know what I could be thinking. It can only be distressing for you to know that you are in danger."

"Er, yes." What was distressing was the bear-hold Matthew had upon her. It was doing far too many things to Penelope's equilibrium, let alone stopping her breath. "Matthew . . . you . . . may release me."

"Balderdash. She is not in danger." Matthew glared at Aunt Clare. "I refuse to believe it."

"That is right," Penelope said weakly. "I'm quite safe. You may let me go."

"You are up to something, Aunt Clare." Matthew paid Penelope no heed. "But I warned you before. I'll not have any of it. Now, I want you to go back to London. . . ."

"Matthew . . ." Faith, but the man was a block.

"And stay out of my life! Do I make myself clear, Aunt Clare?"

"Matthew . . ." An officious block at that. How dare he speak to such a sweet old lady in that manner! And how dare he maul her without it affecting him one whit!

"I will choose my own bride. . . ."

Gracious. So they were back to that! Enraged,

Penelope stomped her heel into Matthew's boot. "Cease."

"Ouch!" Matthew, appearing most stunned, blinked at her. "What the devil!"

"Unhand me, you clunch." Penelope lifted her chin. "This instant, please."

"Oh. Er, yes. " Matthew dropped his arms from about her. He had the grace to flush. "My apologies."

"Now get out!" Penelope shoved at him. At her meager height of five two she was forced to add extra vehemence. It didn't even rock him.

"I beg your pardon?" Matthew reared back then, on his own volition.

That didn't soothe Penelope's temper. She placed her hands firmly to her hips. "I do not know who you think you are, Matthew Severs, but I will tell you who *I* think you are. I think you are an odious, churlish boor. That's who I think you are."

"What?"

"How dare you charge in here, without a by-your-leave, mind you. . . ."

"I heard a scream. . . ."

"And stand there spouting off about how you will not marry me! When I never asked you to do so. Nor will I ever, to be sure. Your conceit is overweening."

"But I . . ."

"Next you attack poor Aunt Clare here. You dare to order her about as if you think you have a right to do so."

Matthew's face darkened. "Poor . . . she is not poor, I assure you."

"She is a sweet old lady and your usage of her is unacceptable. What if she *has* misdirected your brides from your address to mine? It is clear she did it out of some mistaken fondness for you."

Matthew growled. "You do not understand . . ."

Penelope lifted her chin belligerently. "I understand that you have not thanked me properly."

"For what?" Matthew's mouth dropped open.

"For taking in your brides and giving them shelter from the storm."

"That was all Aunt Clare's fault. In truth, I do not want you to shelter them."

"Matthew . . ." Aunt Clare cried.

"No, Aunt Clare." Penelope shook with rage. "You need not explain anything to him. He is a stubborn chucklehead who will not listen."

"And you are no better than a fishmonger's wife, Penelope Lancer! Pealing into a fellow as you do."

Penelope gasped. "Get out! Get out of my house!"

Matthew stood his ground. "I will gladly do so after we discuss the matter of my brides . . . I mean my guests."

"There is no discussion necessary. I certainly do not intend to keep them from your devoted side for long. Indeed, Father ordered me to toss them out on their ears the moment they arrived. However, unlike you, I am not heartless. I will wait for the storm to clear and then I will send them to you."

"I see. You will be kindhearted to them. But *I* am to go out into the rain directly?"

"Correct!"

"You shall rue this day, Penelope. You do not know Aunt Clare!"

"I'd rather know her than you. Now leave!"

"Damn and blast!" Matthew spun. "Shrew."

He said it just beneath his breath, but Penelope heard it.

"I am *not* a shrew. I am . . ."

Matthew strode out the door without a glance back.

Enraged that he had dared to insult her and then ignore her, Penelope tore after him. "I am . . ."

She halted abruptly upon the covered portico. She'd not go into the pelting rain after that beast. Therefore, Matthew made good his escape, striding through the torrent directly toward his awaiting horse.

Penelope stared. Faith, he truly had been in a rage when he arrived to have left his mount in such a fashion outside the door. She knew Matthew for an excellent rider. Indeed, he was the type of equestrian who could make a horse perform phenomenal feats. Regardless, his demand on his horse in this instant was inconsiderate to say the least.

"Good riddance." Penelope crossed her arms. Matthew bolted into the saddle and grabbed up the reins. He pulled on them in command for his animal to turn. Penelope frowned. "He's cramming him frightfully."

Apparently even the heavens believed it to be so. Lightning rent the sky, searing close to Matthew. Penelope cried out as the horse reared high into the air. Matthew flew even higher.

"Matthew!" Fear ripped through Penelope. Lifting her skirts, she dashed down the steps and squished across the drive, the sodden grass and mud tugging at her skirts and sucking at her delicate kid-leather slippers. "Matthew!"

He had landed flat on his back in a huge puddle. He did not move one jot. Shaking with nerves, Penelope crouched beside him. "Matthew? Are you all right?" She received no answer. "Matthew. For mercy's sake, answer me."

She leaned closer, searching for signs of life. She swiftly lost a slipper and her balance in the muck. Instinctively she braced her hands upon Matthew's chest to maintain some poise. Not that she had much, drenched as she was.

"Oof." Matthew's eyes snapped open. "Are you planning to pound the answer out of me?"

"Ah, no." Penelope scrambled away as he sat up. "Though I should. Are you all right?"

"I think so." Matthew groaned and pulled a face. "Confound that infernal horse."

"You crammed him!" Penelope rose. Brushing aside a soggy tendril of hair plastered across her face, she raised her voice above a roll of thunder. "It was not his fault."

"Indeed?"

"*His* behavior has been wonderful, all things considered." Without thought, Penelope stuck out her hand toward Matthew to offer assistance.

"While mine has not been?" Matthew crawled to one knee and took it. The suction between their muddy palms was noticeable.

Penelope dutifully ignored it. "Indeed, yours has been odious . . . ohh!"

Matthew, almost halfway risen, unaccountably cursed and fell back. His weight towed Penelope down with him.

"Ugh." Penelope crawled to a sitting position. Enraged to be wetter, and muddier, she glared. "You beast!

"I am sorry." Matthew's pained expression revealed in a crack of lightning verified his words. "I fear I've twisted my ankle."

"Oh dear, no."

"Oh dear, yes." Matthew lifted his brow. "It is justice for cramming my poor horse, no doubt."

Penelope flushed. She rose quickly. She ran her hand upon her skirts. Which was ridiculous, since both were sluiced in mud. She held it out. "Should we try again?" She controlled a quick twitch of her lips. "Or do you wish for me to go for help in the house?"

"God, no. Anything but that, please." A wry smile crossed Matthew's lips. He slowly crawled to his one knee. This time, when he took Penelope's hand he conscientiously favored his weakened ankle as he stood.

Still, he swayed unsteadily. Penelope reached quickly to grab him about his waist, even as he clutched her. Then both swayed, their balance precarious. Finally then, they gained a firm stance.

"There!" She grinned up at Matthew. "That wasn't too difficult."

"Yes, but dare we move?" Matthew parried.

"I don't know." Penelope looked solemn. "We can remain and pretend to be the statuary in a fountain if you wish. A lake is rapidly growing about us."

Matthew barked a laugh, holding on to her all the more. His eyes warmed. He shook his head wryly. "Gad's, Penn, but I have missed you."

Penelope looked up through the rain. With his laughter, and his look, and his use of her pet name, Matthew captivated her. She found it the easiest thing to confess. "And I have missed you."

They stared at each other. A breathless feeling welled up in Penelope. She bit back a groan. It was that old feeling. That feeling that wasn't supposed to be there these years later.

"You are a sight, you know?" Matthew studied.

Penelope tried to appear indignant. "And what of you, my lord?"

"At my most elegant, I am sure." Matthew's lips turned up into the teasing smile that only he could wear. "I would offer you a proper bow . . ."

"Don't you dare!" Penelope giggled.

She knew they were straying off the inevitable, standing in the rain and bantering as they did, but she couldn't care. The niggling question in her mind was, what was the inevitable? His suffering in pain as they tried to make it back to the house?

"S'death. My Lord Severs!" A voice shouted.

"Blast." Matthew didn't turn his gaze from Penelope.

"Yes. Indeed." Penelope bit her lip. No, that was the inevitable. Being dragged back to reality. And others . . .

Matthew turned his gaze away then, toward the call. Penelope did the same. The portico was filled with people. Penelope sighed. Through the blur of the downpour, the ladies' bright silks shone like a brilliant painting.

"Severs, what are you doing?" one of the men called through cupped hands.

"Oh, nothing much. Penn and I are practicing to be in a fountain, you know?"

"What?" The man's confused expression, even from where they stood, was obvious.

Matthew lifted a brow toward Penelope. "Well?"

"Do not roast the man so."

Matthew laughed. "I guess I haven't put my best foot forward, have I?"

Penelope laughed. "At least you are not wearing your soap-making dress."

"Ah, is that what that delightful creation is? I had wondered." Matthew nodded. They both looked back to the crowd. The group upon the steps was growing in numbers by the second. All were cautious to remain far enough under the roof line to escape the rain.

Aunt Clare smiled and waved from amongst them. "Are you having fun playing, children?"

"What?" the other man shouted once more. "Don't think I heard you correctly."

"I fell from my horse and twisted my ankle," Matthew shouted in return.

The feminine cries were loud and long. And the sympathy of the ladies toward Matthew was truly effective. Effective, that was, after Penelope assisted him all the way back to the dry haven of the house, she noticed.

It must be the sign of a true lady, of which test she failed, that not one of those fashionable ladies had gotten wet. The thought didn't warm her much as the ladies enveloped him with a cloud of perfume and carried him off with soft words, leaving Penelope to stand alone, dripping and muddy.

* * *

Matthew nodded and smiled as everyone said good night at the early hour of nine. In a herd, they crowded from the parlor. Penelope was definitely the shepherdess of the flock as she led them forth. For an impromptu party, she had managed a fine table. Clearly her staff must have been adequate in housing the party, for the ladies had shone in their finery and they had laughed and talked through the evening without complaint. Not an easy accomplishment at any fashionable party of the *ton*, let alone an accidental grouping foisted upon a country manor.

The fact that Jacob Lancer never made an appearance interested Matthew, not that he wasn't grateful that Jacob had refrained from attending. Penelope had declared that Jacob's gout had troubled him, due to the weather to be sure, and that he intended to take his meals within his chambers. Matthew never doubted Penelope had somehow had the managing of it.

Matthew noticed that the ladies glanced at each other covertly and then offered him a much different, beckoning look. Matthew's lips tightened. He had no intention of singling out any particular lady for a parting word tonight. No, he was too intent upon trying to quiz Aunt Clare, who had circulated amongst his prospective brides with what appeared to be random conviviality the entire evening.

God only knew what she had said to them. He had seen by the parents' reactions that they knew who Aunt Clare was. Still, none of them seemed able to keep her from their offspring. Aunt Clare could appear so very innocuous and doddering, they probably thought her their friend and supporter, each and every one of them.

Now, that Machiavellian lady was remaining close under Penelope's wing as they left to retire. Matthew's pained ankle did not assist him in his efforts to overcome her. Indeed, she and Penelope had their heads bent together in serious conversation as he limped in double time up to them.

He cared not that he was rather impolite as he clamped hold of Aunt Clare's arm. "Might I have a word with you in private, Aunt Clare?"

"What, dear?" Aunt Clare looked up at him, wide-eyed.

"A word with you in private?" Matthew forced a grin. "I wish to apologize to you for my earlier behavior."

"Dear Matthew, there is no need." Aunt Clare smiled benignly. "As Garth says, I didn't take snuff." She halted and looked at Penelope. "Garth is my son-in-law, did you know?"

Penelope smiled. "No, I did not. It is clear you are fond of him."

Matthew gritted his teeth. Penelope must have been the only one in all of England who had not heard the fantastic and mortifying story. He simply must take care of Aunt Clare as quickly as possible. He simply must.

"Oh, yes. I helped raise him, you know. And now I am learning so many different words from him since his return to London. He doesn't take snuff at anything, you see." She said it proudly, then considered a moment. "My, but I do like that phrase. Only, it is more confusing when you use it in regard to other men. For they are always taking snuff, in one fashion or another. Then it is difficult to decide if they mean they are not in a pelter, or whether they mean they do not partake of snuff, the substance itself."

"Aunt Clare . . ." Matthew exhaled.

"I know what you mean. But I rather they didn't take snuff." Penelope's gaze sparkled with an impish light as she looked at Matthew. He scowled at her, knowing very well her meaning. "It is a nasty habit for a gentleman to engage in, I believe, taking snuff at every odd turn."

"Yes, isn't it?" Aunt Clare beamed. "I far prefer a

gentleman to enjoy a cigar. Bendford, my brother, does. And though many women say that is a nasty habit as well, I find it rather nice-smelling."

"Aunt Clare." Matthew ground out. "I wish to apologize. . . ."

"But I assure you, there is no reason to do so." Aunt Clare smiled and patted his arm. "Anger should never be held too long, I vow. Nor should an apology, for that matter. Else it become frightfully embarrassing, don't you think? I do not know why, but when someone apologizes extensively, it makes me start apologizing to them in return."

"Aunt Clare . . ."

"Do go with Matthew. If he wishes to abase himself before you, then it is a very good thing, I would say." Penelope patted her shoulder. "I shall go and see to the other guests."

"Of course, my dear, I . . ."

"Let us go back to the parlor." Matthew swung Aunt Clare so swiftly in a circle that she gasped. He dragged her back into the room and closed the doors. He drew in a breath and turned to her. "Now . . ."

Aunt Clare jumped, looking nervous. "Truly, Matthew, I—I would rather you not abase yourself."

"I'm not going to do so. Penn was only roasting me."

"What?" Aunt Clare's brow wrinkled in perplexity.

"I brought you here in order that we may settle the issue at hand. You did receive my letter, I assume?"

"Your letter?" Aunt Clare frowned, and then nodded. "Ah yes, that note, so very brief and crisp, telling me forthwith you did not wish for my services in finding your true love?"

"Yes." Matthew stiffened his resolve. "That one."

"But Matthew, cannot you trust me in this? I will find your true love for you if you will but permit me."

"I do not want a true love, Aunt Clare. I want a wife. A wealthy wife."

Aunt Clare's eyes widened. They became great blue pools of sadness. "Oh, my dear boy, you have claimed that before, I know. But surely you jest. Or you have become disheartened. But you should not. You have a great love destined for you. You cannot marry for money alone, Matthew."

"Yes I can." Matthew snapped. Aunt Clare looked so stricken that he sighed. Walking up to her, he took her hand. "Aunt Clare, I do not wish you to think the worse of me, but I must marry for money. And since I must, I intend to do so in a forthright manner. I want a marriage of convenience. No illusions. No delusions. At least I can retain that much honor."

"No, Matthew." Aunt Clare gripped his hand tight. "To marry in such a fashion would be fatal for you. You have a great love destined for you. You cannot forsake that. Truly, you cannot. You will come about, I am sure. You are resourceful. I would not advise this to anyone else." Aunt Clare leaned forward, her face sincere. "But it would be better for you to become anything else before wedding for money. You could become a highwayman . . . or a pirate . . . or a smuggler."

"No!" Matthew reared back as if she had slapped him. He dropped her hand and strode away. "God. I cannot believe you dared to say that. What I told you . . . I told you under the strictest of confidences."

Aunt Clare nodded. "That means you were taphacket, correct?"

Matthew bit back a curse. "Yes. Exactly. I never meant to . . . to tell you about my . . . my family history as I did."

"I do not understand why not." Aunt Clare looked puzzled. "Not every man is privileged to have had highwaymen and smugglers and pirates as their forefathers. Such talents are uncommon. Indeed, they must be in your blood and you should not ignore that." She dashed up to him. "That is why I am advising you in this. I would not suggest this to just any man. Some do not have such romance in their soul."

"Romance? Talent?" Matthew spun with a growl. "You speak of my family's sins as if they were to be applauded."

"My dear, would you truly prefer to come from a line of ordinary people? People who never drew one jot of attention to themselves while alive? Rather, you have a wonderful family history. It is full of romance and adventure, do and daring."

"Oh, God." Matthew rolled his eyes.

"You seem to want respectability. Truly, it is not what it is touted to be. I know. I have been respectable all my life." Aunt Clare frowned. "I assure you, Matthew. A marriage of convenience would . . . would make you into . . . well, into something you are not to be. Worse, you would not be happy."

"Yes, I would be. And that brings me back to the issue at hand. I want you to curtail any plans you have in my direction. I am going to choose my own bride this very week and I will not permit you to interfere."

Aunt Clare opened her mouth and then closed it. "There is no reason to brangle with you. You are very strong-minded."

"I am glad you recognize that." Matthew frowned. "Now promise me. You will not arrange any more schemes like the one today."

"Certainly not."

"Good."

"So many things went awry."

"Aunt Clare! Do not try and gammon me. They went exactly as you wanted them to go. You've kept my house party from me quite successfully. Though how you could depend upon it to rain is beyond me."

"Oh no, dear, that was not in my plan at all." Her eyes almost crossed in contemplation. "Though I did ask the Almighty to add any advice or improvements he thought necessary. I did not expect the rain. It put me quite behind and I arrived much later than expected. Poor Penelope received all your brides before I could even warn her. She is a dear girl to have accepted them regardless."

"That is another thing. How you could have dragged her into this . . ."

"I told you, dear."

"Yes, yes. She is a friend of mine." Matthew paused. He flushed. "I must have told you that also when I was . . ."

"Castaway."

"Just what exactly did I tell you?" Matthew forced himself to ask.

Aunt Clare's eyes widened. "Nothing much, dear. You merely talked about her. But it seemed to me that you held her in respect."

"Yes." Matthew said it with relief. "Of course I do."

"Now, this foreboding I had," Aunt Clare continued, "I do not like it. I have read about it happening before. Miss Radcliffe's dear ladies all suffer from them, you know. But I never thought that I would. I would gladly accept a migraine before suffering another foreboding. . . ."

"Aunt Clare. You are being ridiculous."

"I must protect dear Penelope." Aunt Clare sighed. Then she brightened. "And while I do so, I can look about for her true love as well."

"What? You cannot do that!"

"Why not, dear?" Aunt Clare cocked her head.

"Why . . . because, because . . . she doesn't need you to do so, I am sure."

"I do not understand. She is not married, is she?"

"No."

"And she has no beau?"

Matthew shrugged. "I do not know if she has or not. That is beside the point."

"She does not have one. She told me so at dinner." Aunt Clare shook her head. "She is such a nice girl, she should have a beau. And she can enjoy him while I decide who is her true love."

Matthew frowned, feeling the oddest pang. He brushed it aside, not wanting to deliberate what it could be. "Weren't you going to find my true love first?"

"You just said you didn't wish me to do so."

"I . . ." Matthew clamped his jaw tight. "Go home, Aunt Clare. You will not divert me, or make me think that you are turning your attentions to Penelope."

"You need not be jealous. . . ."

"I am not!"

"I know I am addlepated at times, but I think if I try my best, I can succeed in finding Penelope a true love while at the same time I find you yours. Indeed, I am becoming far more accomplished at this than when I started with Julia and Garth. I have gained experience now, you see. Your case will be the most important one, of course. I promise I will not let Penelope's case overshadow yours."

"Ha! You admit you have not given up your designs for me!"

Aunt Clare tapped her finger to her cheek. Her gaze grew fuzzy and distant. "Gracious, but I cannot wait to see the difference in Penelope once she finds her true love. She has such a passionate but faithful nature. . . ."

"Passionate?" Matthew blinked. "Penelope?"

"Oh yes, dear." Aunt Clare delivered it vaguely, her gaze definitely somewhere off in another place. It made Matthew nervous. "Very much so."

"I cannot believe it." It shocked Matthew.

"But it is true, Matthew." Aunt Clare looked at him with utmost sincerity. "I would lay any odds you like that Penelope will kiss excessively well. She might need some teaching, of course. . . ."

"Aunt Clare!" Matthew roared in outrage.

"Oh, dear." Aunt Clare's hand flew to her mouth.

Embarrassment traced her features. "Goodness me, I should not have said that. I fear I have learned some very improper things from you boys when you visited with me. And unfortunately, it only seems to grow worse." She shook her head. "Forgive me. I was thinking aloud to myself, you know? I wouldn't truly lay a bet with you upon how Penelope kissed. That would be utterly reprehensible."

"It certainly would."

"You want a marriage of convenience, after all." Aunt Clare nodded. "You cannot be kissing Penelope."

"Certainly not."

Aunt Clare took on that considering look. "Some other man must discover if Penelope kisses well."

Matthew clenched his fist. "Aunt Clare, I forbid you to . . ."

"Hello?" Penelope walked into the room at that very moment, with nary a knock or a by-your-leave.

Matthew blinked. "I beg your pardon?"

She smiled. "No, it is Aunt Clare's pardon you are supposed to be begging. Have you finished your apology yet?"

"No. I . . ."

"It was all a bubble, Penelope." Aunt Clare shook her head. "Matthew did not bring me in here to apologize."

"I didn't think so, Aunt Clare." Penelope smiled gently. "He brought you in here to ring a peal over your head, didn't he?"

"Yes." Aunt Clare's eyes widened. "He did. How did you know? And why didn't you warn me?"

"I wanted to give him the benefit of the doubt." Penelope raised her brow toward Matthew. "After all, he is a man full grown. He might have learned to curb his temper."

Matthew flushed. Then laughing, he threw up his hands. "*Pax*, Penn. I cry *pax*."

"As you should. Aunt Clare, come, let us make our escape. I will show you to your chambers. Your kitties will be pleased to see you, no doubt."

"No!" Matthew stepped toward her.

"No?" Penelope frowned.

He stiffened. "I need . . . I wish to talk to you."

"I see." Her lips twitched.

"Dearest." Aunt Clare scuttled up to her. "I fear he wants to bamboozle you. He will ring a peal over your head as well."

"What, again?" Penelope sighed heavily.

"I was not going to ring a peal over her head, Aunt Clare." Matthew frowned grimly.

"Poppycock," Aunt Clare said.

"Gammon." Penelope concurred. She patted Aunt Clare's shoulder. "Do run along. You can leave me safely alone with the mean old curmudgeon."

"I do not know, Penelope dear, if I should." Aunt Clare shook her head.

"I have been raised by a gout-stricken father, Aunt Clare. I assure you, I am no shrinking violet under a few blasts from a dragon."

"Oh no, dear, I was thinking that I should remain as your chaperone."

"With Matthew?" Penelope stared. She gurgled in delight. "No. You need not concern yourself in that respect." Matthew narrowed his gaze. Why shouldn't Aunt Clare do so? He frowned even more as Penelope waved a dismissive hand. "We have been friends since . . ." She halted, flushing. She shrugged. "Matthew would never go beyond the line, I assure you."

Matthew stiffened. He had not been treated so much like an ineffectual puppy in a long time. He was no rake or cad, but in London he was considered somewhat of a ladies' man. "Certainly I would not."

Penelope flushed all the more. However, she smiled. "The most he will do is give me a good bear-jawing, Aunt. Now do run along."

"Very well." Aunt Clare sighed and left the room.

"Now . . ." Penelope walked over to the settee and sat. "I am prepared. Do proceed with the ranting, Matthew."

Matthew stared. A chuckle escaped him. Faith, he had forgotten how amusing Penelope could be. She appeared the most reserved of ladies, nothing flamboyant about her one bit. Yet, then her humor would flash through—indeed, slice through, to be exact—amusing and irritating a man all at the same time. What Clare had said about Penelope being passionate crossed his mind. He ruthlessly pushed the thought away as he took up the chair opposite her. "No, no. You have quite taken the wind out of my sails. It is decidedly flat when someone is prepared for a fight."

"Do forgive me."

Matthew shook his head. "I do not mean to beat a dead horse, but you simply do not understand the situation."

Penelope turned a level gaze upon him. "No, I do not. I was jesting before. You have never been a man to ride rough and rusty. And certainly never with a lady."

"Thank you." Matthew grimaced. "Though I did act like a bore with you this afternoon."

"I meant Aunt Clare, silly." Penelope laughed. "You have never considered me a lady."

"I have."

She lifted a challenging brow.

Matthew couldn't help it. He grinned. "Very well. I have not always done so. But the last time I saw you, you were not a lady. You were a pert young chit."

A flush rose to her cheeks. "You are right. I was."

A silence fell. The past years, those separated years, seemed to haunt the room. Matthew drew in a breath. "But I did consider you my friend."

"Thank you." Penelope lowered her gaze.

A pause ensued. It became obvious that she was not

going to return the same avowal, not even for politeness sake. Blast that infernal feud. Now that Matthew looked back, he wasn't sure how it had started. It had been between his father and Jacob Lancer. Something to do with a money transaction. His father had vowed that Jacob had fabricated all the accusations. Jacob had vowed that Matthew's father was a liar and cheat. Matthew cleared his throat. "I hope we can be friends again."

Penelope's gaze flew to his. The flare of anticipation within it set Matthew's pulse racing. Then she looked away. "I hope so, too."

"Truly." Matthew stood and without thought crossed over and sat down beside her. He picked up her hand, forcing her to look back at him. "The feud was between our families. I stopped seeing you because I assumed that you would not see me."

"I see."

Matthew could tell that she didn't. God, did she think he had severed their friendship first all those years ago?

Penelope smiled. "Now, tell me why you are terrorizing a dear old lady."

"Rather, she is terrorizing me." Matthew cast Penelope a discerning look. Her gaze was innocent. "Have you truly not heard any of the story?"

"No. You know I am rather behind hand with the news from London. We live quietly here at the manor."

"I know." A guilty twinge passed through Matthew. No doubt Penelope lived even more quietly after the feud, for Matthew had been one of her few close friends. One of the few friends that Jacob Lancer had not driven off before. He released her hand and sprang up. "It is a strange story, I fear."

"Do tell me."

Matthew drew in a deep breath. He might as well confess the most embarrassing part first. "Aunt Clare abducted me."

"What?" Penelope's eyes widened in astonishment. "Gracious!"

At least she had not said *impossible* and *how could that have happened.*

Her gaze darkened in sympathy. "No wonder you do not like her. Whatever caused Aunt Clare to do such a thing?"

Matthew stared at Penelope. Her calm acceptance was amazing. "I had proposed to her niece, Lady Julia. She wanted to keep me from marrying her."

Now Penelope paled. "I see."

"What? What did I say wrong?" Here he had gotten over the roughest ground only to discover a new turn.

"I-I did not know that you had been engaged." Penelope looked sad. "I am so very sorry."

"For what?"

"That you lost the woman you loved. No wonder you will choose a marriage of convenience now."

Matthew flushed. Gad's, this was the most embarrassing part after all. "I did not love Lady Julia, Penn. Aunt Clare knew that. She also knew that Lady Julia did not love me."

"But . . ." Penelope shook her head, bewilderment clouding her clear gaze.

"I was marrying Lady Julia for her fortune, Penn." His words came out fierce and angry.

Penn started back. She finally nodded. "Your family is that far down the river tick then?"

The greatest sigh eased from Matthew. Faith, but Penn was a wonderful fellow. You could always count on her to be nimble-witted, taking things in a calm, no-nonsense manner. "You've hit the nub of it. I *must* marry a fortune. And if I am going to do so, I will be honest about it."

Penelope rose and wandered away. "How great an heiress do you require?"

"Lady Julia was very rich. As rich as you, I would imagine."

"Indeed?"

"But there are very few heiresses with that deep of pockets." He smiled wryly. "I believe I can live with a lady who has a lesser legacy."

"I see." Penelope sounded as if she were choking. "I am glad to hear it, since there are not any other heiresses as well heeled as I."

"Indeed. And that is why you must help me, Penn." Matthew strode up to her and clasped up her hands. "Help me to win one of these ladies. Do not let Aunt Clare destroy my chances."

"Wh-why would she wish to do that?" Penelope gazed up at him with wide, curious eyes.

A thrill passed through Matthew. Penn's eyes had grown greener over the years. And her hair had darkened to burnished brown. Her petite frame was fuller and rounder. He tightened his clasp upon her hand. "She wants me to marry for true love."

"I see." Penelope licked her lips. "Is there something so wrong with that?"

"I must marry an heiress. There is no doubt about that. Else the family will be in debtor's prison." Matthew couldn't seem to take his gaze from her lips. Sweetly curved, he realized. And of the freshest rose. Faith, how would it be to kiss those lips?

"C-couldn't you marry for true love *and* money?" Penelope whispered.

She was so innocent. If any man was to kiss her first, it should be him. As a friend, that is. If Aunt Clare was correct, and Penn was passionate, another man might take advantage of her before she had found her sea legs, as it were. Matthew lowered his head, smiling in pleasure. "Of course not."

"Wh-why?" She lifted those tempting lips even closer.

"Because that would be dishonest."

Suddenly Penelope was all windmilling arms. She

shoved away from him, taking those tempting lips with her. "You . . . you dunderhead!"

"What?" Matthew shook his head to clear it. "What is the matter?"

"Nothing."

"But you just called me a dunderhead!"

"Yes, I did." She lifted her head regally.

It should have looked humorous on such a petite woman. It didn't. Matthew frowned. "Why?"

Penelope stared at him, her eyes flashing. "You really do not know why?"

Determination filled Matthew. Gad's, but he should be the one to kiss her first. She did possess a passionate side. "No, I do not."

"Very well." Penelope's look grew calm. "You are a dunderhead to worry that Aunt Clare could stop you from doing anything you truly wished to do."

Matthew saw it in her eyes. "You are lying to me, Penn."

"I am not." She spoke firmly. "If you do not wish to love someone, you will not. It is that plain and simple."

"You still do not understand. Aunt Clare is a matchmaker of the first water. She—she is devious and conniving and she will do anything to match the couples she believes belong with one another. She abducted her own niece's fiancés to stop her from marrying anyone but Garth."

"And this Lady Julia and Garth are miserable now?"

"No. In fact, they are famous for their love." Matthew cringed. "I did not tell you, but she kidnapped six other men besides myself."

"Six?" Penelope's eyes did pop wide at that.

Matthew shrugged. "They were contestants for Lady Julia's hand. She kept us all in the third story of her house, with her cats."

"Gracious."

Matthew waved it away. "She treated us like royalty.

That was not the problem. Indeed, at the time, I—I grew very fond of Aunt Clare. She—she has a way of making you dream. And talk. And forget what you tell her."

Penelope stilled. "Why are you so set against her now?"

"Because she found a match for five of those other men already, Penn. Will they, nil they, they married exactly whom she wished for them to wed. It is harrowing."

"I see. So *those* men are miserable now?"

"No, confound it. They all smell of June and roses. They swear they are happy, though each and every one of them fought a good fight before that."

"Why is she doing this?"

"Because she promised to find us our own true loves in restitution for taking Lady Julia from us."

"Oh my!" Penelope covered her mouth. A giggle escaped her.

"It is not amusing."

"Yes, it is." She broke out into outright laughter. "Only imagine, all of you men permitting a little old lady to find your true loves for you because you are such dunderheads as to not want to do so yourselves."

"You do not understand, Penn." Matthew stalked up and gripped her by the shoulders. He rattled her slightly. "I must marry for money, Penn. If I married a woman I loved for her money, I could never respect myself. Always she would know that her money had been a driving force in our marriage. How could love last with that thought?"

Penn paled. "A woman marries a man for money and is respected."

"I am not a woman."

"No." Tears welled up in Penelope's eyes. "No, you are not."

He might label himself a cad, but he'd take advantage of her sympathy, for surely sympathy was the cause of her tears. "Will you help me, Penn? Promise me you will send Aunt Clare packing tomorrow. She mustn't be able to stay here and play off her tricks."

"She hasn't asked if she can stay."

He snorted. "She will. I'll lay any odds on it."

"You can't afford to do so, remember?" Penelope lifted her chin. "And I will not promise anything."

Matthew stiffened. He dropped his hands from her shoulders and stepped back. He bowed formally. "Very well, Miss Lancer. I will bid you good night."

"Please do." Penelope said it coldly.

Matthew growled. Clenching his hands, he spun and stalked from the room. Faith, had he actually thought Penelope a good fellow? Worse, he had actually considered kissing her! Ha. That would never happen. Some other poor chap would have to deal with her contrariness!

Three

Penelope stood at the center of the entry hall. Once again, an impressive number of trunks and bandboxes strewed across the floor. The front doors were open to a fresh and breezy morning, washed clean from the storm of the day before.

She eyed Matthew Severs and his court of four ladies as they fawned about him, ruffles dancing, fans waving, and dainty curls bobbing. The noble entourage awaited the last pieces to be loaded into the carriages. Amazing. Yesterday, Penelope had been a baffled and unaware attendant as she had received these completely unknown people into her house. Now she was mistress of ceremonies, privy to far more of the plot than she wished to be. Indeed, she felt she knew more about these people than she desired. Say what they may, there were times when ignorance was surely bliss at its finest.

She grimaced. Faith, that was a very malicious train of thought. She most certainly didn't have an inkling as to who those women truly were, and she knew it. Yet since they vied for the position of bride-to-be to Matthew Severs, she couldn't help but look at them with a jaundiced eye. Jaundiced, certainly not jealous. She cast said jaundiced eye down a mental list of the contestants and sighed.

Now, Lady Estelle Hastings was by far the beauty
amongst beauties. A diamond of the first water with
that glossy black hair, those great brown eyes, and
those dratted classic features. No woman should look
so like sculpted ivory to rival the statue Athena Parthe-
nos. And certainly not at this early hour of the morning. Penelope grimaced as she briefly remembered
those childhood afternoons with Matthew as they
rushed through his lessons in the classics in an effort
to speed up the time till they could tear across the
lawns in freedom. She remembered now. Phidias
carved his Athena with her right arm raised as a statue
of victory. And, certainly, Lady Estelle presented the
epitome of graceful womanhood. Her charm and manner—indeed, everything about her—was that of a lady.
Possibly a victorious lady. At least she would be, if
Phidias had anything to say to it.

Yet, if Miss Cecily Morris had anything to say to it,
Phidias would be sent packing back to the Parthenon.
Penelope glanced at the shining blonde fluttering beside the elegant Lady Estelle. She possessed an elfin
quality that could intrigue one. She stood, burnished
gold beside the cool ivory. The least of the titled list—
her father, a new baron, still reeking of the shop—she
spoke less than the others, though her blue eyes often
sparkled in observation. She seemed to burst with *joie
de vivre*, only restraining it within this noble throng.

As for the ideal representation of demure shyness
and pliable femininity, one could not fault Violet Stapleton. Her looks were those of a delicate water painting with pale silver eyes and hair a soft dove brown.
She patiently stood to Matthew's left and back a step,
delicately waving a dainty Brisé fan, tendrils of willow-
green satin ribbon dangling from its pearl handle. A
madonna in a fawn dimity round gown, a spray of her
namesake flower modestly tucked into a fichu of blond
lace. A man would not have to worry about opposition
within his home if wed to Violet. Of course, as quiet

as she was, he might have to concern himself with over-looking her location about the place on a regular basis.

And to Violet's side, two steps ahead and impatiently tapping her high-heeled kid boot against the marble floor was her opposite. Where Violet was a soft, misty morning watercolor, Lady Sherrice Norton was a vibrant oil painting. She was a striking green-eyed redhead with a flamboyant nature. With aplomb, she successfully presented an ensemble that was daring yet did not push beyond the limits of *bon ton*. Her deep, rich black-green gown sported the fashionable new high skirt that showed a foot of her straw-colored petticoat below. With the flair of a skilled artist she topped her gown with a cape and lapels of carmel-colored satin. On her head she sported a Highland bonnet, made of gold foil and her favored carmel satin, the ends trimmed with a gold fringe. Ruby earrings sparkled in the rays of sunlight, a strikingly unusual choice for a redhead, yet their rich claret a perfect choice as they reflected the gold of her bonnet and cape. The entire effect was to frame her expressive emerald eyes. In truth, women would employ the term "brash" for her. Which would, in turn, translate into the word "challenging" for the gentlemen.

This bevy of femininity surrounded Matthew, surely the inner circle to the deity. Their mothers stood guard about them in a second colonnade, watching with fond approval. Their fathers were suspiciously absent, all attending the demanding job of loading the carriages outside. Their footmen were like ants, moving back and forth through the hall, carrying bandbox after trunk after portmanteau. A steady stream of hatboxes marched by, the liveried limbs of Penelope's servants peeking out below, double-stepping now and then to avoid near-collisions with flustered maids as they inventoried the precious hoard of gems and toiletries entrusted to their care.

Gracious, but would they be at it all day? Penelope

bit her lip. If they did not hurry, her father might very well muster up the energy to come downstairs and attempt to give his noble guests the good caning that he vowed he would administer if they were not gone by noonday.

Of course, since he had offered this threat from his bed, far too hung over to move and actually appearing to enjoy it, Penelope tamped down her concerns. No doubt he would toss out the drought she had given him and would, instead, chase the hair of the dog that bit him. She would have to be firm with him later in the day, but for the nonce, she had more pressing concerns to attend.

Penelope tensed as she saw Matthew murmur to his court and then walk over to stand beside her.

"Where the devil is Aunt Clare?" was his greeting. The man didn't even meet her gaze, but nodded toward his flock with a tight smile.

"She will be down shortly, I would assume. Gathering up her twelve cats cannot be an easy task." Penelope maintained a neutral tone. "Since she is not in your entourage, what does it signify? You may proceed ahead. I certainly have enough staff to serve Aunt Clare in whatever she needs."

Matthew shifted. "I shall wait."

Penelope studied him. "You are still afraid she will not actually leave, are you not?"

Matthew frowned. "With reason."

"You are impossible." Penelope's ire rose. "I tell you, she has not asked to remain. She has already sent her trunks down. Her coachman awaits with the rest. What more could you demand?"

"You are not shot of her yet." Matthew growled. "Only . . ."

"Meow. Brr!" Aunt Clare's huge orange-marmalade cat, Sir Percy, led the advance of the twelve cats into the great hall. They leapt and howled, clearly showing their enjoyment at being let from Aunt Clare's rooms.

"Percy!" Aunt Clare's voice called from far behind. "Do wait, dear."

Sir Percy didn't wait one bit. A feline of action, he meowed with vigor and dashed at a Norton footman. The man, a trunk upon his shoulders, was no match for a mammoth cat playing beneath his feet. The footman cursed, spun, and lost hold of the trunk. It hit the marble floor with a thud, snapped open, and spewed out its trove of treasures.

To the right, an angry shriek arose. Two cats had found Lady Sherrice Norton's satin petticoat and green skirts and were climbing them, leaving a trail of loops and snags behind them on the satin. Her lady mother, an extremely large woman, bellowed at the indignity foisted upon her offspring. She heaved forward to bat at the cats, and smacked her own dear child in the ribs instead.

"Peaches and Cream. No!" Matthew stalked toward them, slowed by the clutter.

Four cats emerged upon Violet Stapleton, who skittered back across the room. She was quiet about the retreat. Lady Stapleton was not. A tall, horsy lady, as forceful as her child was malleable, she clapped loudly from where she stood. "Scat! Shoo! Else I'll take a whip to you, I will!"

Two more cats attended to Lady Estelle Hastings. They pawed and pranced about her. She merely stood, wide-eyed, gripping her hands together. Her mother, an elegant lady herself, entered battle by waving a wispy handkerchief at them. This had unfortunate results. The cats took cover beneath Lady Estelle's skirts.

Lady Estelle did object to this. The elegant statue came to life. Indeed, she screamed. Her lashes fluttered and her eyes rolled up.

"Oh, no!" The signs of an imminent swoon were evident. Penelope dashed toward the distressed girl.

"Dear me, kitties! Kitties! Behave." Aunt Clare arrived in the hall, panting. Her blue eyes widened. "Oh, my. Where are your manners?"

"Gone abegging, I fear." Cecily Morris, eyes brimming with merriment, pointed to two "kitties" that plundered through the contents of the broken trunk. The one, a calico, dragged a frilly petticoat across the floor. The other, a fat Persian, lay squat in the middle of an open powder tin. The strong scent of ambergris and freesia wafted through the room from the perfume bottle beside it, its stopper having rolled across the floor. Clutched between its two front paws a nut-brown, now soggy, frayed cylinder. The cat chewed another strip from its length.

"No!" Lady Norton was diverted from batting Lady Sherrice and cats. She stared at the Persian. "Is that a . . . a cigar?"

"Faith, but it is." Lady Stapleton paced forward with a stride that would have looked better in a riding habit, or, for that matter, riding britches. "Well, ain't that cute. Someone ought to light it for the poor devil."

"Sherrice! How could you?" Lady Norton's face blushed purple. She lifted her hand and thumped her well-upholstered chest.

"Oh, Mother. I only wished to try it." Lady Sherrice shrugged. "Do not fly into the boughs."

"Ah me!" Lady Norton flung up her hands in a manner worthy of the great Siddons. She rocked back and forth.

"Matthew, please catch Lady Norton." Aunt Clare called, though she herself rushed in a completely different direction. "Estelle, dear . . ."

Penelope returned to her own place in time. She grabbed hold of the swaying girl before her. However, Lady Estelle was far taller than she, and Penelope realized that she did not have complete control of the situation.

"Permit me to assist." Another pair of arms enveloped Lady Estelle. It was Cecily Morris on the other side of Lady Estelle. "Let us lower her slowly."

Penelope nodded and they did so; all the while Lady Hastings waved her handkerchief and clucked.

"Alexander and Romeo! Come out from beneath her skirts this instant!" Aunt Clare's voice actually held command. The cats scurried out promptly.

"Oh dear." Lady Estelle's eyes fluttered open. They were large in embarrassment. "Do forgive me. I am so sorry."

"Do not be." Penelope soothed. "Many people are afraid of cats."

"But I am not." Lady Estelle shook her head, flushing. "I—I think I was overcome with the excitement."

"Lady Estelle, dear"—Aunt Clare dropped to the floor beside them—"are you all right?"

"I am fine." Lady Estelle sat up, looking anything but that. "It was s-so silly. I-I do not faint often."

"Yes, dear." Aunt Clare nodded. "But it will happen, I have heard, when . . ."

"For goodness sake, Mother." Lady Sherrice's voice cracked through the hall. "Do get up. You are making a spectacle of yourself."

The girl's tone was such that Penelope could not help but look over in that direction. She stifled a laugh. Matthew sat in a crouch, attempting to hold up the prone bulk of Lady Norton from the floor. As large a man as he was, his face showed definite signs of strain.

"Aren't you glad we chose to help Lady Estelle?" Cecily whispered. Penelope did giggle then. Lady Estelle joined them, color returning to her cheeks.

"Girls, for shame," Aunt Clare clucked.

Lady Sherrice tapped her foot. "Mother, do attend me."

"She can't hear you, you ninnyhammer," Lady Stapleton said to Lady Sherrice. "Yer ma's dead fainted away. Which, I'd do the same if I had a child like you."

Penelope gulped back another laugh. She could not see the intrepid Lady Stapleton swooning over ought.

Lady Stapleton paused. A grin cracked across her thin face. "That was after I whipped you good for it. Your poor ma has mollycoddled you." She clapped her hands. "Who's got hartshorn?"

"I do." Lady Hastings scurried over, waving her handkerchief and digging into her reticule.

"I thought you would," Lady Stapleton snorted. She took the vial from Lady Hastings and snapping it open, bent and waved it under Lady Norton's nose. Lady Norton moaned and blinked.

"Thank you, Lady Stapleton," Matthew murmured.

"That should do the trick." Lady Stapleton stood and handed the bottle back to Lady Hastings. She rubbed her hands. "Well, that was a jolly uproar. Now, let us stop this shilly-shallying. Rupert will be coming back here to see what's going on and then we'll have a dust-up. He detests delays." She looked about with impatience. "Violet, girl, where are you?"

"Oh my," Aunt Clare murmured, her gaze directed to a corner. Her face showed concern and confusion. "How very odd."

Penelope looked to where Aunt Clare peered. Lady Violet Stapleton stood with her back to the wall. She remained perfectly still, staring unwaveringly at the four cats that had sat down in a ring about her. They neither jumped at her nor moved. They stared back with equal intent.

"Come, girl. Don't dawdle." Lady Stapleton waved her hand. "Your father will be waiting."

"Yes, Mother." Lady Violet ducked her head. Picking up her skirts, she tiptoed through the surrounding cats over to her mother's side.

"Gracious. How unusual. I wonder . . ." Aunt Clare's face turned vague.

"Oh, Sherrice. How could you?" Lady Norton moaned. That stricken lady crawled to all fours and then hoisted herself up. Her eyes teared as she looked to her daughter.

"Oh, Mother, do stop the tragedy airs. I only tried smoking once. That isn't even mine!"

Matthew rose stealthily as Lady Norton proceeded to remonstrate with Lady Sherrice, all to the edification of the Stapletons. His panther stride did not bode well as he approached.

However, he smiled as he offered his assistance in helping Lady Estelle to rise. "Are you all right, Lady Estelle?"

"Yes, my lord." Lady Estelle nodded. Her complexion was ghostly. "I-I do not know why I swooned."

"No doubt from such commotion." Matthew glared at Aunt Clare. "Did you plan this?"

"What, dear?" Aunt Clare rose, bewilderment rife upon her face.

Penelope sprang up. "Of course she did not."

Cecily stood with a laugh. "I doubt anyone could have planned such. Your cats are far more entertaining than the horses at Astleys, Aunt Clare."

"Why, thank you, dear." Aunt Clare broke into a proud beam. "Horses are quite useful creatures, in their way, and where would we be without them? But cats are by far the more interesting creature . . ." She halted, since a low rumble emitted from Matthew. "Oh dear. I am . . . I believe I am digressing. I do mean to apologize, Matthew. Indeed I do. I should not have permitted the kitties to run ahead of me. I know their company manners are not up to snuff."

"You could not have realized what would happen," Penelope said firmly. Lady Estelle's gentle assurances and Cecily's vigorous nod should certainly set Matthew back.

"Indeed." Aunt Clare sighed. "It is very lowering. I have tried for years to teach them etiquette. I do not know why you think I would applaud their ill manners."

Matthew had the grace to look embarrassed. "Very well. It is of no significance."

"Indeed." Penelope's good humor returned. She knew very well what nettled Matthew. His future brides and their respective mothers had not exactly shone in the past episode. A smile unwittingly crossed her face.

"What are you smiling about? It is not amusing." Matthew turned his glare upon her in full force.

"What?" Her smile split into a grin. She didn't know why, but she was going to do it. "Aunt Clare, are you positive you wish to return to London at this moment?"

"Penelope, don't you dare . . ." Matthew glowered at her.

Aunt Clare blinked. "Why, no, to tell you the truth. I rarely leave town, and I find the country delightful."

"Then please do consider remaining with me for a visit. I have enjoyed your company tremendously."

"You have?" Aunt Clare's face brightened.

"Indeed. I have not had so much diversion since I can remember." The sad part of the tale was that she spoke the truth.

"I know I-I have been pleased to meet you, Aunt Clare," Lady Estelle said softly.

"I quite agree." Cecily nodded her head. "I've always wanted to meet you after the story my fath . . ." She halted, her blue eyes widening. She peeked at Matthew. "Er . . ."

"Then it is settled," Penelope said.

"Penelope, no!" Matthew spoke so harshly that Lady Estelle jumped. Penelope merely tilted her chin. "You cannot . . ."

"Hello, ladies, we should be finished in a moment, what?" Sir Morris, a short, energetic man strode into the hall. He halted abruptly and peered about. "Would you look at all the pusses." His white, bushy brows shot up to his balding pate. "I say, is that fat cat over there smoking a cigar?"

"No, he needs you to light it for him." Lady Steepleton guffawed.

"Penelope. You cannot permit Aunt Clare to remain," Matthew repeated, and loudly at that.

"What the devil?" Jacob Lancer pounded across the flagstone floor at that moment. Needless to say, he looked worse than normal. His eyes were bloodshot, his face unshaved, and his jacket appeared to be pulled over his nightshirt.

"Father." Penelope's heart sank. Now they were truly in the suds. Until she noticed that he swung his cane about quite adroitly and that there was a spring to his gouty step. Yes, he *had* partaken of the hair of the dog that bit him.

Jacob Lancer glared at her. "B'gad, are you not shot of them all yet? What did I tell you, gal?"

"I am trying, Father." Penelope glared at Matthew. "Only *he* won't go!"

"I will with pleasure, I assure you." Matthew bowed, his face stubborn. "Once I escort Aunt Clare from here, that is."

"She needs no escort," Penelope said firmly. "Aunt Clare is visiting me. She remains."

"What?" Jacob's eye popped wide, showing the web of red veins to a greater extent.

"Yes, Father . . ." Penelope began. She would have to do some quick talking to cozen her father into permitting anyone to remain at Lancer Hall. She couldn't remember the last time they had had guests. But now that she had said it, she truly wanted it.

"Aunt Clare is not staying." Matthew clenched his fists. "I warn you, Penelope . . ."

"Here, now!" Jacob shook his cane. "You ain't going to order my Penelope about, Severs. Not under my roof, confound it. This Aunt Clare, whoever she is, can stay if my Penelope wants it."

Penelope's mouth fell open. Then she clamped it shut with a smug smile. She hadn't needed to do any fancy talking. Matthew had done it all for her. Jacob Lancer might order her about, but no one else dared do so.

"Now get out of my house, Severs, before I take this cane to you!" Jacob lifted it high only to freeze. He blinked, his gaze veering away in distraction. "Gad's, but that cat there looks like he is smoking."

"The devil confound it!" Matthew Severs threw up his hand and spinning, strode from the hall.

It was amazing how everyone scurried then, and without the threat of Jacob's cane. Penelope watched wide-eyed as they all disappeared. The lords. The ladies. The bandboxes and trunks. The footmen.

Then the great hall fell silent. Aunt Clare, Penelope, Jacob Lancer, and twelve cats were the sole remaining occupants.

"Thank God," Jacob Lancer growled. "Perhaps now we can have some peace and quiet. Blast. I'm going to have a calming drink. Me nerves are shot!" The cats all meowed and followed him as he hobbled toward the drawing room.

"Father, you have had more than enough drink!" Penelope cried. Now that the danger was past, she simply must consider his health.

"Kitties! You are not to imbibe either!" Aunt Clare called out. "The gentleman will do fine without your camaraderie, I am sure."

Penelope looked at her. "Never say they drink?"

"They tipple a bit." Remorse filled Aunt Clare's blue eyes. "It is an unfortunate habit they acquired when they kept company with Matthew and the boys."

Penelope stared. Then she laughed. She placed an arm about the dear little lady. "I am so very glad I invited you to stay."

"I am, too, dear." Aunt Clare's voice was sincere. "I did not look forward to instructing Meeker to break the wheel on the carriage."

"I beg your pardon?" Penelope asked. Then she raised her hand. "No, I believe I understand."

"I knew you would." Aunt Clare beamed at her. "Isn't it so very nice when you discover someone to whom you need not explain things?" She sighed. "It seems that these days I am always trying to explain myself. Which is very odd. Bendford says I am a perfect widgeon, and indeed, I am. But I have come to the conclusion that the simpler a person is, the more people will not understand them."

Matthew paced across the library carpet. He glanced at the ornamental clock upon the mantel. Soon Lady Estelle Hastings would be stepping through that door. Soon he would be asking for her hand in marriage.

Gad's, but he could use a brandy. He grimaced. He couldn't very well take a quick nip before Lady Estelle arrived, could he? That would be no way to offer for a lady, reeking of brandy. And Lady Estelle was definitely a lady. Charming, but calm and soothing. She would make a lovely wife, to be sure.

A knock at the door sounded. Matthew stiffened. Straightening his jacket, he drew in a deep breath. "Enter."

The door opened. Matthew blinked as Lady Florence entered instead of Lady Estelle. "Mother, what are you doing here? Lady Estelle should be here at any minute."

"I know, dear." Lady Florence bustled over to him. "I only wished to ascertain whether you were prepared."

Matthew grimaced. "I am prepared as I will ever be."

"Excellent." Lady Florence reached out and straightened his jacket lapels. A frown of concern marred her face. "Are you positive that you wish to propose to Lady Estelle so quickly?"

"Of course." Matthew eyed his mother closely. "Why? Do you wish to change your vote?"

"No, dear," Lady Florence said. "We have all agreed that she appears the best candidate. Only . . . they are to be here for two weeks, if you wished to wait a few more days."

"No. I do not intend to give Aunt Clare a moment to do anything. I intend to move so swiftly that she cannot interfere. I doubt she would expect me to propose so quickly."

Lady Florence's expression was dubious. She looked as if she were going to speak, but then pressed her lips together. She reached into her pocket. "In that case, I do believe you should have this, my love."

"What . . . ?" Matthew clamped his mouth shut as she offered him the family engagement ring. He took it with steady hands. His spirit, however, shook. "Yes. I do not know how I could have forgotten this."

"It is understandable," Lady Florence said. "With so much upon your mind, how could you remember? Everything has been at sixes and sevens, what with you chasing after your house guests and all." She stepped back and studied him. Reaching up, she twitched a fold of his cravat. She sighed. "I am very proud of you, son."

"Thank you." Strange, he felt like a complete cad himself. The engagement ring burned in his hand. In a moment he would offer it to a lady whom he knew little or nothing about. The only thing he knew was that he and his family had sat down and cast votes as to which of the four ladies should be approached first. Lady Estelle had won, all hands down.

"I'd best leave you before Lady Estelle arrives." Offering him a motherly smile, tinged with outright conspiracy, Lady Florence tiptoed from the library, waving before she closed the door.

Matthew sighed and ran his hand across his forehead. Faith, he wished this was done with already. He should not suffer such qualms. He had already spoken to Lady Estelle's father this morning. Lord Hastings had been in high alts and had vowed that Lady Estelle would be, too. They had set this appointment time for Lady Estelle and him to meet, apart from the other guests. Matthew had chosen to arrive early. Now he wondered what he could have been thinking.

He shook his head. There would be nothing to it. This was an arrangement of convenience and naught more.

A knock sounded upon the door. Matthew buried the ring in his vest pocket. "Enter."

The door slipped open. Monica and Christine slipped into the room. Their arms were full. Flowers mingled with boxes of candy and jars of preserves. Christine also carried one large ornamental vase.

Matthew groaned. "Lord, what do you two want?"

Monica glanced around quickly. "Good. We are not too late. We thought you might wish to give these to Lady Estelle." She traipsed over and heaved her armload onto the settee.

"What?"

"Yes." Christine nodded and proceeded to release hers as well. "You should offer a lady gifts, I have heard."

Matthew stared. The assortment was worse than he had imagined. "If I were a traveling tinker I might offer her such, yes."

"We did our best." Monica's voice displayed deep hurt.

"We were rather rushed," Christine admitted.

Matthew shook his head, grinning. "Do not be concerned. Mother was here before you. She remembered the best gift. The family engagement ring."

"Bully for Mother!" Monica exclaimed.

"Yes. We had not thought of that." Christine crossed to him. Very solemnly, she delved in her pocket and withdrew a slip of paper. "Here."

"What is this?" Matthew took the sheet and studied it. *"My dearest, my love . . .* what the devil?"

"In case you become tongue-tied and do not know what to say." Monica frowned at him, very much like a governess. "I wrote it down for you."

"And here is what I think you should say." Christine jabbed another slip of paper at him.

Matthew lifted a brow as he pursued it. *"I will love you and your money for life. I have famous sisters, too."*

"I was trying for the honest approach."

Matthew rolled his eyes. He leveled a stern look upon them. "Both of you out, now!"

The girls knew the look. They scurried from the room. Matthew stared down at the papers. Then he walked to the settee and rummaged through their offerings. They clearly had gone through the house, picking as they went. He worried they might have visited the attic as well.

He sighed. At fourteen and fifteen they were precocious and unmanageable. Their governess had quit four months ago after failing to be paid for the quarter. It was another reason for him to wed Lady Estelle Hastings. Under her tutelage, the girls would learn the full graces of being ladies of the *ton*. At present they were but two innocent hoydens and nothing more. His mother was a dear, but she never stood upon ceremony herself. She also detested society. Lady Estelle could take over the girls' training and fire them off far more appropriately.

Another knock sounded at the door. Matthew grimaced. He supposed it would now be Andrew come to advise him. "Enter. And do be quick about it."

"I-I beg your pardon?" Lady Estelle's gentle voice quizzed with hesitation.

Matthew spun, a chipped statue in his hand. "Lady Estelle. Forgive me. I thought you were someone else."

She flushed. "Was I not to meet you at this time?"

"Yes, yes, you were." Matthew strode over to her,

offering his most reassuring smile. "Do come in and have a seat."

"Th-thank you." Lady Estelle's gaze skittered to the settee. She gasped. "Oh, dear."

"Er, yes." Matthew mentally accepted defeat. He offered her the cracked statue. "These are presents for you from my sisters. And me, of course."

"I see." Lady Estelle, a dazed look to her large brown eyes, walked to the settee. She gazed down at the array for a moment. Her voice was soft and almost inaudible. "Th-that w-was v-very kind of them. And you, of course."

"I am glad you approve." Matthew sighed in relief and moved quickly to her. When she looked up, he sucked in his breath. Tears glistened in her eyes. Faith, but he hated tears. They always unmanned him. He hadn't realized Lady Estelle was so very emotional.

Thinking hard, Matthew dropped the statue and dug into his pocket. If he worked fast, he might escape them. "Er . . . Lady Estelle . . . I-I beg of you . . ." Blast, one tear was slipping down her cheek. "Please, do not cry."

"Forgive me." Lady Estelle choked and dashed the tear away. "I-I do not mean to be a watering pot."

"No. It is understandable. This is a—ah, momentous occasion, what?" Matthew desperately stuck out the family ring. It was a magnificent emerald. It was rather famous for its worth and beauty. It still stunned Matthew that the family had not pawned it before this. He smiled gently as she gasped. "Could this perchance cheer you up? I believe it would look lovely upon your finger. May I?"

"Y-yes, you may." Lady Estelle held out a slim, trembling hand. A wracking sob came from her.

Matthew frowned. "If you do not care for it, we . . ."

"No. It—it is lovely." Lady Estelle wept. "Please . . . please forgive me. I-I am overwhelmed. That is all. Pray, pay me no heed."

Matthew clenched his teeth. She was asking the impossible. He never could ignore tears on a woman. He stepped forward and placed the ring upon her finger. "Certainly."

"Thank you." Lady Estelle broke into a fresh waterspout of tears.

"Ah, sweetings, do not cry." Matthew wrapped his arms about her. She clung to him, sobbing all the harder.

"I-I am sorry."

"No, I understand," Matthew soothed in a strained voice. He mustered a smile. "I have an excellent notion. Why don't you dry your eyes and then you can go and show the ring to your parents and the others." Matthew winced. Gad's, he was treating her like he did Christine or Monica. Lady Estelle choked on another lament. "You do not like that? What? What can I do?"

"N-nothing." Lady Estelle looked up at him, her eyes red. "Y-you are being so very kind. I—I sh-shall go and—and do just what you said."

"That's a good girl." Matthew, relieved beyond relief, bent down and kissed her quickly.

Lady Estelle gasped and drew back, staring at him. Matthew tensed, an unpleasant memory asserting itself. Faith, would she now call him a dunderhead, too?

Lady Estelle merely burst into louder sobs. "I-I will l-leave you know. Thank you. Y-you have honored m-me."

"And you me." Matthew gratefully stepped back and let his new fiancée flee the room. He sighed deeply as the door closed upon her.

"Gad's, but that was rough," Andrew's voice said from the corner of the room. "I would say that a brandy is in order, what?"

Matthew spun about in shock. Andrew stepped out from behind the Oriental screen at the far left of the room. He was about to castigate his brother, until he noted that Andrew held a brandy bottle in his hand. "Thank God, yes."

Andrew strolled forward, his gaze awed. "I thought you might need one after doing the deed. But Gad's, it was worse than I would have imagined."

"Wasn't it, though?" Matthew approached Andrew and commissioned the bottle.

"Forsooth. I never knew a woman could cry so much."

"Neither did I." Matthew gulped from the bottle.

"She cried even when you kissed her. I was impressed with your courage, old man."

"It could have been worse." At least Lady Estelle hadn't called him a dunderhead.

"What is worse than a woman crying when you kiss her?"

Matthew paused. He weighed both situations once more. A wry grin crossed his lips. "Actually, now that I consider it, nothing. And I should know."

"And she cried when . . ."

"Andrew. Enough." Matthew cringed.

The door swung open at that moment. Lady Florence entered. Alarm stamped her face. "What happened? I saw Miss Hastings run past in tears. Never say she refused you?"

Matthew didn't even bother to ask where his mother had stationed herself. "No. She accepted."

"Thank God!" Lady Florence sighed in relief.

"Better not do that yet, Mother, love." Andrew shook his head. "Matthew's bride is a woman of sensibilities, I fear. 'Deed, she's a watering pot. An absolute fountain."

Matthew's head shot up at the last word. Once again, he saw Penelope's face upturned to him, muddied and laughing in the rain. He shook it to clear it.

"Oh dear." Lady Florence rushed over to a cabinet, opening its doors. Within it rested a silver tray, a decanter of sherry, and glasses. She reached in hastily.

"What happened?" Christine dashed into the room. "What happened?"

"Yes?" Monica was directly behind her. "Did she like our gifts?"

"She certainly did." Matthew forced a smile. "She was . . ."

"Overwhelmed," Andrew said solemnly.

Christine glanced to Lady Florence, who was intently pouring herself a drink. She then narrowed her look upon Matthew with the brandy bottle. "It didn't go well, did it? All of you are drinking. What happened? Did you muff it? You should have read what we wrote."

"Gad's, no." It was Andrew who yelped it. "That would have caused a monsoon, I don't doubt."

"I told you we should have eavesdropped," Monica said in too loud a whisper.

"No." Matthew gripped his glass and tried for a reassuring voice. "Everything went well. Exceedingly well."

"Yes. We are merely celebrating, girls." Lady Florence sipped from her sherry. Her face was determined, even as her glass shook. "We will have a new member in the family, after all."

"And just remember," Andrew's crooked grin was irrepressible, "when she droops and sobs all over you, that we aren't in a sponging house and that it's a good thing."

Four

"Oh dear. I do not know what to say." Aunt Clare wrung her hands. "Peaches and Cream have never behaved this way before."

"They have never lived with my father before." Penelope laughed. She clung to the library ladder and looked up. The two cats sat perched two more shelves out of reach, glaring at her. They and Jacob Lancer had suffered a confrontation. In escape they had crawled to the top of the library shelves. Her father had retreated in the opposite direction, stalking out of the library in a rage.

"But they have lived with my brother Bendford, who can be extremely fractious at times. Cross as crabs to be exact." Aunt Clare frowned. "What he has threatened in the past to do to my poor kitties is frightful."

"Your brother and my father should meet, I believe." Penelope climbed one more step. She gazed at the two cats, who burrowed deeper between the volumes of Aristotle and Plato. "Here, kitties. Surely you cannot enjoy such dull reading. Wouldn't a nice bowl of milk be more digestible?"

"Meow," Peaches said, sounding half-coaxed.

"Brr," Cream said, apparently not to be mollified by such paltry fare.

"Bendford and your father will meet, I am sure. I

can only hope, however, that they do not do so too quickly. Bendford has threatened to come and retrieve me. He does not take my absence well, I am pleased to tell you.''

"Aunt Clare, how can you say that?'' Penelope laughed. One thing about Aunt Clare was that she was astonishingly open, so far from Matthew's image of a conniver that Penelope could not meld the two pictures together. Aunt Clare's ramblings clearly came from the heart. Indeed, she would express solicitude over the sensibilities of a poor fly in one sentence and, in the next, voice concern over what the Great Almighty's intentions for the whole of the universe might be. All this without belittling either in her perambulations.

"I know, dear, that I should not be as overjoyed as I am.'' Aunt Clare sighed. "Except, I have always thought that my absence would not be noticed by Bendford if I ever disappeared. That it would be a case of out of sight, out of mind. Still, I left him Ruppleton and Wilson and that was assuredly a great sacrifice. I do wonder if I have not made a dreadful mistake. I do miss them dreadfully.''

"Do you?'' Penelope had discovered these two famous personages were not only Aunt Clare's butler and chef, but also her two henchmen in her matchmaking schemes. "I would have thought with all the missives and messengers sent back and forth from your home to here that you would not.'' Aunt Clare had received more mail in the past three days than Penelope had within her entire life. It could not help but make a girl wistful. Even Jacob Lancer, a determined recluse claiming to want nothing to do with society, whistled over the names of the great, titled gentlemen and ladies who corresponded with Aunt Clare.

"That is helpful, yes. But it is not the same as if they

were here. I can but describe the situations and people to them."

"Miss Penelope . . ." Finch's voice said.

"Yes?" Penelope glanced back. She quickly clung to the ladder. Matthew stood directly behind Finch. She had wondered, after she withstood his anger and insisted Aunt Clare remain a guest with her, if she would ever see him again.

She told herself that her concern about ever seeing him again was no more than a result of Aunt Clare's incessant talk about him for three days straight. And when she did not ramble on about him, she was quizzing Penelope for every memory she had of Matthew. Wild horses would not have dragged it from her, but Penelope had found it a relief to be able to finally talk, and to reminisce, about Matthew. Her father had refused to have the Severs name, or any reference to the House of Raleigh, spoken under his roof following the feud. Indeed, Penelope had talked so much about Matthew these past days that she was sure she had managed to talk him out of her system. She was over her infatuation with him. "Yes?"

"My Lord Severs wishes an audience," Finch offered quickly, his face dismayed. For a proper introduction it lacked proper pacing, but with the object of the introduction breathing down one's back, what was a butler to do?

"Where is she, Aunt Clare?" Matthew brushed past Finch and forged into the library. His expression was direct and dark.

"Where is whom, dear?" Aunt Clare frowned.

"Good morning, my lord." Penelope smiled and nodded as if they were at high tea. "How pleasant to see you. Please do come in. Please do have a seat. It is lovely weather we are having, is it not?"

Matthew halted. He frowned. "What are you doing up there?"

"I am trying to retrieve Peaches and Cream. Father drove them up here."

"I am not surprised," Matthew said curtly.

"Dearest, again, who are you talking about?" Aunt Clare asked.

Matthew glared at her. "Do not play the innocent. You know very well who I am talking about."

"No, I do not think I do."

Matthew growled and glanced back up at Penelope. "Come down from there, Penn. It is dangerous."

Penelope narrowed her gaze. Matthew looked frightful. His eyes were bloodshot, his face unshaven. Instead of his usual pristine cravat, he was sporting a Belcher scarf. His buff unmentionables and his high boots were powdered with dust. "Did you shoot the cat last night?"

"No, I did not. Though I was tempted. Very tempted. I had but one, very well, two, congratulatory drinks." His voice was as rough as he appeared. He moved to the bottom of the ladder. "Did you help Aunt Clare? She can persuade a dead man to assist her. Now come down from there. I will retrieve Peaches and Cream."

Penelope lifted her brow. "Not with that odious temper you are displaying. You'll be paid short shrift. They are not dumb creatures."

"Help me with what, dear?" Aunt Clare persisted. "And who am I supposed to know you were talking about?"

Penelope stiffened. Intuition struck her like a cold wind. A very cold and lonely wind. "Wh-who did you propose to, Matthew?"

"Propose! Oh dear, no." Aunt Clare wrung her hands. "Did you propose already, Matthew?"

"I did," Matthew said curtly. "But you know that. Now come down, Penelope, before I come and get you."

"Yes." Penelope could not fight. She felt drained of

energy. Strange. Stupid. It should not affect her. She had been positive she had escaped her childhood crush upon him. She numbly climbed down. Matthew assisted her from the last rung.

Penelope stood frozen, the ground feeling no steadier. "Who, Matthew?"

"Lady Estelle. And she disappeared this very morning."

"Gracious!" Aunt Clare exclaimed.

"Yes, so very shocking, what?" Matthew's voice was viscious as he grabbed hold of the ladder and climbed it. "Now, where is she, Aunt? Peaches and Cream, come here. This instant."

"When did you propose?" Penelope asked. "When did you have time?"

"Confound it, Peaches and Cream, I am warning you to come here now! I tell you, I will brook no argument from you."

Such was the force of his command, and his voice, that Peaches and Cream moved post haste. They scrabbled from the books and well nigh became flying cats as they jumped to Matthew's shoulders. Penelope's eyes widened—partly due to the fact that the cats certainly had honored Matthew with their obedience, partly due to the fact that such a large, masculine man appeared rather humorous with two felines nesting upon his shoulders, batting the tips of his neck scarf.

"That was wise of you," Matthew murmured to the cats. "Mind you, watch those claws if you are going to accompany me."

Aunt Clare sighed gustily. "He is so heroic, isn't he?"

Penelope bit her lip. She should laugh. Except, as silly as it was, she rather thought so, too. Feeling that warm, weak feeling invade her, Penelope steeled herself. "Matthew, just when did you propose?"

"Yesterday." Matthew backed slowly down the ladder, the two cats swaying.

"Yesterday?" The warm, weak feeling dispersed directly. "Gracious. You did not give poor Lady Estelle one day to settle into your house. What manner of host, let alone suitor, are you?"

"Why did you choose Estelle, dear?" Aunt Clare asked, her voice strong with curiosity.

Matthew descended and turned. Penelope could hear the cats purring. They were clearly feeling rather smart in catching a human carriage down. "She won the . . ." He halted. His gaze grew closed. "I proposed to her after deep consideration and advice from the family."

Penelope well knew his devil-may-care family. His first words were not overlooked. "You . . . you took a vote upon it. She won the vote, didn't she? Matthew, how could you?"

He stiffened. A tendon leapt upon his cheek. "She will be part of my family. Why should they not be permitted a say in the matter?"

"Peaches, scratch him. Cream, claw him," Penelope muttered. She knew how Matthew loved his family. Indeed, the protection of it was clearly a deep responsibility and priority to him. But that he let the family cast votes upon his choice of wife was the outside of enough.

Matthew's gaze turned cold. "Do not make out that I am unconscionable. Rather I ask how conscionable was it of Aunt Clare to steal away my fiancée?"

"She must *like* Lady Estelle," Penelope retorted. "And wished to save her from you."

"Penelope!" Aunt Clare gasped.

"Well." Penelope bit her lip. She was certainly the ill-mannered cat at the moment, and she knew it.

"So!" Matthew's tone dripped triumph. "You did help her steal away Lady Estelle."

Penelope stared. Gracious! How had he taken that turn? "No, I did not."

"Of course she didn't. She is totally innocent. You must not blame her." Aunt Clare exclaimed. Then she blinked. "Heavens, what am I saying? You mustn't blame me, either. I did not steal Estelle. Truly! I did not even know you had proposed to her."

"She thought you might possess more style than to pop the question the first day a poor girl arrives at your doorstep."

"Severs!" Jacob Lancer's voice rang through library. "What are you doing here?"

The cats jumped. As did Penelope and Aunt Clare.

"Soft paws, please, Peaches and Cream." Matthew did not jump and his voice was calm. He turned and leveled a look upon Jacob, who had come into the room without notice. "I am here for my bride, sir."

"What?" Jacob's face turned ashen. He rapped the cane to the floor. "You will never get my Penelope. Never! Do you hear me?"

"No, Father," Penelope flushed in mortification. "Matthew seeks Lady Estelle. She . . . she is his affianced."

"Lady Estelle?" Color ebbed back into Jacob's face. "Who the devil is she?"

"She was one of the ladies who visited us, Father."

"I see. I thought the gel had departed with the rest of the lot. She didn't leave?"

"She did," Penelope said.

"Then why are you here, Severs? We do not have the gel."

"He thinks Aunt Clare stole her," Penelope said with disdain.

Jacob studied Aunt Clare, his eyes brightening. "Good. Bedevil him all you want. Gad's hounds, but I hooted when I heard you had kidnapped Severs before. Now you've made off with his new fiancée. That's good. Very good."

"Father, you knew about Matthew's abduction?" Penelope gasped. "Why did you not tell me?"

Jacob flushed. "I heard the gossip from Theodore. I did not deem it anything necessary for you to know."

"This is no jest," Matthew said sternly. "I proposed to Lady Estelle yesterday afternoon. This morning she has disappeared. I know the story line very well. None of her possessions have been taken. Only she has been taken."

"Oh, no!" Aunt Clare gasped. Her eyes widened and she covered her mouth. "Gracious!"

"Aunt Clare," Matthew said in a threatening tone. "What did you do?"

"I did not do anything . . . much, that is."

"You cannot cast the blame on Aunt Clare," Penelope said vehemently. "She has been here at the hall since the first day. I shall vouch for her."

"She is involved." Matthew nodded toward Aunt Clare. "I can tell by her face that she is."

In truth, guilt was rife upon the lady's face. "Matthew dear, I did not steal away Lady Estelle."

"What did you do with her?" Matthew persisted.

Aunt Clare turned a bright red. "*I* did not do anything with her. But . . . but, I think I know what . . . I mean where, she might have . . . er, disappeared."

"Aunt Clare," Penelope gasped. "Do you?"

"She and I had a small talk that one night." Aunt Clare clasped her hands together, rather in the pleading style of a woman before a hangman. "It was not much of a talk. Truly, just a tiny, tiny talk. Only, I fear I have had what is called a hunch."

"Not a foreboding?" Matthew asked dryly.

"Oh no, dear. A hunch is different. It comes from having certain signs."

"Signs?" Penelope asked before Matthew could.

"Yes. People give them to you. Only signs do not make much sense until there are enough to give you a hunch."

"Really?" Penelope frowned in deep consideration.

"Aunt Clare." Matthew frowned for a different reason. "You are trying to lead this conversation away from the facts. And the fact is you stole my bride and you won't gull me into believing anything else."

Aunt Clare wrung her hands. "I vow I did not. But I do know where she went if my hunch is correct."

"Where did she go then?" Matthew asked, his voice impatient.

"Yes." Jacob laughed. "Where did she run to escape Severs here?"

"Father, for shame." Penelope frowned.

Aunt Clare truly looked as if she were being put to the question by the Inquisitor, rather than merely Matthew and Jacob. "I-I dare not tell you. If my hunch was wrong and I divulge what I had learned from dear Estelle, why, the consequences might be tragic. Not to mention that it would be completely dishonorable of me."

Matthew nodded. "Of course, Aunt Clare. I understand."

Relief flooded her face. "You do?"

"Indeed I do." Matthew's smile wasn't pleasant. "Very neat. I applaud your style. You tempt me with admitting you know where Lady Estelle is, but then inform me you cannot tell me for it would not be honorable."

"That is it." Aunt Clare beamed.

Penelope groaned. Aunt Clare's wits weren't halfway a match for Matthew's distrust. "Aunt Clare, he is being fractious."

"I beg your pardon?" Aunt Clare asked.

"Heh. She's a pip," Penelope's own father said with approval. "She has you rolled up, Severs. The boot is on the other foot. She's cheating you like your father cheated me."

"No!" Penelope said quickly, angrily. "We will have no discussion of the past. And Aunt Clare is *not* cheating anyone. I believe her."

"Thank you, dear." Aunt Clare peeked at Matthew. "If you will go with me, I will lead you to Lady Estelle.

But . . . but I will not tell you now why I think what I think."

"No, Aunt Clare." Matthew crossed his arms. "I am not going to let you make a May game of me. I am not chasing all over the country with you. I know that ploy. Remember, we helped you when you sent Lady Julia and Stanwood cavorting about, hither and yon. Do you take me for a flat?"

"Wait one moment." Penelope frowned. "Aunt Clare is telling you that she knows where Lady Estelle is, your future *bride*, mind you, and is asking you to go with her. Are you truly refusing to do so?"

"That is right," Matthew gritted out.

"Oh, dear." Aunt Clare wrung her hands. "This is all my fault. I did not plan for Estelle to take off to . . . well, never would I have advised that. Never. I . . . oh dear. I do not know what to do now."

Penelope studied Aunt Clare's tormented face. She glanced only once at Matthew's exhausted features. It was more than she could bear and she would not stand for it. "Well, I know what to do. We will go after Lady Estelle. You and I, Aunt Clare."

"What?" Matthew shouted. Peaches and Cream hissed and sprang from his shoulder.

"What?" Jacob dropped his cane.

"You do wish to have Lady Estelle as your bride, do you not?" Penelope asked coolly of Matthew. She would not wait to hear his affirmation. There was only so much a woman should take. "However, you do not trust Aunt Clare and her hunch. Whereas, I do. Therefore, she and I will go after Lady Estelle. If Aunt Clare is wrong, no one has played the fool but she and me."

"No, Penelope, you will not go after my bride," Matthew commanded.

"You cannot leave me," Jacob spouted.

"I will not permit it," Matthew said

"I won't allow it!" Jacob concurred.

Matthew started in astonishment. Jacob jumped back

in surprise. They looked at each other, both expressions appalled.

Penelope stifled a chuckle. "How nice. We are all in agreement for once. Aunt Clare and I are going after Lady Estelle."

"Gracious, it does feel exactly as I have read about." Aunt Clare's face showed sheer enjoyment as she stood ankle-high in the rushing, babbling stream. "I feel just like those heroines in the books. Isn't this a great adventure?"

"It is." Penelope laughed. She should be above it, but she felt the same. This very morning, with carriage piled high, she and Aunt Clare had taken off in search of Lady Estelle. They had successfully brooked Jacob Lancer's fury. Penelope had never done so before and was amazed to discover the world had not ended by her revolt.

Of course, she and Aunt Clare had been somewhat nefarious in taking off that morning. They knew Jacob was still laid low from finding succor in an excellent port—succor from a disobedient daughter. Penelope didn't want to imagine what state of inebriation her father would be in when she returned, but at least the sky had not fallen. Indeed, it was bright and sunny today and surely the brightest blue Penelope had ever seen it be.

Rather flushed with triumph, the ladies had decided in favor of stopping for an impromptu picnic beside a bubbling stream, rather than eating in the traveling carriage. They had packed it specifically that they might make good time upon the journey, wherever it may take them. But they had been in agreement. The moss-covered bank and the rippling waters were just too delightful to ignore for the sake of timeliness.

It had been Aunt Clare's suggestion then that they might wade in the stream which looked so very refreshing as the noon sun heated them. She had dithered on about the country heroines of her favorite novels. Each, sweet and pure, would always be discovered in this bucolic pastime by the reprobate hero. She assured Penelope he would come upon the damsel and fall deeply in love with her, then and there.

Smiling, Penelope hiked the skirts of her sky-blue crepe carriage dress even higher, feeling safe in doing so. Her plaited straw hat dangled by its nankeen ribbons, tied and looped over one arm. She had removed her jonquil-and-white striped fichu from its modest drape around her neck and had used it to tie back her hair. They had sent Meeker, Aunt Clare's coachman, off for a nap farther down the stream. Even the only other male of the traveling party, Sir Percy, was not about, having gone after a bird or squirrel tidbit. "Tell me another of those romantic stories, please, Aunt Clare."

"Have you never read any? Penelope, they are wondrous." Aunt Clare rather danced in place as she kicked up the water. "You should read them, my dear."

"I intend to do so." Penelope had always been so busy about her father's household that the only matter she read had been recipes and the physics' directions. Certainly she had never had time for novels of the romantic bent. Now it seemed so very important that she expand her world. Perhaps it was because of Aunt Clare's presence. The lady had such a youthful exuberance for a woman her age. Which made Penelope realize that she herself had a rather old staidness for a girl her age. She smiled at the picture of Aunt Clare poking a tree branch at a broad-leafed plant growing between two stepping-stones along the brook's edge. Aunt Clare's inquisitive expression was framed by a poke bonnet, its sheer muslin scarf pulled tight across the brim and tied down around her chin in a jaunty bow. The wide brim of the hat rose from its confines of the veil to two exaggerated points, one at each side of her head, the whole effect looking like two pointed ears. Penelope chuckled to herself. Add the *coup de grâce*, Aunt Clare's dove-gray crepe dress layered over tiers of creamy Mechlin lace, and she reminded Penelope of Esther, Clare's gray-and-white tabby. Penelope sighed contentedly. There was far too much in common between Aunt Clare and her. Witness the two of them standing in a stream, feeling positively wicked and free.

"And the Greek ladies were always meeting gods beside the waters for dalliances." Aunt Clare flushed. "They seemed to be caught out in their ablutions far too often. I do not believe I would care for that, even if it were Apollo who came peeking. I am so very glad to be English. We do not tolerate such rudesby behavior."

Penelope laughed. Then she squealed as something flashed through her toes. She hopped up and down as it fluttered at her ankles. "Oh my!"

"What is it, dear?" Aunt Clare asked. Then she, too, squealed and splashed about. "Oh my. Oh my."

"It must be a fish." Penelope started to laugh, but it was cut short. The sound of thundering hooves approaching could do that to a girl standing defenseless in a pond. Her eyes widened as a man upon a gleaming stallion galloped *ventre à terre* down upon them. He held a large Manton high, its metal gleaming in the sun.

"Oh, yes." Aunt Clare breathed. "Just like that, dear Penelope. That is how the hero arrives."

Penelope could only nod, her voice gone for a moment. Brilliant blue eyes blazed beneath dark, flaring brows. He did look saturnine, and yes, his heart was cold and jaded. Oh, if he would only be her hero. And if only he could fall in love with her as she stood, the innocent country lass in the stream.

Aunt Clare frowned. "However, he should be wearing a flowing cape."

Penelope chuckled. "Surely not in this heat, Aunt? That would make him addlepated."

"Just what the devil are you two doing?" The hero spoke with suppressed exasperation. The gleam in his eye did not look at all loving.

"We are wading in a stream," Penelope said sunnily. "Please do not shoot us, sirrah—we are but simple country lasses."

Matthew's brows flared high. "I beg your pardon?"

"Please, sir." She dipped a slight curtsy. "Spare us our lives."

"No, no." Aunt Clare murmured. "Those words would be for the villain, Penelope dear."

"Drat." Penelope looked to Matthew. "It must be the pistol that is confusing me."

"Penn, do cut line." Matthew barked a laugh. "I discovered your coach abandoned. Then I heard screams. What was I to think?"

"You came to our rescue, you dear boy." Aunt Clare sighed. "Wasn't that famous of him, Penelope?"

Matthew raised a sardonic brow and dismounted. "What, pray tell, were you two screaming about?" He leveled a stern glare to Aunt Clare. "And do not say you have suffered another foreboding." He uncocked his pistol, shaking his head. "Faith, it is I who have a foreboding. I will no doubt expire from your fits and starts. Done in by anxiety, in truth."

Penelope flushed with warmth. Matthew cared for them. He had followed them, and he was concerned.

"How very chivalrous of you." Aunt Clare beamed. "You came to save us from bandits and cutthroats. That is most charming."

Matthew, grinning, offered as grand a leg as any a chevalier could offer, even though lacking a cape and plumed hat. "I am at your service, my ladies. Now, where are the villains? Forsooth, I shall shoot them dead. Indeed, I would run them through, but I forgot my sword. A terrible oversight."

Penelope's lips twitched. "Did you bring a line and hook perhaps? It would suffice just as well."

"No, I did not." Matthew's brow rose. Then they snapped down. "No. Do not dare to tell me you were screaming in fright from fish, Penn, else I will . . ."

"Very well. It was a serpent," Penelope said solemnly. "A large sea serpent which attacked us."

"Ah, that is better." Matthew strolled down to the water's edge. He frowned narrowly. "Now if you will stand very still, I will shoot the monster."

"No!" Penelope exclaimed. She flushed then to notice that Matthew hadn't even raised his pistol. "I . . ."

A large bellow interrupted her. Penelope gulped as Meeker, Aunt Clare's coachman, came charging out of the woods. He flayed a large stick and ran full tilt at Matthew.

"Hello, Meeker," Matthew greeted calmly, not moving a jot.

Meeker skidded to a halt. His face worked in comical dismay. He lowered the stick and hid it behind his back. "My Lord Severs! Forgive me. I thought . . ."

"Do not tax yourself, old man. I know exactly how you feel." Matthew nodded, his voice kindly commiserating. "These two can give any man gray hairs. It will be an onerous task to protect them upon this journey."

Meeker broke into a large, relieved grin. "Thank God you have come, my lord. I begged Miss Clare not to leave without male escort. Begged and begged, mind you, but she would have none of it."

"Meeker," Aunt Clare said, her voice reproaching. "This was a secret escape from Lancer Hall. We couldn't very well take all of Mr. Lancer's footmen. That would have been most improper."

"Whereas two lone ladies careening about the country by themselves is not?" Matthew gazed at Penelope, a teasing glint in his eyes. "And stopping to wade with hiked skirts is proper, too, I suppose? I never knew you possessed such shapely ankles, Penn."

"You cannot see . . ." Penn looked down. She gasped. She had been so involved she hadn't noticed, but she was indeed displaying a goodly portion of ankle and leg. Mortified, she dropped her skirts, regardless that they fell into the water. "Oh, dear!"

"And Aunt Clare." Matthew shook his head. "If you permit other men to spy your ankles like I have, you will be wed before me."

"Matthew, naughty boy." Aunt Clare giggled.

"I do not mean to be critical," Matthew said, his tone mild, "but is this how you two intend to find my fiancée? Is that what Lady Estelle confessed to you, Aunt Clare? That she wished to go fishing?"

"No, dear Matthew, though I wish she had." Aunt Clare waded from the stream. "It would be ever more pleasant."

"Ah, she confessed her secret desire for a picnic luncheon?" Matthew persisted.

"Do stop roasting us." Penelope picked her way cautiously to land. "We merely stopped because . . . very well, because it is a lovely day."

"That it is." Matthew offered a hand to each. "Is there any food left for me, perchance?"

"No." Penelope flushed. "We did not know you were coming."

"You should have." His eyes sparkled as blue as the sky above.

"Please, do not start with it again." Penelope tried for an irate tone. "Aunt Clare did not plan this . . ."

"No, Penn. Do not fly out at me." Matthew's voice turned gentle. "I only meant that you forced my hand. Do you know how churlish I looked, having you go after my fiancée rather than me?"

"Gammon." Penelope laughed, her spirits soaring. "I am sure you simply could not tolerate the festive atmosphere of your party and made good an escape."

"No. I assure you. My cook heard it from your cook about the ruthless escape you two ladies concocted.

My cook told my mother's maid and mother told me."
His grin twisted. "I will confess, however, that I did
not bruit that about. I informed Lady and Lord Hastings that I felt driven to go in search of Lady Estelle.
I feared Lord Hastings would wish to accompany me.
However, he could not leave Lady Hastings, who is
prostrate with grief."

"I can only imagine," Aunt Clare said. "How very
dreadful this time must be for her."

"Well, I like that," Matthew said. "I am sure you did
not have that much sympathy for my family when you
abducted me."

"But dearest, you were quite safe and sound with
me," Aunt Clare said, her tone reasonable. "I knew
exactly where you were and that made all the difference, don't you see?"

"Yes, Aunt Clare. Certainly." Matthew cast a wry look
to Penelope. "Regardless, I am here. You two ladies
may do the leading. Poor Meeker and I will do the
guarding."

"Wonderful." Aunt Clare clapped her hands together. "This was going to be such an adventure. But
I am sure it will be even nicer with your company."

Matthew cocked a questioning brow at Penelope.
"What do you think, Penn? Can you tolerate my company?"

"I believe so," Penelope said, presenting a demure
image. "Due to the danger of sea serpents, you understand?"

"Indeed." Matthew laughed. "I will keep this pistol
armed and at the ready. I'll not let any serpent harm
you, I promise."

"How very kind." Penelope focused upon adjusting
her skirts. It wasn't sea serpents that she feared. Now,
the thought of being in Matthew's company did make
her tremble.

Five

"What is keeping Aunt Clare?" Penelope said, her voice truly innocent as the servants left the private room of the inn. A large dinner lay spread before them. "She said she forgot her shawl but would be down directly."

"Do not concern yourself." Matthew smiled. He tried to keep the smugness from it. "We'd best not wait for her. Let us eat before it grows cold."

"I beg your pardon?" Penelope looked astonished.

"She is merely playing her games, Penn. She has . . ."

". . . planned this." Penelope sighed. "So you say."

"I am sorry, but she has." Matthew reached for the green beans. "She did this with Lady Julia and Stanwood. She kept sending them notes as to where they were to go. She sent them to the most romantic places until they simply succumbed and fell in love."

"Would you cease?" Penelope's voice was tight. "We are not Julia Wrexton and Garth Stanwood. Not by a long chalk."

Matthew stiffened. "Forgive me. I have offended you."

"No." Penelope looked down. "Forgive me. That was ungracious of me."

"Why have I overset you?"

Penelope glanced up. The amused candor which was very much a part of Penelope showed through. "To tell you the truth, I cannot be as blasé as you. This . . . this *is* an adventure for me. I do not often travel anywhere, let alone after an abducted bride. And though you are sure of the outcome, I am not."

"I see." Matthew frowned.

She lowered her gaze. "Also, your continual reference to two people who did love each other and who Aunt Clare did match together is very lowering." She looked directly at him then, her green eyes soft and luminescent. "Unlike you, some of us *would* like to find true love. I know I would."

Matthew swallowed hard, feeling as if he had been delivered an astonishing blow. Aunt Clare had meandered on over such, dropping insinuations hither and thither, but until now he hadn't thought of Penelope as a woman desiring love. Why not? Because he had left a young girl five years ago, and while they had been separated, she had grown into a woman. His heart twisted. She had grown up, his friend. The girl who had followed him about with wide and adoring eyes was now a woman. "Forgive me, Penn."

"I do," Penelope said, her voice calm. Her lips tugged up into a smile. "I should not be so very snappish. Perhaps I do need to eat." She picked up her fork and delved into her boiled leeks and potatoes. "In fact, if you promise not to constantly liken us to *them*, I would care to hear more of what happened. It amazes me to find that Father has heard the story and has never told me."

Matthew wished to kick himself. She offered him polite conversation now and naught else. "Why *haven't* you ever married, Penn?"

She shrugged, her features controlled. "When and where would I be able to meet a suitable man?"

"True. You live an extremely secluded life." Matthew frowned. "Which can be laid at your father's doorsteps.

He has never permitted you to socialize. He has driven away all the local men. Men who *are* of good virtue and worth. With your fortune behind you, he should have hied you off to London for a season. Instead, he's done everything to keep you tied to him."

"Perhaps." Her discomfort was obvious.

"Please, do not take me wrong," Matthew said quickly. "I have always respected your faithfulness in caring for your father."

"Thank you."

Matthew watched the warm blush rise to Penelope's cheeks. She looked down, not in demureness, but in actual embarrassment of a compliment. "It makes you unique and special, Penn. And you are wrong—I could in no way liken you to Lady Julia. Or any other ladies of the *ton*. You are not worldly or jaded, as they are."

"I do not think Lady Estelle is jaded. Do you?"

"No, no. That is true." Matthew sighed. "But she cries."

"What?" Penelope asked.

Matthew started. What an ungentlemanly thing to have confessed. "Pray, do not heed me."

"If you wish it." Penelope gazed at him with steady, open concern.

Matthew surrendered to that look. "I should not speak of this, but . . . confound it, Penn, I do not know what to make of it. Lady Estelle cried all the way through my proposal."

"She did?" Penelope's look of astonishment soothed Matthew's wounded confidence. "Gracious."

"That is what I thought." He frowned. "Perhaps you can explain it to me. I can make no sense of it. She actually cried, and copiously at that. A veritable watering pot."

"Some women cry when they are happy." Penelope's look was dubious. "I-I would imagine that is what happened."

"I suppose that is the answer." Matthew nodded.

Then he shook his head. "You do not really think that, do you?"

"No. I mean, yes, I do hold that to be so. Surely she was overwhelmed. Many women do cry from the sheer emotion."

"That is what she said."

"There, you see?" Penelope nodded, clearly fond of the theory now. "It makes sense. I myself do not cry often, but I find I am not a lady of sensibilities."

"You do not cry?" Matthew pounced on that.

"Well, perhaps once in a while, I do."

"When is once in a while?" he asked, hoping for enlightenment.

"Oh, when I prick my finger, or stub my toe." Penelope twirled her fork on her plate and her voice lowered to a mumble. "Or maybe late at night."

"Why do you do that?" Matthew asked. Rather, he growled it.

"Do you never have sad dreams?" Penelope glanced up. "I know you would not cry about them—you are a man, after all. But do you have sad dreams sometimes?"

"Of course." Matthew admitted it with a frown. Somehow it was not as bad for him to have them as to know that Penelope suffered them, and that she cried in the middle of the night. "But . . ."

"Tell me about the other couples," Penelope said quickly.

"I beg your pardon?"

"You said that Aunt Clare matched the other men with their true loves as well. Tell me about them?"

Matthew narrowed his gaze upon her. She presented an innocent look as if she hadn't blatantly veered off course from their conversation once again. However, there was just enough tension in her look for Matthew to concede to the detour. "Very well. Aunt Clare proceeded to match the couples in the order that she abducted each of us. Which, in truth, was in the order in which we became engaged to Lady Julia."

"And you were . . ." Penelope stopped. Matthew gritted his teeth when she gasped. "You were number *six*. How could that be? You were . . ."

"Yes," Matthew said, crisply. "I was Lady Julia's sixth choice. Not her first. I did not rank high."

"I did not mean that. But . . ." Penelope gave out an exasperated sigh. "Just how could you have proposed to a woman who had already been engaged so many times before?"

"I did not know she had been engaged that many times," Matthew said in defense. "She . . . once Aunt Clare had abducted her first and second fiancé, removing them from the scene, Lady Julia . . . well, she went upon a proposing jaunt, as it were."

"I beg your pardon?"

"She proposed to *us*, Penelope," Matthew explained with patience. "She did it all in one day and never told any of us she was proposing to and accepting the betrothal of the others as well."

Penelope blinked. She blinked again. And again. Then anger, unmitigated, at that, sparked her eyes. "Do you mean all she had to do was t-to . . . t-to ask you to marry her and you *accepted*. *That was all that was required?*"

"Yes. She is an extremely wealthy heiress." Penelope looked as if she were about to explode. "Why are you so angry?"

"Because I—I am a such a widgeon. A complete ninnyhammer." Penelope's eyes glittered to an emerald green, though no jewel could hold the fire that burned within them. "I did not know it was that simple."

A nervous feeling entered Matthew. "What is that simple?"

Penelope glared at him. "I didn't know that all an heiress need do was propose to a man and snap, she could have herself a husband."

"Now, Penn. Lady Julia is very different from you. You couldn't . . ." Matthew froze at her threatening look.

"What? Have a man, no make that *men*, accept me like Lady Julia did? Why? Because I'm not worldly, or jaded, or as Aunt Clare says, *up to snuff?*" She stood abruptly. "Excuse me."

"No, Penn." Matthew sprang up. "Wait. I did not mean it like that. You know I did not."

"No, I do not know it," She said hotly. "I only know that for days you have spent every moment making me aware that I cannot be considered an eligible female for marriage and that it would take the best of Aunt Clare's schemes and connivance to snag me a husband."

"Penn, I . . ."

"This, even though I have a fortune as great as Lady Julia's!"

"Penn . . ."

"All she had to do was ask, and you accepted, even if you were but sixth on her list! She is an heiress, after all. While even if I am an heiress, I could not hope to . . ."

"Damn it, Penn." Matthew, enraged, circumvented the table in a flash to stand before her. He grabbed hold of her shoulders. "Stop. I never meant to make you think that. You can get a man to marry you within a moment if you wish it!"

"Thank you." Penn's smile was odd. Matthew didn't like the look of it. "That is what I wanted to hear you say. I have but to take a leaf from Lady Julia's book then."

Matthew felt as if the carpet had been pulled out from underneath him. "But you . . . you wouldn't, couldn't do what lady Julia did. You said you wanted to marry for love, did you not?"

"Yes." Penn pouted out her lower lip. She sighed, and her anger disappeared. "I did. And I-I do."

"Then do not be angry with me," Matthew coaxed. He lifted his hand and brushed back an errant tendril from her forehead. The smoothness of her skin tempted him and he reached out to gently touch her cheek. She gasped and gazed up at him with stunned eyes. "My sweet Penn. Why such a tempest? You are innocent and honest and kind. Forgive me if I cannot liken you to Lady Julia."

A bemused smile crossed her lips. "When you speak like that, I cannot fathom how Lady Julia did not ask you first before anyone else."

Matthew chuckled. "I am glad to know you'd cast your vote for me."

She looked down, her lashes hiding those beautiful green eyes. "Yes, I-I would. It is unfortunate that you would not do the same and cast your vote for me."

"But I do. I respect you, Penn, more than any lady I know. You would never accept a fortune hunter and I am glad of it."

Penn stiffened. Matthew drew in his breath. He could sense it as she looked up. Indeed, she had drawn away from him again. The word "dunderhead" floated through his mind.

The door opened at that specific moment and Aunt Clare entered. She presented the most innocent of expressions, though no shawl graced her shoulders. "Hello, children. I am sorry I am so late. But I have news. We are clearly on the right path. I thought to stop and ask about Estelle from the proprietor. He said a lady of her description stopped here sometime at noon, though she did not step from the carriage. A gentleman accompanies her now."

"Really?" Matthew muttered, still studying Penn. "Ruppleton or Wilson, no doubt."

"N-no, dear. I w-wouldn't think so," Aunt Clare stammered. "We are farther behind her, er, them, than I would wish. The landlord said they were taking the North road."

"That is nice," Matthew said curtly.

"I beg pardon?" Aunt Clare frowned. Her eyes widened. "Forgive me, have I interrupted ought? Please do not say that you two have been brangling?"

Matthew dropped his hands. He returned hastily to his chair. "No. Of course not. Penn and I had a misunderstanding, that is all."

"However, it is settled now." Penelope drew in her breath and turned. "Aunt Clare, I wish to make a request."

"Certainly, dear. What is it?"

"Matthew does not wish for you to find him a true love. But . . . but I do. I mean, I wish you to turn your, ah, *skills* toward me and find *me* a true love instead."

"Penn!" Matthew stared at her, shocked.

Penn lifted her chin and looked Aunt Clare directly in the eye. "I am as rich as Lady Julia, truly I am. And I would like to marry. But I would never marry a fortune hunter, or . . . or anyone like that, so would you help me? I would appreciate it far more than Matthew, I assure you."

"Why, dear, I would be proud to do so." Aunt Clare blinked. "Indeed, I had told Matthew that I was considering doing just that. But then, he said he didn't think you would wish it."

"What?" Penelope looked to Matthew. "Why did you say that?"

"I didn't say that exactly," Matthew gritted out. "Of course, I did not know you were hanging out for a husband at that point."

"Gammon!" Penelope returned inelegantly. "You have been quite frightened that I wished to snag *you* as a husband, have you not? Else you wouldn't have felt it necessary to warn me at every turn and sneeze as you have. Indeed, it has become the most drawn out of litanies that you would never marry me. You said not a half-hour past, that you thought Aunt Clare was planning to make a match between us as she did with Lady Julia and Lord Garth."

"Forgive me." Matthew felt unfairly bedeviled. "I was wrong. I was puffed up in my own conceit. I was . . ."

"No, Matthew." Aunt Clare's voice was kind. "You were quite right."

"What!" Matthew exclaimed.

"What?" Penelope gasped.

"Oh dear, what a muddle." Aunt Clare shook her head and sighed. She looked to Penelope. "I do think, dearest, you are right. I should employ my services on your behalf instead. I have quite muffed it with Matthew, I fear. I will confess that I am at point nonplus."

"How so?" Matthew frowned. He should be overjoyed with her speech. Rather, it nettled him.

"I fear I may have, ah, fibbed a tad, dear. I told you I did not intend for you to choose Penelope as your bride. That was completely true. However, if I had been honest, as well as truthful, I would have admitted that I planned for you to fall in love with her and that you would marry her, regardless of your first intentions."

"I knew I was right!" Matthew's confidence returned full force. "Ha!"

"Aunt Clare." It was Penelope who looked as if the rug had scuttled away from beneath her. "How could you?"

"My dear, I had to see for myself that it wouldn't fadge. I wished to be sure that *you* were telling me the truth."

"Truth?" Matthew raised a brow. "What truth?"

Aunt Clare smiled benignly. "Why, that she is indeed over the *tendre* she harbored for you when she was young, Matthew."

"Aunt Clare! Please," Penelope gasped, clearly mortified.

"What?" Matthew looked quickly to Penelope. His

heart raced, no doubt from surprise. "You had a *tendre* for me?"

"I did."

Matthew drew in a breath. Of course, those adoring eyes of hers. Hadn't he been just thinking of them? Why hadn't he known? Although, if he were as honest as Aunt Clare, deep down, he *had* known it.

Penelope's chin lifted. "However, I grew out of it."

"You did?" Matthew shook his head to clear it. He had gained and lost, all in one moment.

"Of course," Penelope said, her tone indignant. "What? Do you think I have been pining for you all these years? I assure you I have not."

"I know that. Now, that is." Aunt Clare sighed. "Only before, well, dearest, it was your *name* that is at fault. It completely bamboozled me. It has turned out to be nothing but a red herring to be sure."

"I beg your pardon?" Penelope asked, eyes wide.

"What the devil are you talking about, Aunt Clare?" Matthew frowned. "Penelope is a charming name."

"Yes, dear, it is. But do you not remember the Greek myth? It came to mind immediately when you spoke of Penelope. Penelope was Ulysses' wife, you see. She remained at home while he gallivanted off on tour, stealing fleeces and fighting bullish creatures. Indeed, he was so busy at it, that those at home thought him dead. And since Penelope was a *rich* widow, she had every buck and dandy vying for her hand. And since she was a princess, there was no doubt she must marry. Only, she didn't want to marry any of them. She wanted Ulysses. And being pluck to the backbone, she told those suitors that she would marry them after she was finished knitting . . . no, not knitting, it was weaving—that is, what they did in those days—a tablecloth or . . . a mantel cloth . . . no, a tapestry . . . or whatnot. Oh, I cannot remember, but it was an important matter and they permitted her to do so. So she would weave it every day and then unweave it every night.

She did this for years. I would say that those suitors were a great bunch of clunches. 'Tis no wonder she waited for Ulysses, even if he were a bit of a here-and-there in my opinion."

Matthew's temper soared. "Just what does that story have to do with Penn? It makes no sense."

"I understand," Penn said. Matthew glanced at her. She was rather pale.

"I thought Penelope was like the other Penelope," Aunt Clare said. "I thought she was waiting there at home for you. I believed that is why she never married. You must admit, with her fortune and her looks and her passion . . ."

"Aunt Clare . . ." Matthew narrowed his gaze.

"Oh dear, I forget how you dislike that subject." Aunt Clare moved to the table and finally sat, or rather fell, into the chair. "Gracious, but confession makes one hungry. And being so far from the mark about matters can make one positively famished. In point of fact, fair gutfounded, as Garth would say."

Matthew frowned. He disliked being brushed aside so quickly, and for food at that. "Do you mean that all you have done is because of a *Greek* myth."

"Yes, dear. But I have seen the error of my ways, I promise you." Aunt Clare at least had the grace to turn her gaze from the roasted hen for a moment. "I own I am the most addlepated of ladies, but even I can see that this Penelope is not like the other Penelope. There is simply no spark between the two of you. No fire. And now that I have discovered that, I am all at sea as to whom you should marry."

"I see," Matthew said rather stiffly.

Aunt Clare looked to Penelope with glistening eyes. "Can you ever forgive me, dear?"

"For what?" Penelope's smile was small, even self-deprecatory. "You have nothing to apologize for, Aunt Clare."

"But I do. I set your house at sixes and sevens, my

dear, for nothing. Or as Matthew just pointed out, I did it because of a myth."

Penelope's smile widened. "I enjoyed the house at sixes and sevens. It's been a mausoleum for too long."

"And I have involved you with chasing after poor Lady Estelle. Another very unfortunate turn of events. I did not abduct Estelle, but after talking to the innkeeper, I fear I am correct in my hunch. A pity. I am correct in what I don't want to be correct about and wrong in what I wished to be right about. Yet if we hope to be at all successful with Lady Estelle, we must press on. We have no extra time to turn back and return you to your home, dear."

"I would not return, even if you wished it." Penelope hastened over to the remorseful lady, placing a gentle hand upon her shoulder. Matthew didn't know why, but he felt as if he were the one who should be comforted. "I might be here by your . . . misconceptions, but this is an adventure for me and I intend to see it through. In truth, you would be forced to send me back kicking and screaming, and you wouldn't want to do that, would you?"

"You are such a dear child. And . . . knowing all this . . . that I have bungled with Matthew so frightfully, do you truly wish for me to find you your perfect match?"

Stars entered Penelope's eyes. Matthew flinched. That was how she used to look at him five years ago. "Oh, yes. Ever so much."

"Thank you, dear." Aunt Clare patted her hand, clearly recovering. "You have helped restore my confidence. I know I should not feel so blue-deviled about Matthew, but I do. However, I have successfully matched six others, you know?"

"I know." Penelope gazed at Matthew. Her eyes told him nothing. "I would be grateful if I was the seventh person you matched with *her* true love."

"Wonderful, my dear. I will do it up properly, I

promise you." Aunt Clare nodded with a solemnity. "I will make restitution for the trouble I have caused you, I promise."

Matthew cursed. He knew Aunt Clare. Once she promised restitution, she would do it!

The carriage rocked gently. It was now dark outside, offering the sense of intimate camaraderie to the three travelers within. Sir Percy could not be counted, for the only thing he offered to the conversation was a snore from where he lay stretched across Aunt Clare's lap.

Penelope would never have imagined that a day could pass so quickly even though confined to a carriage. However, the conversation of her companions had kept her intrigued. She glanced at Matthew, who sat across from her and Aunt Clare.

His face was appalled as he stared at Aunt Clare. "Gad's. Are you telling me that 'the boys' have been assisting you with finding each others' true loves?"

"Certainly, dear." Aunt Clare nodded with pride. "I could never take all the credit. No, without their assistance, I could never succeed. It was Garth who directed me to Lady Clementine, avowing that if there were to be a match for Charles Danford, the Marquess of Hambledon, it would be she. Of course, he believed it to be a good match, because the Lady Clementine is as much an inveterate gambler as is Charles. And, she is an adorable rogue. I felt it would be a perfect match, for Charles, left to his own devices, can be rather a dull dog." Aunt Clare patted Penelope's hand. "Garth calls him that. And I must admit, he needed someone more lively. Someone who would informal his formality, so to speak."

"Lady Clementine does that." Matthew's tone was dry. He looked at Penelope. "Her entire family are spendthrifts and are drowning in the river tick more than Charles or me combined. However, Clementine and Charles seem to be repairing both their fortunes now. They have had the greatest streak of luck at the E.O. tables London has ever known."

"They also secretly own several gambling houses." Aunt Clare nodded.

"Truly?" Matthew's eyes sparkled. "Gad's, Charles has lost his starch to be sure."

"And it was dear Charles who espied Giles's lady for me," Aunt Clare said. "Melinda Chestercort. She was the daughter of one of his most frequent customers. Her father decided to take ship to the Americas and quite forgot to take her with him. I worried, at first, that Giles would not come up to scratch. He is rather a care-for-nobody. But he became the most forceful of men when he met Melinda."

"Aunt Clare arranges situations that demand that a man appear heroic," Matthew murmured aside to Penelope.

"Then Melinda, now the new Lady Mancroft, along with Clementine, found a conceivable match for Lord Reginald Beresford. A match which I quite supported. She is lady-in-waiting to the Princess. She is quite the dearest thing and positioned as she is, Lord Beresford need not fear from his past . . ." Aunt Clare flushed. Her hand fluttered. "Dear me, I dare not say that. Suffice to say, she is in a higher position of influence than other . . . er, women."

"Who was responsible for Lord Harry Redmond being matched with Lady Celeste?"

"Ruppleton discovered Lady Celeste. And Lord Beresford assisted in bringing her to town."

Matthew looked at Penelope. "Harry Redmond considers himself the best whip in all of England. Now, I do not know Aunt Clare's plotting and how she managed it, but Harry felt pressed to challenge the unknown Lady Celeste to a race. Turns out she was a neck-or-nothing driver worthy of the Four-in-Hand

Club, had she not been a woman. She beat him all hollow."

"We did not have to contrive *that* part at all." Aunt Clare smiled. "But yes, it took some assistance from us to make Harry challenge her to the race. He is a dear and a gentleman. But he also needed to be completely challenged, I fear, if he were to truly love and respect his mate."

"Whereas Lady Delia is the exact opposite, I would say." Matthew looked to Penelope. "She married the Viscount Dunn. Harrington is a manmilliner of the worst degree. She never contradicts him. Indeed, she thinks him the smartest thing for his fashion sense."

"Yes. And she delights in permitting him the designing of her clothes." Aunt Clare sighed. "Lucas discovered her for us. He is one of my best advisers, don't you know. His mind is quite devious."

"Lucas Monteith? Never say so." The fear entered Matthew's eyes again. "Faith, the traitor. Does he not know that he will be after me upon the list? I might forgive the others. They are insane in love at the moment. It makes sense that they will wish to draw men into the same hole they have fallen into. But for Lucas, a free man, to do so, b'gad, he is a bounder."

"No, dear. He is not." Aunt Clare shook her head. "Do you not remember? He believes he has met his true love and has lost her. He thinks he will never love again and that I will not be able to help him."

Penelope bit her lip, even as hope flared in her. That sounded rather like her situation. "Do you think you can help him?"

"Oh yes, dear. I already have his match waiting for him. Only I wished to settle Matthew here first. I am trying to make restitution in an orderly manner, you see."

Matthew frowned. His look turned positively evil. "Out with it! Who helped you in regard to me?"

"No one, dear." Aunt Clare flushed. "I told you my

feelings on the matter. And why I erred in that matter. I should not have gone off half-cocked, as it were. Only I felt so . . . positive about it all that I did not turn to the others."

Penelope bit her lip. She now recognized the names of the different personages whom Aunt Clare had received letters from in the past few days. She clearly was receiving advice from them.

"Indeed, I have been rather eager to make the match ever since we talked about Penelope."

Penelope sat up. "When was this?"

"I was castaway," Matthew said quickly.

"I see." Penelope sighed, definitely put in her place. He'd only spoken of her in some inebriated ramblings. Penelope knew how those went. No doubt Matthew had mentioned her directly behind his confession to seeing a purple rabbit or what not. Penelope forced a smile. "Well, I feel I must be fortunate, regardless." She looked sincerely to Aunt Clare. This Penelope was done with weaving and unweaving her own cloth. "I will be glad to take Matthew's place. And I do not mind one wit if all these others assist you."

"I am so glad—love is such a worthy destination. Truly, even helping others discover their ideal love is . . . why, my dear, it is so rewarding." She sighed. "In truth, I think any time that you are involved with working for love, it will make you happy. My life has been completely changed since I helped Julia and Garth. I never, ever thought I had any sort of special part in life. But now I do. That is what love does."

Penelope shivered suddenly. It was a shiver of excitement. "Indeed."

Matthew narrowed his eyes. "What will be your steps in finding Penelope's true love?"

"We do not need to discuss that." Penelope blushed.

"No." Matthew's tone was firm. "You really must give Aunt Clare clues as to what you look for in your perfect match."

"Matthew is right." Aunt Clare nodded. "I need to know what your dreams are if I am to find you your true love."

Penelope allowed herself to imagine a moment. "Pray, do not laugh. But I would like someone . . ."

"Yes?" Aunt Clare leaned forward.

"Very well. Someone very much like you spoke of in your stories, Aunt Clare. Someone who is dashing. Since I am anything but, I would like a man who does take action. One who will take risks."

"Gad's!" Matthew murmured.

"Hush, Matthew." Aunt Clare's eyes sparkled. "I think it famous."

Penelope didn't even heed them, so caught up was she in her vision. "I would like a man who could . . . steal my heart away. He would be so in love with me that he would carry me away."

"Ah, yes," Matthew drawled. "You would wish for a highwayman, or a pirate, Penn?"

Penelope started from her reverie. Matthew's gaze upon her was dark, his face stern in the shadows of the coach. At that moment, he looked like a pirate himself. She swallowed hard. "In certain ways . . . yes."

"Did you tell her, Aunt Clare?"

"Tell her what, dear?" Aunt Clare asked.

Penelope leaned back against the cushion of a sudden. Matthew not only looked like a pirate, but a fierce one. "Of my family's history."

"Gracious. Is that what you meant?" Aunt Clare cocked her head. "No dear, I see what you mean now. No, I would never have told her, for that, too, was in confidence. Besides, what would it serve? Indeed, it would be a sad thing. Penelope's dream man would have been one of your forefathers. And they are passed on, don't you know. I would never wish her to fall in love with . . . well, they would have to be ghosts, would they not?"

"What are you talking about?" Penelope frowned.

She couldn't help feeling a bit miffed. She rarely spoke of her dreams to anyone, and now when she did, it all but caused dissent amongst the ranks.

"Since you take it so very much to heart, dear, you must tell her," Aunt Clare said. "I will not."

"Very well." Matthew turned a cool gaze upon Penelope. "As you know, my father was a confirmed gambler."

"Yes," Penelope said. The entire village knew that Matthew's father had been an impossible gamester. It was he who had run the estate into the ground before passing on. That had been three years ago and it was clear Matthew could still not steer the family's fortunes about because of it.

"What you do not know is that he may very well have been the least wicked of my family. My great-great-great-grandfather was a pirate, Penn. He all but stole the Severs title."

"Faith." Penelope stared at him. "Why did you never tell me this before?"

"I do not find it anything to boast about." His lips twisted bitterly. "Now, great-grandfather and grandfather ceased pirating upon the seas. They settled for the far more genteel occupation of smuggling. 'Gentlemen of the Coast' would be their title."

"Truly?" Penelope asked, wide-eyed.

"Yes, truly." Matthew snorted. "You appear awed." She flushed. "I-I am."

"I thought it very exciting myself," Aunt Clare nodded.

"You ladies may do so because it is not *your* family you speak of. You are dreaming of some romantic flights from one of your Gothics. This is, rather, the stark, god-honest truth of it. I come from a long line of cutthroats and blackguards. They have taken what they want and damn the consequences." He snorted. "Or better yet, leave the whole infernal mess to their ancestors, the poor flats. Ah, the wages of sin . . . a crumbling estate which is a rambling torture chamber in and of itself and enough debt to bury an abbey."

Pain stabbed through Penelope. "Matthew, I am so sorry."

"It is not a legacy I wish to pass on to my sons and daughters." He turned a stark look upon her. "Nor will I. That I vow. I cannot vouch for the blood I pass to them, but they will know of honor."

"Yes, they will," Penelope whispered.

Matthew looked away, staring out the darkened window. "When Jacob accused my father of cheating in that transaction, I fear I could not help but believe him. My father swore he was innocent—to his dying day, in fact. Father was a gambler, but before that I had believed him to be honorable in his play and in his life."

Penelope sat frozen. There was nothing she could say to soothe his deep pain. Worse, she understood Matthew's illogical drive to marry only for wealth and not for love. He feared deception within his life.

She started as he looked at her once more. "I fully understood when Jacob told me I was never to see you again."

"He told you that?" A numbness filled Penelope. "I-I did not know."

"No doubt he wished to protect you." He frowned. "Though at the time I thought you were in agreement with him."

"No. I thought it was *your* decision to end our acquaintance. I thought you did not wish to see me because my father was so very insulting to your father. I—my father is quick to judge and that without mercy."

"True." A ghost of a laugh came from Matthew.

Penelope smiled hesitantly at him. "My family has its own sins, I fear. Please, do not eat me, but I would far prefer that my family wealth came from pirate ancestors, rather than from crusty curmudgeons who gained theirs from pinching their groat and everyone else's around them. You may have bad blood within your veins, but I fear my father still has my great-great-great-grandfather's first ha'pence. And that is not a legacy I wish to pass to *my* children, I promise you."

Matthew barked a laugh. Penelope nodded. "That ha'pence can just very well remain in that strong box of Father's. I refuse to take it with me if ever I wed!"

Six

The ship rocked back and forth. Waves pounded against its hull. Penelope gazed out over the wild ocean. Her pirate lover commanded his crew to fire the cannons upon the ship that followed them. He had abducted her. She prayed those who followed, those who would take her back, would not catch them. She prayed that her pirate lover would fend them off. Then she and he would escape to love and happiness.

Suddenly the ship slowed, as if a great anchor dragged at it. Fear rose in Penelope. They would surely be caught.

She heard a cat meow. She looked about in bewilderment as the ship jerked to a halt in the middle of the ocean. Sir Percy stalked toward her. So did Aunt Clare. She sported a yellow eye patch on her right eye and a green parrot on her left shoulder.

"I am so very sorry, Penelope." Aunt Clare shook her head. "They are gaining on us. My foreboding has come true."

"No! No!" Penelope's heart sank. She must run to her pirate lover. She picked up her skirts . . .

"Penelope, wake up," Matthew's voice called.

"What?" Penelope snapped her eyes open. Then her heart truly leapt. Matthew sat next to her, his face close to hers. She stared into his eyes, disoriented. Slowly, reality came to her. She was in the carriage. She must have fallen asleep.

A deep, unreasonable disappointment filled her. She

had desperately wanted to see her pirate lover. Now she stared at Matthew. "Hello."

"What were you dreaming?" he asked softly.

"Oh, nothing. Nothing at all." Penelope sat up and peered about blearily. "H-how long have I been asleep?"

"For the last hour or so." Matthew nodded. "You must have been dreaming something exciting if the expressions on your face proved aught."

Penelope groaned. "Y-you were watching me?"

Matthew started. His face turned rueful. "Perhaps. You—what were you dreaming of?"

Penelope was too sleepy to resist. She knew Matthew's streak of determination too well. "I will tell you only if you promise not to laugh."

"Yes. Of course."

"Promise me."

"I vow it, Penn."

"Very well. I—I dreamed about a . . . a pirate lover."

"Oh Lord, no," Matthew choked.

Penelope glared at him. "Yes?"

"N-nothing." Matthew was silent, but his shoulders twitched suspiciously.

Penelope shook her head. "Very well, go ahead and laugh before you hurt yourself."

Matthew did. Loud and long.

"It—it was due to our discussion before, no doubt," Penelope murmured. She peered about. She and Matthew were alone in the carriage. The door stood open and the sound of people and horses came from without. "Where are we, by the bye? Where is Percy? And Aunt Clare?"

"We have stopped at an inn. As to where Aunt Clare and Percy are, I am not sure. While you have been sleeping, Percy woke up and has been meddlesome. He sprang out the minute Meeker opened the door. Aunt Clare is trying to call him to her side. She should let him run it out, I say."

"I see." Penelope brushed a hand across her eyes. She could not shake off her dream. Who had *they* been who chased her?

"Come." Matthew's tone was gentle. He climbed from the carriage and offered his hand.

"Thank you." Penelope clasped it and alighted. She gasped as shooting needles attacked her feet, and her knees gave out. They evidently were as sound asleep as she had been.

"Steady on." Matthew wrapped his arm about her, which didn't help Penelope's balance one whit.

An unearthly, keening howl rent the air. Then a jungle cat cry. Or so it seemed to Penelope. Clearly she had not forsaken sleep after all. A huge dog of unknown antecedents pelted toward her from out of the dark. Directly behind was no tiger from the Royal Exchange, but one battle-scarred, marmalade cat, Sir Percy.

Dream or not, Penelope cried out as the dog closed in upon her, his howl one of fear. "Oh dear, no!"

Before the beast could knock her down, she was lifted in strong arms. She breathed a sigh of relief as Matthew held her safe above the furor.

"Damn it, Percy, lay off the poor cur." Matthew whirled as the dog attempted to hide behind him and Percy circled after. The dog yelped as Percy swiped a claw at him.

Unfortunately, the horses took exception to the hubbub. The lead horse reared, snorting out his disfavor.

"Gad's!" Matthew leapt back. Penelope clung to him, burying her head in his shoulder. It simply was too discombobulating when just fresh from sleep. She received a steady and impressive stream of invective in her ear as Matthew turned and bolted across the darkened inn yard, away from the rioting horses and toward the torch-lit entryway. Penelope found herself grateful. Grateful for once that her stature was small, and grateful that Matthew's was grand.

Penelope heard Matthew chuckle. She refused to lift her head. "Is it safe now?"

"Yes. They are gone." Matthew laughed all the more. "The horses. The dog. Percy. Aunt Clare. And Meeker."

"What?" Penelope lifted her head in surprise. She just barely saw Aunt Clare and Meeker chasing away into the night. "Oh dear."

They both laughed. Slowly, it subsided. For a moment they merely smiled at each other. Penelope noticed that Matthew did not release her. She rather enjoyed the cozy feeling of his arms holding her. His scent of Joppa soap and cigar drifted to her befogged brain. She sniffed happily.

Then she flushed. "Er . . . thank you for saving me."

"Saving you? Yes, I was quite dashing, wasn't I? First it was fish, and now it is dogs and cats. I progress."

Penelope's lips twitched. The brilliance of Matthew's gaze teased her. "Yes, so you do. But you mustn't forget horses, too."

"Minx," Matthew chuckled.

He kissed her then. Just like that. Swiftly. Surely. Like lightning moving fast across the sky. Indeed, the effect upon Penelope was as strong as a natural force. Penelope blinked as Matthew drew back. His eyes widened in shock as he gazed at her. Truly, he looked as if it had been she who had leaned over and with one earth-shattering move, kissed him. "I beg your pardon."

"No, no, that is quite all right." What was the matter with her? She sounded like a wanton.

At least he didn't take her at her word. Matthew still looked at her as if she were the innocent. Yet a lady who had felt so much with the touch of another's lips upon hers could not be totally innocent and Penelope knew it deep inside. Worse, she would adore it if he kissed her again.

Matthew frowned and then the light of humor lit

his eyes. Ah, more fatal than even a kiss to Penelope was that gleam in Matthew's eyes that asked her to laugh with him. "I am merely preparing you. As a good friend should, don't you know?"

Penelope's brow rose. She laughed already, merely from his look. "Preparing me for what? As a friend, that is."

"For that pirate you dream of. For any man . . . who dares to kiss you." Matthew's voice grew husky, fierce, as he lowered his lips to hers slowly. So slowly that a woman could not act coy, astonished, or unprepared. So slowly that it seemed forever in those few seconds.

Yet as their lips met, softly, gently, met as if every moment of their lives before led to this very one kiss, Penelope *was* astonished. Bowled over. Knocked so very far from the wicket that her heart almost failed her. This was far better than her dreams. This was not possible.

Impossibility fled as Matthew deepened the kiss. It felt so real. His lips taught hers to dance within a second, to meet with open desire and no embarrassment. Dimly, with the first passion tormenting her, Penelope was aware enough to be glad that Matthew held her aloft. If she had been standing, she surely would have fallen.

"Er . . . ah hum . . . pardon me?" a hesitant voice asked.

Penelope's toes, which did not need to touch earth and therefore reality, tingled away. As did every other part and particle of her being.

"Please forgive me . . ." There was that intrusive voice again!

Penelope gasped in grief as Matthew drew back. She could only stare at Matthew in passionate awe. Slowly, because of the discreet coughing and ah-hming, she then noticed a man standing before them. Short and thin, he was clearly nervous.

The man bowed. "I would not wish t-to discommode

you, b-but . . . my establishment is a discreet one. Could you p-possibly refrain from . . . er . . . *doing* such in the public yard?"

"Yes. Certainly," Matthew said it with a cool aplomb for which Penelope was grateful. She knew she was ready to sink and wouldn't be able to muster even speech. "We need a room."

"That is very clear." The proprietor nodded. "Very."

"No, I meant rooms. Suites, of course. Two separate ones, please." Matthew quickly dropped Penelope to her feet.

Penelope well nigh toppled. He swiftly put a bolstering arm about her. She flushed. "It—it is not what you think, sir. I do have a chaperone."

"I see." The diffident proprietor clearly did not, but was being polite.

Mortified, Penelope tried to clarify the situation. "Aunt Clare, who is my chaperone, is chasing her cat . . . who was chasing a dog . . . which made the horses bolt and My lord . . . er . . . saved me."

The proprietor's eyes widened appreciatively at that, but not exactly with belief. "If you say so, mam."

"That is the . . . truth," Penelope trailed off.

"You may lead us to the chambers now." Matthew's tone was curt.

"Oh, yes. They are th-this way." The proprietor bowed, and turning, scurried ahead of them. Penelope found she could not speak through their entire progress. She choked doubly when the proprietor finally stopped before a door and opened it. "This is one of the suites. Will it be to your satisfaction?"

"Yes," Penelope squeaked before any of them could enter the room.

"Indeed." Matthew nodded, solemnly. He did not take a step either.

The proprietor was the only one to enter the room. His face showed concern. "D-do you not wish to inspect it?"

"No." Somehow walking into the room with Matthew would be quite embarrassing now. The memory of his kiss still seared her lips.

"But . . . ?" the proprietor began.

"That will be all," Matthew said.

"Yes, my lord." The proprietor jumped slightly and then hastened out of the room.

He was far down the hall when Matthew frowned. "Hello. What of my suite?" He apparently did not hear, for he did not turn back. "Blast it."

Matthew looked at Penelope, his smile wry. Penelope looked down, unable to meet his gaze directly. He did not speak. Finally, she was forced to look up out of sheer curiosity.

His gaze was steady upon her, his blue eyes filled with concern. A gentle smile tipped his lips. "Thank God. For a moment I thought you would never look at me again."

Penelope smiled, despite herself. "Idiot."

Matthew's eyes flared with amusement. "No. No. *Dunderhead.* I consider that your proper term of endearment for me, you know?"

"Do you?" Penelope blushed all the more.

"Will you forgive this dunderhead?" Matthew asked softly. "I-I do not know what came over me, Penn. All I can do is beg your . . ."

"No. Please, do not apologize. I—understand," Penelope said quickly. Which was a great lie. The power of his kiss was still a mystery to her.

"It was the height of dishonor since I am an engaged man," Matthew continued with a frown. "But I vow, it will not happen again. I-I do not want you to feel that you cannot be safe with me."

"No, I-I understand." Penelope attempted to hide her disappointment. "After all, it cannot . . . must not happen again."

"That is true." Matthew nodded.

"Very true," Penelope sighed.

Matthew looked at her intently. "You sighed. Why?"

"I didn't sigh."

"Yes, you did."

Penelope stared at him. She couldn't very well say that his kiss had rocked her to her core and she wanted another. Therefore, she said the next closest thing to it. "As a friend to friend, y-you might understand that . . . I was quite half asleep. I only wish that I had been more prepared for it. Since it was my first kiss, you understand."

"Penn, you rogue," Matthew barked a laugh. "If that is how you kiss when exhausted . . ." He stopped promptly. Then he sighed himself. "Blast! I see what you mean."

"Mm, yes." Penelope nodded. She drew in a breath. "However, that . . . that is all right. I mean . . . we cannot try again and that is that. I must simply wait for some other pirate t-to teach me more."

"Penn, confound it!" Matthew stepped toward her, placing large, warm hands to her shoulders.

"Yes?" Penelope shivered.

"Meow. Brr—grr."

Matthew jumped. He dropped his hands from her as if he had been caught pilfering, which in a manner of speaking, he was. They both glanced quickly to the call. Percy stalked down the hall toward them. He settled down to stare at them with unblinking sphinx eyes.

"Oh, thank heaven." Penelope breathed. "Aunt Clare will be here in a moment. That—that is a good thing, isn't it?"

"Yes." Matthew nodded, even as she saw him clench his teeth. Then he groaned. "Oh, Lord, Penn. We are in the suds. You know how lax Aunt Clare is about her duties as chaperone. Percy here would be far better at it, I don't doubt."

"Oh dear." Penelope swallowed hard. She forced a smile. "Well, it should not be too difficult. W-we will simply have to be our own chaperones, will we not?"

***

The carriage stopped before a small blacksmith shop. The coach that they had followed for three days was drawn to the side of the building. By all calculations, Lady Estelle and the mystery man who traveled with her should be within. Discovery should be imminent. The fact that this particular blacksmith resided within Gretna Green could only add piquancy.

Matthew glanced at the two ladies across from him. Aunt Clare ran nervous fingers through Percy's fur. Her blue eyes held a fine blend of guilt and anxiety. Penelope, on the other hand, was subdued. She had been so ever since they had made that final turn which left no doubt as to their destination.

He quirked a brow. "Would anyone care to lay bets as to who and what we will discover once we enter?"

"No." Penelope shook her head. "No, I would not."

"I presume then you would cast a vote for the plot that follows so—Lady Estelle has fled with her lover in a mad attempt for a runaway marriage in Gretna Green. She has arrived to this blacksmith shop, probably one with an anvil priest within. Indeed, an anvil priest ready and willing to wed them for the shilling, as we speak. However, you are being too polite to say so."

Penelope gazed at him steadily. "What would you do if it were true?"

Jump for joy a, small voice whispered within his head. Matthew clenched his teeth. What a dishonorable thought. He also knew better. This was another of Aunt Clare's keenly crafted plans. And since it was, he determined that the least he could do was to offer the finest of dramatics to his susceptible audience. "Why, I shall take her back. I will not be balked of yet another rich bride. She is mine!"

"Oh dear," Aunt Clare moaned and fell back against the squabs.

Sir Percy sat up and showed interest. "Meow?"

Penelope paled. "W-would you?"

"I would." Matthew grinned. "But what if she is with a man who is, indeed, her abductor and we have come upon them only by virtue of a broken axle? Perhaps they may have stopped merely because the scoundrel had need of a blacksmith. A villain whom I must save her from? What then, Penelope?"

Indecision streaked through her green eyes. Her chin tilted up. "We must discover the truth. That is why we are here, is it not?"

"That's my girl," Matthew murmured huskily before he realized it. He frowned direly to cover the slip. "Come. It is time to recover my missing bride."

Matthew swung open the carriage door and clambered down. He turned and assisted Aunt Clare and Penelope to alight from the carriage. He turned on one heel and brushed past Meeker industriously trying to contain an armful of one large and impatient marmalade cat. Matthew did not wait for Sir Percy. He did not wait for Aunt Clare and Penelope. He was determined to take the measure of the situation before they entered.

He barged through the doorway. He paused but a moment as he spied Lady Estelle and a man standing within. No one else was present. He heard rather than saw Aunt Clare and Penelope enter behind him.

"Aha!" Matthew strove for a dramatic tone and stance. Aunt Clare had set a scene and he vowed to do it justice. If a romantic hero was required, so be it. "There you are, my love. I have come to save you!"

Lady Estelle turned. She fell back, gasping, her face drained to white. "Lord Severs. No, oh no!"

The man who stood beside her spun. A fair young man, he flushed red. His eyes burned, however, in anger. "No! You will not take Estelle from me. She is mine."

Faith. Matthew started back. Aunt Clare had found

a rare actor for the performance. The boy's fervent delivery of the statement was eloquent with emotion. It demanded Matthew to throw himself into the dialogue with equal vigor. "You have stolen my fiancée. For that you will pay."

"If—if it is a duel you desire, sir, you shall have it."

"Duel? You young puppy. I would not duel with you." Matthew totally lost his character. The gasp from all about warned him that he had mistaken the script. To regain focus, he roared, "And there are no swords or pistols here. What shall you do about that, cub?"

"I-I . . ." The young man was at a loss, his eyes desperate as he looked to Lady Estelle.

"I will take Lady Estelle now." Matthew squelched his laughter. Aunt Clare's actor was not as prepared as he ought to be. "Do not think to stop me."

"No!" the youth roared. Apparently forgetting any dialogue written, the young fellow charged at Matthew, hands actually outstretched. Clearly he had been trained in dramatics and not in the science of fisticuffs. Yet, he had obviously been trained in the art of the stage. His face was so contorted as to go beyond that of an amateur thespian.

"Good show!" Matthew choked, as much from surprise as from the young man's hands wrapped around his neck. The lad was overdoing it, to say the least.

"Dear God, no. Peter, no!" Lady Estelle screamed. Matthew, gurgling, glanced at her from the corner of his eye. She swayed, her hands clasped in that of prayer.

"Indeed!" Performance or not, Matthew was not going to die at the hands of an overzealous actor. He chopped the lad sharply on the arms, breaking his hold. He then retreated into a defensive crouch. "Don't you think you are overplaying it somewhat?"

"Damn you, you fiend!" The boy charged at him. "Estelle is mine!"

Prepared this time, Matthew sidestepped him with

the greatest ease. While the boy stumbled past him, he said sternly. "Aunt Clare, do call your boy off."

"Oh dear, I was afraid of that." Aunt Clare's voice was worried. "He is not my boy, dear . . ."

"Matthew!" Penelope waved frantically. "Behind you!"

Matthew whirled about. The lad had grabbed up a pitchfork and looked intent upon employing it to advantage, and from the hot look in his eyes, not upon the straw, either. "Faith. Now you tell me!" Matthew dove and rolled swiftly, the tines of the fork far too close to him. By the time he came to his feet, the infernal boy had spun about and was prepared. "Who is he?"

"I truly do not know his name." Aunt Clare jumped up and down. Sir Percy, for once, did not advance, but sat before his beloved mistress, hair raised, ears back. "Ask Lady Estelle."

"Lady Estelle, who is this young fire-eater!" Matthew dodged the pitchfork successfully again. "Fiend seize it, woman! Answer me!"

"Don't you dare raise your voice to her, sirrah!" The boy whipped about and charged again.

"She cannot answer, Matthew," Penelope called. "She has fainted."

The boy flinched and hesitated.

"See what you have done." Matthew sought reason. "You have caused her to swoon. This is quite improper behavior, and in front of the ladies, too."

The boy responded to that logic by improperly charging again at Matthew with the pitchfork. Matthew sidestepped it. The procedure was becoming quite redundant, in his opinion. He grabbed hold of the pole as the boy fell past him. He jerked it from his unsuspecting hands. Rage flaring high, he tossed the pitchfork aside. "Now let us talk, damn it. We are men, not farm animals to be stuck. Just who the devil are you?"

"Mister High and Mighty," the boy sneered. It was

ruined by his panting and high color. Now, why had Matthew thought him a good actor? "You act as if you do not know who I am."

"That is because I do not," Matthew answered in a reasonable tone. "Is there any reason I should?"

It clearly was a question most undiplomatic. Howling, the boy spun and snatched up a wicked-looking fire iron.

"Blast! Aunt Clare," Matthew growled and glared at her. "Cannot you bend your vow of secrecy before he bends that over my head?"

"Oh dear. I am sorry," Aunt Clare cried. "But the first plot, plot number one, is correct. He is Lady Estelle's lover."

"What?" Shock froze Matthew.

"No!" Penelope shouted. Matthew whirled. His momentary pause might very well have proven fatal. The "lover" was advancing far faster than anticipated and far more adroitly than previously. A movement flashed in the corner of Matthew's sight as he crouched in preparation of the onslaught.

Matthew did not receive a poker to the skull. Rather, the advancing boy received a bucket of water to his face. He halted as it clearly dashed his vision.

"That was good, Penelope," Aunt Clare's voice approved.

Not waiting for another moment, Matthew bolted forward. He jerked the poker from the sputtering and spitting lad. Now that Matthew knew the fight was in honest, he would not pull his punches. He drew back and delivered a flush hit to do Gentleman Jackson proud. Just as he planted it, he heard Lady Estelle scream.

The lad, his eyes stunned, whispered, "Estelle!"

He crumpled to the ground. Lady Estelle screamed again. Matthew spun and groaned. Deathly pale, tears streaming down her cheeks, Lady Estelle stood a tragic figure. Of all times for her to come to!

"Peter!" Estelle ran to him. She flung herself upon the lad's recumbent form. With one last sob and his name upon her breath, she swooned atop him.

"Good Lord." Matthew stared. He felt like one of the watchmen standing over the fallen Romeo and Juliet. "I-I never thought he'd fall so readily. Or her, for that matter. I did not intend . . ."

"Of course not, dear." Aunt Clare rushed to his side and patted his arm. "That is a famous left you have, dear. Rattled his bone-box, as Garth would put it. And, it did not appear that Sir Peter intended to concede. One can accept being mauled by just so many pokers and pitchforks before objecting."

"As for Lady Estelle," Penelope came to stand by him upon the other side, her voice soft, "it is very common for ladies to swoon when in her delicate condition."

"What!" Matthew stared at her.

"Am I right, Aunt Clare?" Penelope asked softly. "Is Lady Estelle *enceinte*?"

"That is my hunch, dear." Aunt Clare nodded. "But Estelle did not tell me that. That is why I dare not say it if it were not true."

"Oh, Lord!" Matthew knew himself to be a strong man, but at this particular moment, he wouldn't have objected to joining the other two in a faint. A faint of sheer relief, that was.

A servant entered into the smithy with a man who wore the collar of the clergy beside him. The servant gasped. "Oh no, Sir Peter. Sir Peter." He looked at Matthew, paling. "What have you done to m'lord."

"Never mind what I have done." Matthew pinned his gaze upon the preacher. "It appears we are here to attend a wedding. Aunt Clare and Penelope can be the witnesses. And I shall give the bride away. It is only fitting."

* * *

"Oh, Percy! Percy, dear kitty?" Penelope called, imitating Aunt Clare's voice. The night sky was star-hazed and silver-mooned. Penelope waded through the high meadow grass, a skip to her step. It was a wondrous night.

"Why call him?" Matthew strolled beside her. He cast her a lazy grin. "Percy goes wandering far too often. I believe Aunt Clare actually hopes he will. I think she likes the excitement."

Penelope laughed and drew in a deep breath. It made her dizzy. "Whoo!"

"You do not drink champagne often, do you?" Matthew's eyes glittered in the moonlight. His tone was quite condescending.

"You do not need to act so very haughty. Are you not tipsy yourself?"

"Yes, b'gads, I am." Matthew grinned. "I have never been more light-spirited upon a mere three glasses of champagne than I am now. I am a four-bottle man, I will have you know, but tonight three glasses have done it."

Penelope giggled. "And I am a two-glass lady, I will have you know."

"Then it was the third that has done this?"

"No." Penelope flung out her arms and lifted her face to the sky. "No, it is having everything turn out s-so neatly."

"Hmm, yes. I must agree," Matthew said. "Now I know why Lady Estelle always cried. I am relieved to know that it was not due to any lack of style on my part."

Penelope refocused her gaze upon Matthew. He was overlaid with the stars she had just studied. It was only right, to her way of thinking. "I thought the dinner you arranged for Lady Estelle and Sir Peter famous. And you soothed their fears so very well by pledging to tell her parents for them."

"It will be my pleasure, I assure you," Matthew

growled. "Though I will have a few other choice words of my own to add."

"And franking a honeymoon on the Continent for Sir Peter and Lady Estelle was a charming notion as well. Surely their parents will calm by the time they return from Paris."

"And, we will have the gossips' guns spiked by the time they return. Until then, they shall be a nine-day wonder, to be sure." He shrugged. "That is unavoidable. But it does not mean they must be present for the entirety of it. And, as you pointed out, Lord and Lady Hastings will have time to grow accustomed."

"They better grow accustomed," Penelope said indignantly. "They were wicked to try and force Lady Estelle to marry you. Especially when they were aware of her condition. And just because they held a poor opinion of Sir Peter, thinking him not elevated enough for their daughter."

"Yes. They would rather fetch an impecunious earl for their daughter than an honorable 'Honorable' whom she loved. It is the way of the world. They counted upon the fact that as they would be the ones paying the piper, so to speak, I could not cavil if a child arrived early." He cringed. "Gad's, what a close call."

"Only imagine," Penelope said with wonderment. "True love has won out and it is all due to one small conversation. To think all this transpired because Aunt Clare told Lady Estelle that one must always follow her heart and *never* permit anyone to destroy that love within one."

Matthew shook his head. "I hate to own it, but I owe Aunt Clare for that. She saved me from a terrible misstep."

"No, *true love* saved you," Penelope said, a glint in her eye. "Lady Estelle's love for Sir Peter actually did it. If she had not decided to call Sir Peter to her side . . . or if he had not come at her bidding . . . and if he had not come and stolen her away . . . and if neither had been brave enough to make a dash for Gretna . . ."

"I would be in the suds. For life." Matthew shook his head. "The Hastings have a lot to pay for, b'gad."

Penelope shook her head. One could not help but count her own blessings at a time like this. "My father is many things, but I know he would never force me into such a marriage."

Matthew laughed. "Lord, no. Your trouble will be quite the opposite. He'll not accept anyone, I fear, who vies for your hand, Penn."

Penelope's chin tilted out. "He will simply be forced to do so . . . once I find my true love."

"Penn, he will be difficult, I must warn you. He had every right to request I not call on you, for I am not an eligible party . . ."

"Why? You have a title and we do not. Look what the Hastings did for that?"

Matthew snorted. "You know your father. A title does not mean much, not if he were to be forced to open his strongbox to support it. As long as Jacob Lancer has control of the fortune your mother left you, he will hold it, and hold it tightly."

"Cease." Penelope waved her hand airily. "You can not dampen my spirits. I shall deal with Father when the time comes. It will be a snap."

"The kitten who roared?" Matthew's brow quirked high in challenge.

"Exactly. Yes." Penelope grinned. "This kitten will roar. I will take lessons from Sir Percy, if I needs must."

"Oh Lord, no. Pray, do not become one of those battle-axes."

"I will not." Penelope laughed. "But I vow, things are going to change. I have sat about weaving for far too long."

Matthew stilled. "What?"

Penelope swallowed. She spun and dashed ahead.

"Oh, Percy. Where are you, dear kitty? Come here, kitty."

"Penelope!" Matthew called, stomping toward her. "What did you say?"

Penelope glanced about. The entire field lay before them. Smiling, she drifted to the right. "I said nothing of any significance, my lord. After all, I am going to marry for love. And Aunt Clare is going to find me a dashing pirate. What do you say to that, sir?"

"I say bully." Matthew veered and paced toward her. "Just bully. It will keep her distracted."

"And who are you going to wed now?"

"I do not know. I shall have to see who remains at the house party."

"I see." Penelope halted. She pointed a stern finger at him. "Stay where you are, Matthew."

"Why?" Matthew's grin was wolfish.

"Because, because . . ."

"I am no longer engaged, Penn. Do you realize that?"

"And neither am I." Penelope's heart fluttered. It might be the champagne, but if it was, Penelope did not care. Tonight was different from any other night, and this moment would never be again. "Of what significance is that?"

Matthew wagged his brow. "Come here, wench!"

"No!" Penelope crossed her arms. "I wish to be swept from my feet, do you not know?"

"Fie. That is no way to talk to a dangerous pirate." Matthew frowned.

Penelope stuck her nose high into the air. "If you do not make haste, I am sure I will become engaged before . . ."

Matthew growled and charged at her.

Laughing, Penelope picked up her skirts and raced across the field. Matthew's strong arm grabbed her about the waist. He spun her about and, encircling her waist with large hands, he lifted her straight up into the air. He spun her round and round. "Are you off your feet high enough, milady?"

"Matthew! Stop. You are making me dizzy!"

"What do you say, wench?"

"Let me down?"

"No. That is not it."

"Please let me down?"

"No. Try again."

Penelope didn't have to think too hard upon the riddle. "Kiss me?"

"That I will." Matthew then lowered her slowly, the fabric of their clothes brushing as he did. Penelope lost her smile as she stood, their bodies melded against each other. Matthew's gaze grew solemn as he cupped her chin gently and kissed her.

Penelope shivered and closed her eyes. Silver flashes shimmered about, even with her lids closed.

Matthew drew back. She heard a ragged sigh come from him as she opened her eyes. He slipped one hand to her hair and drew her close, laying his chin to her head. Penelope felt a tremble course through his large body.

"Matthew?" she whispered in awe. Inexperienced as she was, she was aware that the tremble she felt was for her.

"Ulysses was very rich, you know?" Matthew's voice sounded very calm, rather like a lecturer.

"I beg your pardon?"

Matthew released her. Penelope stood dazed. And lost.

"I know very well the myth of Ulysses and Penelope. Aunt Clare, er, brought it rather up to date, but she had the gist of it right." He took up Penelope's hand. He began to walk and Penelope followed him. She did not need to ask where they were going. Not while he held her hand. "When he returned from his jaunting about he was still a rich man, that I will tell you. His father hadn't gambled his inheritance away. Nor did he have a family who, though they are dear to him, will never understand thriftiness. It is his duty to turn their ship about, you know?"

"I know." Penelope now did not like where they were going, but she could see no reason to turn back.

"I am sure Ulysses had Penelope's father's blessings." He halted and looked down at her. His smile twisted. "Ulysses *was* a clunch to travel about while Penelope sat and weaved at home. But . . . but it has worked out for the best, I have no doubt."

"Indeed?" Penelope flushed.

His gaze was dark, but determined. "I know it is good for you to find yourself a husband who loves you."

Penelope's heart lurched. "Yes."

"And . . . confound it, Penelope," Matthew sighed. "All I can say is . . . I am proud that for a while at least, I had someone weaving a tablecloth for me."

Penelope nodded. Gracious, but it was going to be difficult. She almost wanted to return to that loom. But Matthew was setting his course away from her again. "Thank you."

He lifted her hand and kissed it in a courtly manner. "I shall not forget this adventure, Penn."

Penelope smiled. Whatever sadness came in the future, she had more to remember now than she had had in many years before. Yes, she could see the stars shining again, shining brightly. "Nor will I."

Seven

Matthew paced the library floor. He awaited the arrival of Miss Cecily Morris. He paused a moment. Stepping over to the Oriental screen, he peered behind it.

"Excellent." He had forced Andrew to a vow not to hide himself behind the screen, or anything else, this time. Matthew wanted no audience. Furthermore, Andrew had been a dissenting vote to Cecily's case. He would not put it past his brother to try and throw a spanner in the works.

Matthew frowned. He wished the family vote had been unanimous. He knew it had been too much for which to hope. While he had been chasing after Estelle Hastings, his family had been left to entertain the remaining three ladies. It had only been natural that they had begun to know the women and to have their particular favorites.

It was Christine and Monica who had cast the two *yea* votes for Cecily Morris. They declared she was far more fun than the others. For this reason, they wanted her as a sister-in-law. She and her father might smell of the shop, but at least she was lively and kind.

Andrew, in an odd about-face, had thrown his support for Lady Sherrice Norton. He had not been kind in regard to her at the first election. Yet, now that Estelle Hastings was not a runner, he had placed Lady

Sherrice first upon his list. Monica and Christina had all but hit him, so enraged were they. They vowed that Sherrice Norton was a haughty cat. Matthew smiled wryly. He did not know about that, but the notion of sitting down to his wife smoking a cheroot was far too odd for him.

Lady Severs had cast her vote for the dark horse, Violet Stapleton. She declared that she had not met such a sweet and demure girl in an age. Andrew had wrangled over that, saying Violet was not demure, but insipid. He further informed them that Lady Stapleton boasted that she had named Violet after her favorite mare. The mare had broken a leg and Lady Stapleton had put the horse down herself. Andrew vowed that Violet shrank so because she no doubt feared that her mother might do the same to her one day. It was no wonder she was reticent in developing anything so risky as an individual personality.

Matthew winced. He could very well hear what words of wisdom Penn would have to say to him about this. Here he was about to propose once more in accordance to his family's vote. But blast it, what was he to do? He was fortunate that his house had still been full of prospective brides when he had returned home from the Gretna Green adventure. He grimaced. Ulysses stole golden fleeces on his travels, while Matthew simply lost brides. He certainly was not made of heroic material.

As he had told Penelope. A smile touched his lips. For a moment, he was in that field again, with Penelope laughing and running from him. He had to shake himself and force his attention back. What was the matter with him? He needed to stop daydreaming and apply himself to a successful proposal.

He wondered if Aunt Clare was sending out letters to the "boys" requesting them to start searching for Penelope's groom. Matthew ground his teeth. He shouldn't feel betrayed, but somehow he did. Which

was ridiculous, since he was not going to marry
Penelope himself. She had sworn that Jacob would accept whom she married, but if it was Matthew, Jacob
might very well disinherit her. That would be a pretty
pickle. He would then be taking her down with him,
as well as his family.

On the other hand, Jacob's blessing upon the marriage would be no better. Matthew wasn't certain he
could live with Jacob's constant antipathy toward him
and his family, and Penn would be caught in the middle. No, Penn and he were friends. A man did not
marry a friend for her money. Just like he could not
marry a woman who loved him for his money.

A knock sounded at the door. Matthew jumped. It
was time, then. "Enter."

The door swung open. He held his sigh of exasperation as the two girls sprinted in. "Yes. What is it? Miss
Cecily will be here at any moment."

"We know." Monica's eyes were large.

"We came to . . . well, to tell you that we are glad
you are following our advice. She suits us to a cow's
thumb," Christine said.

"You won't regret it," Monica added solemnly.

"Truly." Christine gulped. "We do not know why
Andrew did not vote for Cecily. We thought he liked
her just as much as we did."

"That Sherrice Norton is spiteful." Monica nodded
firmly.

Matthew studied the two girls. He smiled and put
an arm around both of them. "Do not take this so to
heart. Remember, *I* am the one proposing. This is not
your responsibility. Not anymore."

A knock sounded upon the door. The girls squeaked
and Matthew looked up. "Who is it?"

"It is I," Lady Severs called. "May I enter?"

"Certainly."

The door opened and Lady Severs all but tiptoed
into the room. She froze with astonishment. "What are

you two girls doing here? Did you forget that Matthew is about to propose within seconds?"

"Yes, they know. They were offering their last-minute council. And what are your words of advice for me, Mother?"

Lady Severs flushed. "I wanted you to know that I have changed my mind and am throwing my vote in for Cecily. I have considered it deeply. I think, in truth, that Violet Stapleton might be too reticent and retiring for a family like us."

"Thank you, Mother dear."

"Then the vote is unanimous," Christine said happily. "Well, practically. Except for Andrew, that is. And I think he must have been jesting when he voted for Lady Sherrice."

"Indeed." Monica nodded quickly. "That must be it. Before you returned, Cecily and Andrew were rubbing along together quite well. They must have had a tiff to make him change his vote. He will come about. You should not let that concern you."

"Thank you, girls." Matthew's lips twitched even as his heartstrings were pulled. This was why he was willing to marry for wealth and wealth alone. Insolvent they might be, but no man could have a better family.

Another knock sounded at the door.

"I will lay odds that is Andrew!" Monica exclaimed. "Coming to say that he votes for Cecily Morris, too."

Matthew smiled. "Enter."

The door opened and Cecily Morris, the lady of the hour, entered. Everyone in the room gasped. Except Matthew. He groaned.

Cecily started back. "I am sorry. I . . ."

"No, no," Lady Severs said quickly. "We—we were just leaving."

Lady Severs and the girls scuttled out of the room.

Cecily peered at Matthew. Her eyes were solemn but steady. She clasped her hands in front of her.

Matthew drew in a deep breath. "Good afternoon, Miss Morris."

"Good afternoon, my lord."

Matthew waved a hand to the settee. Now that the moment had arrived, it unnerved him. Perhaps some conversation first would be appropriate. After the debacle with Lady Estelle and her parents, it would serve him well to ask a few home questions of her first. "Would you care to sit, Miss Morris?"

"Not particularly." Cecily clasped her hands together. "I-I find it difficult to sit when I am on tenterhooks."

Matthew chuckled. "I fully understand. I thought, however, it would be . . . nice if we could converse a bit. I know we cannot come to know each other in one conversation, but it might lead to a better understanding between us."

"Oh dear, no." Alarm crossed Cecily's pixie face.

"I beg your pardon."

"Forgive me. I only meant . . . I am far too nervous for discussion. And I have never cared for roundaboutation." A becoming flush painted her cheeks. She was an attractive girl, in truth. She drew in a breath. "Therefore . . . the answer is yes."

Matthew started. "What?"

"I am sorry." Consternation washed her face. "Father told me you wished to propose to me. Is that incorrect?"

"No. I did," Matthew said quickly. He shook his head. "I mean, I do. Yes, that is it, I do."

"Very well." Cecily nodded briskly. "I accept."

"I-I am honored." Matthew bowed for lack of what else he should do. "Quite honored."

She studied him. "You do not look it."

"No. I am." Matthew forced a laugh. "Only I suppose I feel like I should have perhaps said something more before this."

"Oh no. I could never have . . ." She halted. Before

Matthew could fathom what she was about she dashed across the room. She flung her arms around him and standing upon tiptoe, kissed him squarely upon the lips.

Matthew, stunned, finally kissed her in return. This was his future wife, after all, and it behooved him to rise to the occasion.

They both drew back at the same moment. They stared at each other. Inside, Matthew groaned. Obviously he had not managed to rise to the occasion. It was there within her eyes.

Worse, he knew she could see the very same thing reflected in his own gaze. Sheer disappointment. The kiss had possessed no vitality. If Aunt Clare thought he and Penelope lacked a fire between them, he and Cecily didn't even have a flint of a hope.

"Well." Cecily offered up a very brave smile, Matthew thought. She was a game one. "I-I thank you, my lord. I am very excited. I must go and tell my father the good news."

"Yes. Please do that." Matthew nodded, determined to maintain sangfroid equal to that which she had just demonstrated.

She turned and hastened from the room.

"Good Lord." Matthew stalked over and poured himself a large brandy. "That was dreadful. Even worse than before. What is your problem, old man?"

The door opened without notice. Matthew looked up wearily. Andrew slipped into the room, his expression unreadable. "Have you proposed to Cecily yet?"

"Yes." Matthew shot back a hearty swig. "I think I have."

"You *think* you have?" Andrew asked in astonishment.

"We are engaged, that I do know," Matthew sighed.

"I see." Andrew's smile seemed tight. "I must congratulate you then."

Matthew smiled. "Thank you, Andrew. I-I know you were against Miss Morris . . ."

"No! I-I think her a wonderful woman." He shrugged. "I do not know why the devil I did not want you to marry her. I hope you will be very happy together."

Matthew nodded. He knew his own emotions colored the words, but they sounded more like a dirge than anything else. "Thank you."

Andrew frowned. "What is the matter?"

"Hmm, What?" Faith. He should never have kissed Penelope. Aunt Clare was right in holding that they were not destined to wed, but she was wrong about there not being a spark between them. The difference between Penelope's kiss and Cecily's kiss was frightening.

"You look . . . rattled."

"Do I?" Blast it, what did it matter how each lady kissed? There was more in a marriage of convenience than that.

"Are you sure everything went well?"

"Oh, yes." Matthew forced a smile. He should look on the bright side, confound it. "Miss Morris did not break into tears when I kissed her. That is an improvement, is it not?"

"You kissed her!" Andrew exclaimed, his face darkening.

Matthew blinked. He felt confused. He could not seem to stay focused on the conversation. "Yes, I did. Or, in truth, she kissed me."

"What!" Andrew exclaimed.

Matthew frowned. "Yes. Why?"

"Nothing." Andrew strode over and poured himself a drink. "Very well. She kissed you. And . . . you may tell me. I-I can face it."

"Face what?" Matthew asked.

Andrew flushed. "It was wonderful, wasn't it?"

"Wonderful?" Matthew sighed. "Not precisely. But it was all right, I assure you."

"Just all right?" Andrew's brows shot up. He shook his head. "No, that does not sound at all right."

"What?" Matthew shook himself from his reverie. He must stop thinking about Penelope. He was an engaged man once more.

"Oh, nothing. Only, well, with Cecily, ahem, Miss Morris . . . are you sure she hasn't captured your heart?"

"What?" Matthew lifted a teasing brow. "Are you perchance turning romantic on me, old man?"

"Perhaps." Andrew returned a wry smile. "This notion of you marrying without love, well, confound it, it doesn't sound as good as I used to think it. Are you positive you do not love her?"

Matthew's heart filled with warmth. "Andrew, do not fret yourself to flinders. You are the last one I would expect to turn coat at this juncture." He threw down his drink. "The deed is done and I can but hope that Cecily and I wed promptly and without ceremony."

"You do?"

"I do. For I will confess, it is growing harder and harder to throw my heart over the fence. Every proposal is worse than the one before. This one simply must stick."

"Heavens, I cannot understand it, but I am quite exhausted." Aunt Clare sat upon the parlor settee, her face bewildered. All twelve cats were present, but to the casual observer, unaccounted for. Unless one looked for a furry tail brushing from beneath the chair, or a paw slipping from around the back of the grandfather clock, or a whiskered face peering out of the arrangement of fresh peonies, they would be overlooked.

Penelope bit back a wry smile. The cats were effectively in hiding. Indeed, so were Aunt Clare and she. Jacob Lancer could not have found any better retribution to punish Penelope's disobedience than to have called upon his brother, Theodore, and his wife, Aunt Susan, to come to him in his hour of need. They had arrived swiftly at his plea and were well entrenched by the time Penelope and Aunt Clare had returned home from their adventure.

Penelope wondered at what sort of metamorphosis she had undergone in the past weeks. When she had arrived home to discover Aunt Susan and Uncle Theodore present, her first emotions had been guilt and self-condemnation. Guilt that she had caused such turmoil within her family. Self-condemnation that she had indeed forsaken her invalid father.

However, when Aunt Susan had said the same thing directly to her head, berating Penelope as an undutiful and selfish daughter, the oddest rebellion had arisen in Penelope's breast. Indeed, it had felt uncommon, and rather refreshing. Penelope realized not only had she been sitting at home weaving at an imaginary cloth on the imaginary loom of the dutiful daughter and the wistful dreamer, but that she had never made a push to have her own life. Otherwise, a mere jaunt like she had embarked on would not have caused such a family crisis. And, apparently, a crisis it had been. Things were not as they should be.

Matthew might declare that Jacob would not tolerate any contender for her hand, but in truth, Penelope had never given her father any cause to think that he would need to do so. Penelope bit her lip. In truth it was not Aunt Susan's outright attack that had made her see it, but rather her Uncle Theodore's behavior.

Uncle Theodore was quite one of her favorite relatives. He was different from his wife, though Penelope could see how he was the ideal match for her. Where Aunt Susan was strident, Uncle Theodore was amiable. He was as relaxed and easygoing as a summer breeze.

She was a crisp, blunt winter wind. She directed him like a general, but he never took it amiss. Where she was tall and gaunt, Uncle Theodore was broad and a good foot shorter than his wife.

Where Aunt Susan openly berated Penelope for her unfilial behavior, Uncle Theodore had but teased her about her madcap lark. He jovially treated the situation as if she were still a child pulling a naughty prank. Indeed, it was one that he felt certain she would repent of. All in all, it had been an eloquent testimony to the fact that the family did not think of her as a woman full grown in need of husband and children.

Penelope shook off her irritation and eyed the mound of sewing beside her. She had sought hard and long to gather a pile of such proportions as to take Aunt Clare and herself from the vicinity of the drawing room for a goodly while. Aunt Susan had accepted the project with dour approval. Now, Penelope and Aunt Clare had their feet tucked up on footstools, and with thread and darning bobbin in hand were set for a comfortable coze.

"I do hope you will not take this amiss, Penelope dear." Aunt Clare struggled with her thread. Sir Percy, fiend to the canine kingdom, lay snoring beneath the shirt she worked upon. "But your Aunt Susan is . . . well, she does keep a person frightfully busy. Which I am sure is only right. For she is a very *good* woman, is she not?"

"Positively a saint." Penelope nodded. She watched Aunt Clare's guilty and nervous reaction in amusement. "She is a leader in I do not know how many charities in London."

"Yes, dear. She told me all about them." Aunt Clare flushed all the more. "It is wondrous, to be sure."

Penelope stifled a chuckle. Aunt Clare's reaction was not unusual. Indeed, Aunt Susan had that effect upon most people. She did much good, but in such a strict and industrious manner that a person couldn't fathom why they wished to hide from her the minute she stepped into a room. "But what should I not take amiss?"

Aunt Clare blinked. "Ah, yes. Well, even though I have learned that dusty corners put you in danger of hell's gates . . ."

"Aunt Clare!" Penelope's eyes widened.

"That was what your Aunt Susan said, dear."

"I see." Penelope shook her head.

"Which I would not want for Lancer Hall. I am prepared to do what I can . . . for she is such a *knowing* lady. If she says the Almighty likes well-waxed banisters and polished silver, I am sure he does, but . . . I fear that it has thrown us from our own purpose. We simply must turn our attentions back to Matthew."

Penelope's heart leapt. In truth, her attentions had never strayed. She had thought about him day and night. "Indeed?"

"He has not called upon us in three days. I remember distinctly when he bade us farewell that he affirmed he would call upon us. Did he not?"

"Yes," Penelope sighed. She forced herself to speak her deep fear as if it were a casual thing. "I do not doubt he has become engaged once more."

"Dear me. I suppose you are right." Aunt Clare sighed. "I do wish he would stop and give us a moment to—to breathe. And think. I cannot help but feel pressed. Here we have been doing our level best to scrub your house into heaven, so to speak, and Matthew is out stealing a march upon another *wrong* bride. I—it is shameful, but I cannot help but feel miffed. And he is always saying it is I who am underhanded."

"Auntie, just who is the *right* bride for Matthew?"

Aunt Clare flushed. "Well, dear. I believe I know who she is, only please do not ask me to tell you more. This time I will not say a word until I am absolutely positive. And even when I am sure, I must inform you that I will not be able to tell you."

"Why not?"

"Because if you knew you would tell Matthew, and then he would be set against the lady ere he met her, which would make matters far more difficult, don't you think?"

"Than they already are, you mean?" Penelope tried to rein in her hurt. "I would not tell Matthew if you confided in me."

"My dear Penelope. You are very much like me." Aunt Clare nodded. "Or you are like how I was before I realized that people should not always be told what is good for them. They become quite nervous over it. Especially when it pertains to men and their true loves. But I promise you, dear, you will like her very much. Indeed, if you are not pleased to dance at their wedding, well . . . I shall be very surprised."

"I-I . . ."

"Hullo, there." Uncle Theodore stuck his head into the room. "Have you two charming ladies seen my dear heart?"

"No, Uncle." Penelope smiled. "She is supervising in the kitchen at the moment. She has called the fishmonger in for an accounting. She declares he has been pressing the scales in his favor."

"That is my beloved, to be sure." Uncle Theodore nodded. He winked. "One of the reasons I married her, you know? My Susan can ring a proper peal over those miscreants, while me, I never could build up enough energy for it, what?"

"True." Penelope smiled. In truth, she always thought Theodore had married Susan because Penelope's father had rather pestered him into doing so. Aunt Susan and Jacob Lancer were similar in attitudes when it came to the husbandry of the pound. Aunt Susan may run the great charities of London, but what actual donations that came from her own vast fortune were never deep enough to put even a crimp in it, which was exactly how it should be in Jacob's opinion.

"I never doubt we will have a different fishmonger before the day is out."

"Probably so, probably so. That will teach the chump." Uncle Theodore slid his entire bulk into the room. He wore a fawn-colored coat with yellow unmentionables.

"My," Aunt Clare gasped. Her eyes grew wide as she studied the boutonniere Theodore sported. It was an exotic, bright yellow blossom of some sort. He was always proud of his boutonnieres. "What kind of flower is that, Mr. Lancer?"

"This is *chilidanthus,* Miss Wrexton. Fairy Lily. It is appreciated for its lemon-like scent." Theodore trod over and lowered his form into a creaking chair. He sighed and in an absentminded manner rubbed his jacket lapel. "Well, now. What are you two ladies chatting about?"

Penelope laughed. She lifted a brow to Aunt Clare. "Auntie, I seem to remember you saying that you are accustomed to your brother smoking a cheroot and that you do not hold it in aversion."

"Why yes, dear, that is exactly what I said. You have such a wondrous memory." Concern swiftly crossed Aunt Clare's face. "Unless you are intending to take up the habit like Sherrice Norton. I pray you will not. I know I am dreadfully old-fashioned, but ladies should not blow a cloud. At least, Matthew's lady should not. But for men, I believe it quite proper. Indeed, Bendford smokes quite religiously." She jumped and peered at Theodore. "Do forgive me. I would not wish to offend you."

"No, no." Theodore grinned. "Not at all."

Penelope laughed all the more. "Do proceed, Uncle Theodore, before Aunt Susan discovers you."

"You are a darling puss." Theodore slipped his hand into his jacket to draw out a cigar. "Ah, yes."

Penelope winked at Aunt Clare. "It is Uncle Theodore's only vice. Unless you consider his penchant for boutonnieres of every exotic type, that is. I think he wears the flowers to disguise the odor of the cigar."

"Here now." Theodore grinned. "You wound me, niece. Cut me to the core, don't you know. And after I called you a darling puss at that."

Aunt Clare's lap stirred. "Meow."

"Egads!" Theodore jumped. "What in blazes?"

Other meows occurred. Theodore peered about, his face astonished.

"It was your employing the term 'puss.' They put all ears to attention at that word, you see," Aunt Clare said solemnly.

"Gadzooks. I thought we were alone. But they are all over, aren't they?"

"They do not mind if you smoke. Do you dislike cats?"

"Forsooth, no." Theodore shook his head. "Only it unnerves a chap to realize he has all eyes upon him and he didn't even know it. I . . ."

A din of no small effect occurred directly outside the parlor door. Voices, raised to battlefield levels, fought and contended.

"Gracious, whatever is happening?" Aunt Clare sprang up. A large thump and indignant howl occurred. She had, for once, moved more swiftly than Sir Percy. "My stars! Do forgive me, dearest."

"Hold the nonce!" Theodore froze, cigar in hand. He cocked his head to listen. Then he popped the cigar back into his mouth. "Susan's not involved. That I know."

Penelope narrowed her gaze. "Father is involved, though. That is clear."

Theodore puffed his cigar and nodded. "And your butler, Finch."

"Hmm." Aunt Clare squinted in concentration. She broke into a grand smile. "Why, Matthew has come to call. Finally!"

"Severs, you mean? Well now, that would explain the

brouhaha. Jacob won't forgive the lad his father's sin."
Theodore settled back into the large chair as the din
came closer. A look of interest crossed his features.
"Here, now. There's another voice I don't recognize.
What do you say, Penelope?"

"It has a certain familiarity . . ." Penelope laid down
her sewing as the parlor door burst open. There was
a roar as two bodies struggled to enter within the same
space. Jacob Lancer, due to his lethal employment of
his cane, toppled inward first. The other man was not
far behind and just as unsteady upon his feet.

"Sir Morris." Penelope blinked. "It is Sir Morris,
Uncle Theodore."

"So it is." Theodore nodded. Then he frowned.
"But who is Sir Morris?"

"There you are, you . . . you *abductress,*" Sir Morris
trumpeted and pointed a shaking finger at Aunt Clare.

"Hmm." Theodore drew in another puff. "He is
dressed like a cit. A well-to-do cit, mind you, but a cit
regardless. Who the devil is he?"

Jacob Lancer gained a steady stance. He rattled his
cane like a saber. "He is one of Severs's guests. B'gads,
I want him out of here."

"I am not leaving." Sir Morris visibly shook. "Not
until *she* tells me where my Cecily is!"

"Oh dear! Cecily is gone?" Aunt Clare clasped her
hands together. The cats crawled from everywhere to
circle about her.

"Who is Cecily?" Theodore asked.

Sir Morris glared at Aunt Clare. "Do not play the
innocent with me. Where have you taken my Cecily?"
He stepped forward with menace, only to have Sir
Percy "brrr" and pace toward him. He stopped.

"Confound it. Why is the fellow acting so addlepated?" Theodore complained. "Who is this Cecily
chit?"

Penelope shook her head, her heart wrenching.

"Cecily is the daughter of Sir Morris . . . and newly affianced to Matthew, if I do not mistake the matter."

At that moment Matthew stepped quietly into the room. Their gazes met for only a moment. "You do not mistake the matter."

"Matthew, dear, never say so," Aunt Clare exclaimed, her face stricken. Penelope hoped hers did not appear as openly the same.

"Of course it is so," Sir Morris roared. "Why else would you abduct my daughter? Heh! But you will not get by with it this time. You have Harold Morris here to contend with, madame. I am no namby-pamby aristocrat that you can gull."

"That is for sure," Theodore said, *sotto voce.*

"I'll not let you abscond with my daughter or stop her from marrying the earl. Do you hear me?"

"Gadzooks. Everyone hears you," Theodore complained. "Severs, I'd congratulate you, but I fear you have made a mistake as well as a misalliance."

Aunt Clare wrung her hands. "Sir Morris, I did not steal away your daughter. I did not even know that dear Matthew had proposed to her as yet."

"You heard her, Morris." Jacob Lancer shook his cane. "Now leave my house. Gad's, but you are an officious fellow, Severs. Just because you can't keep hold of a fiancée, it doesn't give you the right to come running to us at every turn."

"I am going to find my Cecily," Sir Harold shouted, a wild glare to his blue eyes. "You'll not play any tricks off on me. I'm no flat. I know you are hiding her here and I am going to find her!"

Theodore sighed and stood. "Why don't you do that, old fellow. Jacob, have Finch show the Bedlamite about, what? It is the best way!"

"Blast it, Theodore!" Jacob Lancer hopped up and down. "I won't allow him to ransack my house. Let him ransack Severs's house, bedamn."

"We have already looked this morning," Matthew said quietly.

"Well then, look again," Jacob snapped.

"My brother Andrew remains at home to do just that, Mr. Lancer." Matthew bowed gravely. "But we have found nothing amiss, except that Miss Morris has vanished. However, not a single item of hers has been taken. If you could . . ."

"No!" Jacob cut him off. "I am not having this jumped-up merchant search my house, I tell you!"

"Jacob, the man's dicked in the nob," Theodore said. "If you toss him out, he'll only toodle back around. We'll never have any peace from this Bedlamite."

"No! I say no!"

"Very well." Theodore sighed heavily. He walked over and offered his cigar to Penelope. "Be a good girl and take care of this properly, will you? I will show the cit around."

"I said . . ." Jacob roared.

"Cecily!" Sir Harold spun and lunged back through the door. "Cecily, where are you?"

"The poor, poor man." Aunt Clare's eyes teared. "I only wished I *had* abducted the dear child. Wherever could she be?" With that, she drifted out the door, her cats trailing behind.

"I am going to give that man a good drubbing, see if I don't!" Jacob Lancer vowed

"Yes, Jacob. But have a care with your foot while you do." Theodore took up his brother's arm and escorted him from the parlor. "Do let us have done with this before Susan is done with her fishmonger, else our gooses will be cooked. Or should I say our cod, ha?"

Penelope looked at Matthew, her heart pounding. Mustering all her reserve, she strolled over and held out Theodore's cigar to him. "Here. You can deal with this properly, I believe."

Matthew lifted a brow. "What is *properly?*"

"Why, douse it and then hold it for Uncle Theodore until he can return for it, of course. And whatever you do, do not permit Aunt Susan to find it." Penelope turned away from him and hastened to the door. She paused. "That was tottyheaded of me. You can always claim it as yours—something I cannot do as a female. Unless I am Lady Sherrice Norton, that is."

"Er, yes." Matthew stepped froward, his gaze dark. "Penelope, a thousand apologies."

Penelope glanced back, lifting her brow. "For what?"

"For this brouhaha Sir Morris is causing. I tried to stop him, truly I did."

"That is nice to know. Though I seem to remember you causing just as much of a stir with Lady Estelle," Penelope said it as levelly as she could. Faith, but Matthew looked exhausted and miserable. She squelched her sympathy with difficulty.

Following the racket, Penelope soon caught up with what now was a retinue of various beings. It consisted of the men, a trail of felines, and . . . Aunt Clare. The butler, footmen, and maids had joined the seekers as well. Theodore employed himself with translating bellows and cries from Sir Harold, directing the servants as to where that meant they were to look.

Penelope trailed them for as long as she could. However, she could feel her grasp upon her composure slipping. Sir Morris's mad bolt up the stairs and his repetitive lunge into each room with a bay for Cecily brought it down to the last thread. Seizing her chance, Penelope nipped into the closest bedroom before anyone could see her come undone.

Matthew watched as Penelope disappeared into a room. Concern overwhelmed him. Was she overset? Who would not be with such a mortifying investigation transpiring?

He paced softly to the door and peered into the room. Penelope sat upon the bed. Her hands covered her face and she shook. Matthew tensed, preparing to rush to her aid.

Then she lowered her hands and fell back upon the bed. She emitted a howl. Pain was completely absent from it. Indeed, it was a howl of sheer mirth.

Matthew's lips twitched. As he stood, Penelope's laughter washing over him, his own wrath dispersed. Gad's, how had he permitted this all to vex him to such a degree? He had well-nigh lost his sense of humor this past year. Above all things that he might be forced to give up, his sense of the absurd had best not be amongst them. Life would be far too dull without that commodity.

Drawing in a great breath, Matthew stalked into the room and roared, "For shame, Penn!"

"What?" Penelope jerked up as if strings had tugged at her. The consternation and guilt writ across her face was a sight to behold. Then the warmest relief sparkled within her green eyes. "Matthew. It is only you. Thank goodness. What are you about, frightening me like that?"

Her welcoming look lightened Matthew's heart. "You *should* be frightened. How dare you laugh upon this dreadful occasion. My second bride has gone missing."

"I am sorry." Penelope bit her lip like a truant child. Only she must have caught Matthew's mood. She smiled. "It is only that Sir Morris's opinion of where Aunt Clare might have hidden Cecily is rather miraculous. He will have it that Aunt Clare has merely dropped poor Cecily into a room and left her."

"He might be imagining her chained to a chair, or the wall, for the truly Gothic."

"Gracious. I had not considered that." Her eyes flared with amusement. "Does he not know that

Lancer Hall was built by bookkeepers with little imagination? They lay claims against people, not chains. Now *your* home would be far better equipped for such purposes."

"Penn, don't you dare put that suggestion in his mind." Matthew cast her as stern as look as he could. "Gad's. Sir Morris would be at it for years if he proceeds the way he is doing here. Did you notice that he even looked up your fireplace? He doesn't miss a trick, what?"

"Or crevice." Penelope stood. "But that's because he is no flat and Aunt Clare is a wily one, you know?"

Matthew cast her a mock frown. "Yes, I do, and it is not amusing."

"Of course not." Penelope pulled a grave face. She tapped her chin with one slim finger. "Hmm. This room has not been searched yet. Only think of the possibilities. Aha! I know." She strode over to the window and pulled up the sash.

"What on earth are you doing?" Matthew asked.

"Perhaps Aunt Clare hid Cecily out here over the edge." Penelope put her head out the window. "Cecily dear, are you hanging about?" She drew back in and sighed. "She is not there. A pity. There is a lovely view from here that she could enjoy."

"No, no. You have it all wrong," Matthew said, diverted by Penelope's diversionary play.

Penelope's eyes teased and she put her hands to her hips. "Do I, now?"

"Yes, you do." Enjoying the challenge, and how Penelope's gaze remained upon him, Matthew strolled over to the large armoire and opened it. "Aunt Clare is far more clever."

"No, never say Miss Morris is in the armoire. It is just too dull."

"No." Matthew pushed the clothes aside and rapped upon the interior wood. "Hmm. Rather too sound."

Penelope laughed. "Now you have me stumped."

"Come, Penelope, think." He crouched down then and opened its lower drawer.

"I am. And Cecily is far smaller than I remember."

"No widgeon." Matthew chuckled. "We are search-ing for a hidden compartment which then leads to a hidden staircase, which in turn leads to a hidden room. Now *that* would be Aunt Clare's favorite choice." He reached into the drawer, shoved the con-tents aside, and knocked on the drawer's bottom. "No such luck!"

"*Now* who is the great gapseed?" Penelope's voice was pure mischief. "But I have a notion. I know where Cecily Morris is."

"Hmm?" Matthew asked in abstraction. He had just taken note of the contents he had brushed aside. How could he not? They were the sort of papers all too familiar to him. He recognized them all too well. And there were stacks of them.

"Aha! I found her! Oh, and six pence, too!"

"What?" Matthew jerked around. He blinked in as-tonishment. All he saw was half of Penelope, a very trim posterior half of her, in fact, from beneath the bed. Laughing despite himself, Matthew closed the drawer. Standing, he strolled slowly over to her. "Hmm. Now this view is much fairer than the one from the window."

"Matthew!" Penelope's scandalized voice squeaked from beneath. The charming posterior half wiggled and squirmed.

"Much fairer."

"Ouch!" Penelope stopped writhing. A nervousness tinged her voice. "Er, Matthew, could you perhaps as-sist me?"

"Why?" Matthew grinned. "I do not mind if you and Cecily have a chat down there. I will stand watch here. Indeed, it is my pleasure."

"N-no." Penelope paused. She squirmed once more,

then halted. "Drat it, Matthew. I am stuck. You must help me."

"Must I?"

"Yes."

"You wish for me to get down upon my hands and knees and crawl under a bed? There is dust, I make no doubt."

"It is not *that* dusty." A stifled sneeze sounded. "Aunt Susan has not found this corner, evidently."

"I am sorry, Penn. It is quite below my dignity. I am an earl, do you not know? I cannot go crawling about like that."

"You may have the sixpence for your help."

"Ah. Now we are talking. A bribe of sixpence." Grinning, Matthew knelt down and clambered beneath the bed. He was quick to see where Penelope was stuck. Rather, *snagged*, in truth. Her hair had become caught within the springs. She turned her head cautiously to look at him.

Matthew feigned disappointment. "I thought you said you had found Cecily. What a hum."

"Matthew. Please do untangle me."

"Certainly." He shifted closer to her and dutifully untangled her hair from the rope. "You are released, milady."

"Thank you." Penelope began inching backward.

"Wait one moment." Matthew put up a staying hand. A wicked thought crossed his mind. It must have been due to the exasperating morning, and the need to escape his duties and concerns. Surely it did not have anything to do with Penelope's disheveled state and her sweet closeness. "Do not think you can squirm out of this so fast, Mistress."

"Oh, yes." Penelope smiled wryly. She unclasped her hand. "Here is your sixpence."

"No, no. I require more payment than that."

"What?" Her eyes widened.

Matthew forced a frown. "This is far dustier than I expected."

"For shame. We made an agreement."

"No, you misled me. I demand a higher price." Matthew lifted a brow. "A kiss will be a proper levy, I believe."

"Matthew!" Penelope's eyes widened. Color flared in her cheeks. "I cannot kiss you. You are engaged again."

"Am I? I would say my engagement has been delayed for the nonce." Penelope's flustered look was beguiling. "It is a perfect time to collect my reward."

Her eyes darkened in confusion. Matthew, not wishing to see it, or think of it, leaned over and kissed her. Unfortunately, they were both at such an angle that their lips barely touched.

Frustrated, Matthew drew back. "I fall short yet again."

"What?" Penelope frowned.

"Nothing." Matthew sighed. "Is not losing another bride enough? You must own my luck is at low ebb these days."

"I see. Then we must not tarry. We must search for Miss Morris." Penelope shifted and shimmied, knocking into Matthew. "Oh dear. My direction is amiss, I fear."

"Penelope, what are you about?" Matthew halted. The look in Penelope's eyes was laughter and desire, innocent delight and hidden wish. "Rather, what am *I* about? Do permit me to assist you."

He shifted toward her. After much twisting and turning, they were uncomfortably ensconced in each other's arms. Matthew cared not a bit, eager to kiss Penelope. When their lips met, reality faded away as he knew it would. No matter the conditions, when he kissed her, it was like coming home. It was like settling before a warm fire.

Then Penelope breathed a soft moan, and that warm

fire flared into desperate heat. The confined quarters but made each small movement of their bodies against each other more seductive, more intimate.

Penelope tore her lips from his with a gasp. "Is your luck improving?"

"Indeed, it's high tide of a sudden." Matthew knew he should release Penelope upon the instant. He barred the thought, however, employing the excuse that they were good and well stuck. He kissed Penelope again. The taste and texture of her was a never-ceasing amazement to him. How many times would it take before . . .

"What's this?" A muffled voice called from above. "Hello? Is anyone down there?"

Matthew drew back, astonished. What an untenable position in which to be discovered.

Penelope gasped, a flush rising swiftly to paint her cheeks. "Uncle Theodore?"

"Yes. That is who I am. Penelope, is that you?"

"Yes, Uncle Theodore." Penelope stared into Matthew's eyes, hers as large as saucers. "Ah . . . who is with you?"

"I am alone."

"Thank God," Penelope breathed. Matthew sent his own gratitude heavenward. If the entire search party had discovered them . . . zounds, he didn't even wish to consider it. Now Uncle Theodore, he was far too complacent a man to enact a tragedy over them.

"What of you, Penelope? Who are you with?"

"I am with Matthew. I mean, Lord Severs. We were . . . ah, looking for Miss Cecily."

"Pon rep. That's a good one." He chuckled. "I meant . . . I never thought of looking *beneath* the bed. Was that your notion, Severs?"

"No, Theodore, it wasn't." Matthew winked at Penelope. "It was Penelope's."

"Then you truly meant it? Tare an' hounds, Penelope, have you lost your mind like the rest of them?

Do you know that cit is searching every armoire, for some infernal reason? Such rot. I presume your fiancée is a girl, Severs, and not a jacket?"

"Yes, sir." Matthew grinned. Penelope made a face at him. He pinched her for it.

"Ohoo!"

"What happened?" Theodore's voice called.

"Nothing." Penelope frowned at Matthew severely. "It's just very difficult to move under here."

"Yes," Matthew called. "We have been having the devil's own time of it."

"I never doubt it, old man." Theodore's voice was muffled, but sounded rather amused. "You are fortunate I discovered you. Think what it would be if I had sat upon the bed. Penelope would be oohing far more. Now, would you two care to come out?"

"After you, my dear," Matthew whispered.

"Villain," Penelope hissed. She started to crawl away from Matthew. He bit back a groan. What blood of his hadn't been stirred before was now successfully set to boiling from Penelope's innocent wiggles.

Drawing in a calming breath, Matthew then made his own escape from under the bed. Penelope stood rather nervously, unable to meet his gaze. Faith, she appeared as guilty as the day was long.

Matthew turned a bland expression upon Uncle Theodore. "Well now, what brings you here, Theodore?"

"Nothing much." Theodore smiled. "Only this *is* my room, old man. Was I intruding?"

"No. No." Thinking quickly, Matthew reached into his pocket and drew out Theodore's stub of cigar. "Would you care for this now?"

"Forsooth, but I would." Theodore took it. "I am totally exhausted."

"We shall leave you then," Penelope squeaked.

"Why don't you do that." Theodore trod over and lowered himself into a wingback chair. "You two are

young enough to keep up the hunt for hours, what?"
He lit his cheroot and leaned back. "Hope you find
your fiancée, Matthew. But if she is ever discovered
beneath a bed, I will . . . well, I will give up my cigars
forever."

Eight

Penelope fought the urge to turn and run. She stood beside Aunt Clare before the large entrance doors to Severs Hall. Spanning to either side where they stood was a stately facade of red brick with white stone courses and cornices. The smooth Georgian front of Severs Hall belied its medieval heritage as home to the Severs family since the early 1600s. Indeed, it had survived ups and downs through a history of owners with a penchant for gambling on life as well as cards. Now, at this time, its calm, serene exterior was fighting off the attack of a garden out of control. No extra funds had been invested in cutting back ivy or trimming the gallery of myrtle trees. But it had survived worse.

Penelope gulped a deep breath as she looked up at the graceful portico above them. She and Matthew had stood under this portico that birthday when he had received his first pony. Another year later, they had pretended that its huge curved landing was the bow of a ship as they brandished wood sticks, fighting off pirates. The Hall had seen a series of generations. Indeed, some had been perfect citizens. And some, according to what Matthew had disclosed in the carriage on their return trip, had simply been denizens in the brotherhood of punting on what opportunities life offered at the moment. For a few generations of Severs it was a turn of the cards. For others it had been as privateers, sanctioned by royalty Matthew had explained, or as pirates . . . unsanctioned, need he say more. And for some, it had been just by the good fortune of looking the other way when one royal raced through their home, escaping the clutches of another royal.

"Are you sure we should do this?" Penelope asked as Aunt Clare lifted the knocker.

"Why, certainly, dear." Aunt Clare employed the knocker with vigor. "It is a perfect time for us to look for *signs.*"

"Let me see if I have this correct." Penelope frowned. "Signs come from people and their behavior. Signs are not to be confused with facts."

"Right, dear." Aunt Clare beamed at her. "The men are going to try and find the facts. That is why they have gone for the authorities. Which I own is a good circumstance. Men seem to find facts, all sorts of them, with great ease. I personally do not care for facts. They always seem so dull, and are quite misleading at times, in my opinion. But signs, now. They are ever so intriguing. Men, however, overlook them more often. We ladies are much more proficient at them, I believe."

"I hope Matthew will understand it better than I." Penelope sighed. "Else he will take our visit here in the worst possible light, I fear."

"Yes. But that is a chance we must take." Aunt Clare sighed herself. "Dear me. I vow it is far worse to be accused of stealing away Matthew's brides than it ever was when I actually did abduct dear Julia's grooms. Though, of course, no one accused me then, since they thought me innocent. Yet the simple truth is that it is far more taxing to *find* misplaced persons than to help *misplace* them."

Penelope smiled. "I would imagine you are correct."

One of the huge doors creaked open and Matthew's butler stood before them. Penelope found herself mumchance. Thank goodness, Aunt Clare dithered for the both of them quite nicely when she identified herself, told him of the longstanding friendship she had formed with her dear Matthew in London, and requested to see dear Matthew's family. The butler, his face impassive, bowed and led them directly to the drawing room. While they waited outside, he stepped into the room and announced their names. He returned and ushered them into the room.

Penelope halted. Aunt Clare had requested an interview with Matthew's family, and the butler had as if by a miracle accomplished just that. Not only were Lady Severs, the two girls, and Andrew present, but so were all of Matthew's guests. Those who still remained, that was. Lady Sherrice sat by Lady Norton upon the settee. Lady Violet sat next to Lord and Lady Stapleton.

"How wonderful." Aunt Clare wafted into the room. "We are just in time for a family discussion, are we not? May we please join? I do not mean to be so brash, but rules should be broken once in a while when things are important."

"Certainly." Lady Severs smiled with an easy grace. "You are Aunt Clare, are you not? We have heard so much about you." She looked to Penelope, who tensed. Her smile brightened all the more. "And Penelope, dear, it is such a pleasure to see you again. You have grown into a very lovely lady, I see."

"Thank you, mam." Penelope blushed. She had worried what manner of reception she would receive from Matthew's family for naught. They apparently did not concern themselves with the past contretemps.

"Please, do have a seat," Lady Severs said and waved to the filled room in a vague manner.

"You may have mine, Miss Wrexton." Monica sprang up. She grinned. "I am Matthew's sister. Could you tell me just how you abducted Matthew? He will not say."

"Thank you, dear." Aunt Clare moved over and took up the offered chair. "And you may call me Aunt

Clare. Everyone does, you know. But I do not think I should break a confidence."

"Rather," Lady Sherrice drawled, "you should ask her how she kidnapped Cecily, don't you think?"

"Sherrice, for shame." Lady Norton frowned.

"Well, it would be more to the point, would it not?" Lady Sherrice smiled a sweet, feline smile. "Though you will not hear a complaint from me. You may keep Cecily Morris tied up, with my blessings."

Aunt Clare blinked, a rosy hue coloring her fair skin. Her blue eyes were horrified. "Oh, dear, no. I-I never tied anyone up. That I vow. And I must tell you now that I do not have Cecily Morris."

"Oh, this is dreadful." Lady Severs sighed. "If you do not have her, what could have happened to the poor child, do you think?"

"Where are Matthew and Sir Morris?" Andrew asked. "Did they visit you?"

"Oh yes." Aunt Clare nodded solemnly. "They visited us, most thoroughly. In point of fact, they visited every room in Penelope's house. Then every outer building, and then even the acreage as well. Now they have gone to the authorities. I think they shall arrive here within an hour or two."

"What?" Andrew shot from his chair.

"Famous." Monica clapped her hands together. "Isn't that thrilling?"

"It will be ever so interesting," Christine chimed.

"Brats." Andrew shook his head and shrugged. "I am sure you are going to be disappointed. You know what Squire Wilson is like?" He strolled toward the door. "I cannot abide the man myself. So if you will pardon me, I will abstain from the entertainment."

"But Andrew!" Monica called. He did not stop, however. "Well, I never knew him to be such a spoilsport."

"I believe . . ." Aunt Clare stood. "That it would be an excellent notion for us to search for Cecily before the authorities do."

"Why?" Lady Severs blinked.

"Why? Because . . ." Aunt Clare looked bewildered.

"Because it will be fun, that is why." Monica sprang up. "Christine and I will help you, Aunt Clare."

"Indeed. We like Miss Cecily." She glared at Sherrice. "We want her to marry Matthew."

Lady Sherrice glared daggers and leaned back into her chair. "You may count me out. I refuse to spend my time looking for a cit's daughter. She no doubt ran off to Gretna Green with the farmer down the road."

"Oh no, I do not think so," Aunt Clare said solemnly. "Cecily had no beau or any particular man of whom she was enamoured. I ascertained that the very first night we met at Penelope's. And I do not believe her to be a dishonest girl."

"Indeed?" Lady Sherrice performed a delicate yawn.

"Violet will help hunt, won't you, gel?" Lady Stapleton said. "She ain't hoity-toity like some chits. *She's* a good and kind girl. She ain't sour grapes over losing the Earl. And if Cecily Morris doesn't appear, just remember my Violet wasn't the one who acted like a cat."

Lady Violet shrunk back, her eyes huge. "I shall go and search now."

"It will be like hide-and-go-seek," Monica said.

"Yes." Lady Violet could barely be heard.

"Penelope and I will go together," Aunt Clare said. "Come, dear."

Penelope found herself forced to sprint from the room, so fast did Aunt Clare move. "Aunt Clare. Where are we going?"

"I am not sure, dear. But there is a maid. Let us ask her." She drifted up to the maid with the sweetest smile. "Pardon me, dear. Did you see where young Andrew went? We must speak to him."

"Yes, madame. He went up the stairs there."

"Thank you." Aunt Clare lifted her skirts and bolted upstairs. Penelope, sighing, chased after her.

At the top Aunt Clare halted. Penelope came to a stand, almost bumping into her. "There he is," Aunt Clare whispered.

"Are we chasing Andrew?" Penelope asked. "And why?"

"Did not you see the *sign*, Penelope?"

"What sign?"

"I wondered this very morning, and now it is obvious."

"What is obvious?"

"Dear, didn't you think it odd that Andrew had chosen to remain here this morning?"

"No, I didn't."

"Ah, my dear, only consider it. Andrew does not appear the sort of lad who wishes to miss out upon any excitement, unless there is something even more exciting to be had. Shh!" Aunt Clare tiptoed after Andrew, who strolled along the hall. He appeared quite natural, and in truth, rather devil may care. Penelope tiptoed after both of them. They proceeded through three more corridors in this cloak-and-dagger fashion, now and then darting into alcoves. Penelope did not find it intriguing. She merely wished to scream.

She had not seen any signs. Why were they so secretively chasing after Andrew?

They paused, peeked, and then turned the next corner. Penelope frowned. Andrew appeared to have walked into an alcove that had been ahead of them, but now it was empty. "Drat. We lost him. Where did he go?"

"Oh, how terribly exciting." Aunt Clare clapped her hands together.

Now Penelope really wanted to scream. "Aunt Clare, we lost Andrew. He must have gone the other way."

"I do not think so dear." Aunt Clare walked with purpose up to the end wall, all but snubbing her nose upon it. She bounced back, only to begin thumping and thwacking upon it.

"What are you doing?"

"I am looking for a secret passage."

"Of course." Penelope drew in her breath, nodding. Her good humor returned. Gracious, but how she would love to tell Matthew the story and see his brilliant blue eyes sparkle with amusement. Matthew had teased her about Aunt Clare, pretending to find secret doors and halls just that morning. He apparently understood dear Aunt Clare well. Rooms and closets would be too banal for her. Better to opt for the Gothic and go for secret doors and hidden passages. Penelope quirked her head. With the history of generations of Severs riding the seas, perhaps Aunt Clare wasn't far off the mark. Penelope strode over to the wall beside Aunt Clare's choice and thwacked it heartily. "Forgive me, I had *not* considered it."

"I understand, dear." Aunt Clare continued to thump, bump, and pound. "You are not at all of the secretive mind. I own, if I had not read so profusely upon the matter, I would not have considered it either."

"Indeed?" Grinning, Penelope rested her weary hand, and leaned against the wall she had been investigating, a portion that portrayed on its plastered surface a mural of the fall of Adam and Eve. It moved. She jumped. "Gracious!"

"Ah, you clever girl. You found it. How delightful." Aunt Clare peered into the crack that had opened.

"Er . . . yes." Penelope reclaimed her balance, but not her credulity. "I cannot believe it. That must be a secret staircase. I wonder where it leads."

"We must find out later, I fear." Aunt Clare sighed.

"What?" Penelope exclaimed. *Now* she was intrigued and it was just too bad of Aunt Clare to say they must put it off. "But why? Shouldn't we . . . er, strike while the iron is hot? Discover if Andrew used these stairs. See where it goes? Perhaps . . ."

Aunt Clare's eyes sparkled. She lifted a finger to her

lips. "Shh. We must return tonight when all are asleep and we need not fear discovery. . . ."

"What? How shall we do that?"

". . . Whatever we do, we must not tell anyone about this as yet. Especially not Matthew."

"Why?"

"The dear boy has enough upon his plate, do you not think? Besides, we discovered this ourselves. I think it only fair that we investigate before anyone else. Matthew seems to be in the testiest of moods these days. Indeed, I would not put it past him to put a damper upon the entire escapade."

"Yes, you are right about that." Penelope peered into the dark crack. Her pulse beat faster with the fantasies of where this secret passage could lead. "Why would Andrew use a secret passage?"

"I do hope it is for an exciting reason, and not for something commonplace. I shall be quite disappointed if he uses it every day merely to go to his room by the fastest way."

Penelope again peered into the crack. "No. I cannot believe that."

"Neither do I. I think this is going to be an adventure. I can just feel it. Only imagine, how fortunate we are to have another adventure, and all in one week."

Penelope smiled. "I believe I can feel it, too, Aunt Clare. I can feel it, too!"

"Now, let us close this and return to the house party. Lady Severs appears the kindest of ladies. I do hope she will permit us to remain as guests—it will make everything far simpler, to be sure."

Penelope prowled about the blue room that Lady Severs had appointed to her. Excitement coursed through her. She paced impatiently up and down the blue-and-white floral carpet. She was learning that when Aunt Clare set her dithering heart and wondering mind to a purpose, things happened. Witness that she had secured invitations to remain the evening with the house party.

Lady Severs fully understood Aunt Clare's deep concerns that dear Cecily be found. Indeed, she was so much in sympathy with Aunt Clare that she vowed that Penelope and she must remain as long as they wished. Both ladies seemed to think that if Aunt Clare lived under the Severs roof it would be testimony to the fact that Aunt Clare could not be engaged in anything havey-cavey.

Lady Severs had also openly laid a bet on Aunt Clare being the first to find the lost fiancée. Monica and Christina had bet against their mother, claiming that they would find Cecily Morris first. Andrew had refrained from the bet but offered to keep the books. Lord and Lady Stapleton had laid their money upon Violet and they would prefer Andrew *not* keep the books. Indeed, this was understandable. They had bet heavily, warning them all that their Violet was the cleverest of girls and if she chose to ride to hounds no one would beat her. Everyone accepted the bet with great diplomacy, since Lady Violet had sat wide-eyed and mumchance, clearly not eager to ride to hounds after the missing Cecily. It was agreed; Matthew was the acceptable choice to administer the books. The betting was closed.

Matthew had not been pleased with any of it, either with the betting or with Lady Severs's invitation that they stay. Penelope frowned. She did not know why he should be in such a disagreeable mood. Aunt Clare had vowed it was merely that poor Matthew was burnt to the socket, what with Squire and the authorities questioning everyone and searching all about the Hall.

Penelope snorted. Matthew was in no manner *poor* in Penelope's opinion. Not with all the attention he was receiving. Sherrice Norton and her mama had fawned over him the entire evening. Lady Violet's parents had also put their bid in to be charming, though with Lady Stapleton, that meant a plethora of horse stories. Faith, even the shy Violet had been casting sheep's eyes at him over the dessert. Though, to be fair, that might have been Penelope's overactive imagination.

She grimaced. Very well, it might not exactly be her imagination that was overactive, but rather her jealousy. It had taken all she had in her to sit through the dinner and withdrawing to the music room afterwards, all the while pretending to be calm and collected. It was in no way felicitous to kiss a man in the morning, only to realize that it meant naught to him by the night.

Indeed, it was lowering, very lowering. Poor Cecily Morris was not even a day cold in her abduction yet, and already the other misses were maneuvering to take her place. Penelope's chin jutted out. She, at least, was not in that category. She was not chasing Matthew to gain a ring. True, she had kissed him this morning. But that was because . . . because he had appeared so very downcast. She had wanted to comfort him, and make him laugh, and make him happy.

Penelope stopped in her tracks. What a perfect ninnyhammer she was. She would cast aspersions upon the other ladies for chasing after him with matrimony the purpose while she, she was so pathetic as to have no other scheme in mind than to amuse him when he was low, and die in his kisses when he offered them.

She shook herself. It must stop, truly it must. She nodded briskly and continued pacing. "It will stop. I refuse to be used so shabbily."

A knock sounded at the door. Penelope jerked to attention. "Yes?"

"Penelope, it is I," Aunt Clare's voice whispered. "May I come in?"

"Oh yes, please do!"

The door opened and Aunt Clare entered.

Penelope's eyes widened. She was shrouded in a long, dark cloak. She held something concealed beneath it, the effect making her look very disfigured. She peeked about the room. "A-are you alone?"

"Yes." Penelope flushed. "Of course I am."

"I thought I heard you speaking to someone."

"No. No, I wasn't." Penelope bit her lip. She couldn't very well say that she was giving herself a strong lecture. "What do you have beneath your cloak?"

"Meeker delivered it when he brought us our trunks." She flipped back her cloak to reveal an ancient torch and a cloak. "Isn't it marvelous?"

"Yes, it is." Penelope blinked. She forced her thoughts back to the moment. Faith, they were going to have an adventure, and here she had let Matthew cast a pall upon it. "I had not thought of a cloak."

"Yes, dear, I expected that. You have not read *The Mysterious Warning*. That is why I brought this one as well. In all the books, the passages are quite drafty."

"Thank you." Penelope's spirits lifted tremendously as she took the cloak and put it on. "What do you think we will discover tonight, Aunt Clare? Do you . . ."

Another knock sounded at the door. Penelope looked up, staring wide-eyed at Aunt Clare. Aunt Clare stared wide-eyed back.

"Who is there?" Penelope asked, her voice tightening.

"Penn. It is me, Matthew."

"Matthew!" Penelope hastened to the door and lowered her voice. "What do you want?"

There was a pause. "Are you alone?"

"Yes," Penelope said. "Of course I am alone."

"I thought I heard you talking to someone."

"I was just talking to myself" Penelope blushed. She was doomed to make that confession in one manner or another. "What do you want?"

An even longer pause ensued. "I wish to speak to you."

"It is very late." Penelope glanced back over her shoulder. Aunt Clare had tucked the torch back beneath her cloak and was looking about in alarm. Penelope motioned her to remain still. "What is it that you need? I mean . . . what do you wish to talk about?"

"I wish to make certain that you are all right."

"Of course I am all right. Why wouldn't I be?"

"You were not acting like yourself tonight."

"Yes, I was. Indeed, I was." Penelope clenched her teeth. "And I am. I mean . . . I am all right."

"Then open up this door and show me that you are all right."

Penelope groaned. There was suspicion in his voice, and determination. "No, Matthew."

"Penn, you seemed overset and . . . unhappy. Was it because of this morning? Was it . . ."

"Be quiet!" Penelope snapped in embarrassment.

"What?"

"I mean . . ." Penelope cracked open the door and slipped out, shutting it firmly behind,

Matthew frowned. "Why are you wearing a cloak? Are you leaving?"

"No, of course not."

"Good." Relief entered his eyes. Then suspicion took over. "Then why are you wearing a cloak?"

"I . . ." Penelope thought swiftly. She lifted her chin. "Because I am prepared for bed. What would you expect? And . . . and my maid did not send a wrapper."

Matthew's eyes flared in amusement and his smile grew wry. "Forgive me. I know it is improper that I have sought you out, but I did not think you would pay heed to it."

"What?" Penelope's new resolve forged to the front with his careless comment. "Why would I not pay heed to the conventions? Do you consider me so very improper, then?"

"No!" Matthew eyes widened in astonishment, and then consternation. "No, Penn, certainly I do not. I meant that I did not think you would stand upon ceremony with me."

"Well, I do," Penelope said with a pugnacious tone. "I mean, I intend to do just that from now on."

Matthew shook his head. "Do what?"

"Stand upon ceremony with you." Penelope drew in a deep breath. "Strict, formal, proper ceremony, at that."

Matthew studied her and clear understanding entered his gaze. "You feel guilty about this morning, do you not? I feared as much. It was clear to me by your behavior at dinner."

"No, it was not clear by my behavior at dinner," Penelope countered ruthlessly. Something in her heart had warmed that Matthew had been watching her and had cared about her sensibilities. Yet that was the rub, for when something warmed in her heart with Matthew, she always ended up in the suds . . . or his arms, whichever came first. "And even if you were concerned, coming here now is . . . is completely vile."

"What?" Matthew reared backward, his expression rather that of a tiger being stung by a wasp.

Penelope flushed. "You know very well that we do not behave properly when we are not chaperoned. Therefore, for you to come here tonight . . ."

"Means that I came here to seduce you." Matthew's brows snapped down, his gaze incredulous and angry. "Is that correct?"

Penn lifted her chin. "You must own you have become somewhat of a . . . a rake."

"What! Me a rake!"

"You kissed me this morning, but you were quite happy to have Lady Sherrice and . . . and the shrinking Violet throw their caps at you tonight."

"Ridiculous." Matthew stared at her. The infernal man then had the brass to grin, and grin very smugly at that. "Penn, you are jealous. That is what this tempest is all about, isn't it?"

"I am not jealous!"

He chuckled. "You must be if you think that poor Violet . . . I mean sweet Violet, was casting out lures to me. Next you will be warning me that she is a Jezebel."

"No." Penelope could very well kick herself. She did look like a pea goose. "Very well, you may laugh at me all you wish. However, what this 'tempest' is all about is to warn you that I am serious in my demand for . . . for propriety. I do not want you to kiss me ever again. Do I make myself clear?"

"Very clear." Matthew's eyes now flared in anger. "I assure you, now that I know they are abhorrent to you, I will never again force my attentions upon you."

"Good," Penelope said curtly. The wicked beast, he knew that in no manner could his attentions be considered abhorrent to her. He was attempting to seek her denial, weaken her resolve. "Re . . . regardless of . . . the quality of your attentions, they should be held in reserve for your future fiancée."

"Penn, forgive me." Matthew said it quickly, his expression instantly contrite, and far too disarming. "You are right. My behavior has been . . . reprehensible. I-I have made a mull of it by coming here tonight. But never doubt that I-I . . ." He straightened and his gaze became guarded. "You *are* my friend and I *am* concerned for your welfare."

"Thank you." Penelope swallowed her pain. They were such lukewarm words compared with the heat of what she harbored for him. "But you need not take it so to heart, Matthew. I am quite able to take care of myself. I do not need you, I promise."

Matthew flinched as if she had physically slapped

him. "Of course. It was quite foolish of me to concern myself, I see."

"Yes, it was." Penelope felt it. She was close to breaking. Then she would beg his forgiveness for acting like such a shrew, and probably confess that his attentions were wonderful to her. That would never do. Without another word, she jerked open the door and scurried back into her room. She slammed it, leaning against the wood for support, closing her eyes against the emotions.

"Are you all right, dear?" Aunt Clare asked.

"Oh!" Penelope jumped. She snapped open her eyes. "Aunt Clare . . . forgive me. I quite forgot . . . ah, never mind."

Aunt Clare cocked her head to one side. "What should I not mind?"

"Nothing, nothing at all." Penelope forced a smile. "We have an adventure to go upon, do we not?"

"Indeed we do, dear Penelope." Aunt Clare beamed. "I am glad to know Matthew did not throw a spanner into the works. You were so long with him, I feared you had let the cat out of the bag, so to speak."

"No." Penelope winced, her sharp words coming back to her. "That was not the particular cat that came out of the bag, I fear."

Penelope's excitement increased. They had followed the winding stone stairs down and down. It had grown colder and damper. Her anticipation had grown equally with each step.

"Wherever can this lead?" Penelope whispered and held the torch high.

"I do not know, dear. But it is a very long passage, is it not? Though in good repair and quite clean." Aunt Clare's voice held disappointment.

"Aunt Clare, what would you have it be? Grumbling and mice-ridden?"

"I suppose not. But . . . I read this famous book where there was a skeleton . . ."

Penelope shivered. "Aunt Clare! Do not even mention such."

"You are right." Aunt Clare giggled. "I think I would rather read about a heroine coming across such a thing than actually doing so myself"

Penelope halted of a sudden. A breath of a breeze wafted to her. Within it, she could smell salt. "I know what we will find!"

"Oh, yes. The water!"

Both ladies, though prepared, could not help but gasp as they stepped from out of the passage onto a rough and craggy overhang. The view of the sea was breathtaking, even void of stars and moon as it was. A mist rose and swirled about them. "How lovely."

"Isn't it?" Aunt Clare sighed. "Imagine being able to come here every day or night if one wished."

"Yes." Penelope frowned. "I do not think Andrew frequents here for the excellence of the view, however."

"No, indeed not." Aunt Clare peered to the right and left. "I will lay any money that there is a cave somewhere close by."

"Cave?" Penelope shook her head. "Just why would you think there would be a cave here?"

Aunt Clare didn't answer, but wandered off. Penelope shrugged and took what appeared to be a path. This was an adventure, after all. If she were to hunt for a cave, hunt she would.

Her heart leapt as she discovered an opening behind two straggling bushes. "Aunt Clare! I believe I have found it."

"Have you, dear? How famous." Aunt Clare came stumbling out of the mist. "Gracious, I do hope we find what I think we should find."

"What do you hope we will find?"

"No, dear, I am not going to tell you. If I am mistaken I will have only raised my own hopes to no purpose, and not yours as well." Aunt Clare plunged into the cave.

"But how did you know about the cave?" Penelope followed behind in curiosity.

"It is something I remember Matthew telling me." Aunt Clare's voice was proud. "He told you, too, if you consider it, dear."

"Told me what?" Then Penelope gasped.

"It has to do with his family history. Remember?" Aunt Clare's voice was eager as they all but loped through the cave, the torch casting flickering, thrilling shadows upon the wall. "His great-grandfather was a free-trader . . . oh my!"

"What?" Penelope collided into a frozen Aunt Clare. Unfortunately, that sent Aunt Clare stumbling forward directly into a large, well-lit enclosure. The space was tight due to rows and rows of kegs. And the bountiful lighting came from other torches, not their own.

"As is his brother," Aunt Clare whispered. Why she did so, however, was a conundrum. For Aunt Clare's tumbling entrance had been duly noted. Andrew was the first to spin toward them. Then five other men bent their gaze upon them. And then one lone woman offered them her attention.

"Cecily Morris!" Penelope squeaked. She then covered her mouth, noting the rather nasty expressions upon the five unknown men. Their features were as coarse as the clothes they wore.

"Yes, dear." Aunt Clare sighed. *"She* was supposed to be the surprise. Not . . . er, Andrew's ventures."

"Blast it to hell, Severs. What's this?" The largest of the men, and clearly the leader, jerked out a pistol from his waist and pointed it at Penelope and Aunt Clare. "A bloody swooooree?"

Aunt Clare scuttled back directly into Penelope. "Oh my. I do not believe I like this. Not at all."

"Lower that gun, Merston," Andrew ordered, his tone haughty. Holding Cecily's hand, he drew her with him, strolling over to Penelope and Aunt Clare as if he'd not a care in the world. He was equally blasé about placing himself between the ladies and the unwavering pistol. "These delightful ladies are friends of mine."

"What have ye been doing? Opening your chaffer to everyone about our lay?" Another man, outstanding for his ugliness, stepped forward. He drew out an even uglier pistol.

"No, Treeble. I was only hiding Miss Morris here for the nonce." Andrew frowned with severity. "She is here upon my wishes and with my permission. While you chaps, are decidedly *de trop*. Hell and the devil confound it, this load was not to be stored here for another week. Were you attempting to pull the wool over my eyes? Get the Scotch whiskey to France early, return with the shipment of muslin and brandy without my knowledge, and cut me out in the middle? You get the ready. I outrun the constable."

"Andrew . . ." Cecily murmured.

"Well, I will have none of it. Our partnership is over."

"Is it now?" Merston puffed out his chest and blustered. "It's not you, guv'nor, who can say it's over."

"It's us who can!" Treeble, responding far more concretely, cocked his pistol. Every lady shrieked.

"Don't, you bloody fool!" Merston swung his hand at his insubordinate partner. It set Treeble's aim off but a jot as the pistol fired. Andrew jerked and crumpled to the cave's floor.

"Andrew!" Cecily threw herself upon him. "Are you all right? Please speak to me." He didn't. "Oh God, please do not let him be dead."

"Treeble. You bacon-brained clunch," Merston growled. "Look what you've done now."

"Blast you, Tom, ye near ruined my aim." Treeble lumbered forward. His face showed eager malice as he looked at the fallen Andrew. "Here I have been just waiting to kill the cocky bastard and you go and spoil me sport. I wanted ter do it in one shot like."

Penelope's stomach turned queasy, and her heart rocketed to her throat. There was cold blood in Treeble, very cold blood. Stumbling forward, she ruthlessly shoved Cecily aside. Treeble wasn't to get to Andrew again if she could help it. "Wait! Cecily, do stop your crying. Maybe he isn't dead." Her hands shaking, Penelope placed her fingers to Andrew's neck with great drama.

"Is he . . ." Cecily clasped her hands together in prayer.

"Well? Is he?" Treeble rumbled.

Penelope couldn't speak a moment as she felt a flutter of a pulse against her fingertips. She swallowed and with as much anger as she could muster, she glared at Treeble. "Yes, you fiend. He is dead. You killed him!"

"No!" Tears rolled down Cecily's face, her blue eyes stricken. "My Andrew."

"I am sorry." Penelope teared in sympathy. She reached out and clasped Cecily's shoulder to force Cecily to look in her eyes. "Treeble killed him . . . all right and tight. With only one shot, there is nothing we can do."

"Ha!" Treeble broke into a frightful grin. He looked at Merston. "You didn't ruin my aim after all."

"Oh dear." Aunt Clare's hand fluttered to her chest. "I-I have never felt like I would faint before, but . . . but . . ."

"Eeks!" Cecily shrieked. Penelope jumped and looked at her. She was staring at Andrew as if he had bit her. Penelope paled. His lashes were fluttering. Cecily looked back to Penelope, her eyes wide with wonderment and understanding. A slight smile tinged her lips before she flung herself on top of the awakening Andrew. "Oh, my Andrew, you are dead! You are dead!"

"Well, it's a good thing ye didn't waste yer shot, Treeble." Merton's voice was bitter. " 'Cause now we gots to kill these here gentry-morts, too. You can't kill one of these flash gentry and not the others. They'll widdle the whole scrap. If you had any wits ye would have thought of it, before going off half-cocked. Think how it's going ter slow us down with four bodies to dispose of. One ye can leave anywhere, but four ye gots to do something with, damn it."

"Damn." Treeble's look of dismay would have been comical if Penelope didn't cherish the four bodies under discussion. The three other men glared at Treeble and added their complaints and curses.

"I am sorry, dear." Aunt Clare wrung her hands. "This was not the adventure I-I planned. Matthew will be so furious with me. And Bendford will be absolutely livid." She paled. "Oh dear, I suppose that won't matter if I am dead, though."

"Bendford!" Penelope murmured. A glimmer of hope flared within her. She tried for a nervous expression. "Shh, Aunt Clare, do not mention your brother."

"What, dear?" Aunt Clare blinked.

"Andrew, you are dead," Cecily cried. She was an affecting sight as she hugged her departed love. She shook him so with her grief, however, that any stirring of the corpse's own volition would be difficult to notice. "You have departed this world forever."

Penelope raised her voice over the distraction. "You know, he is too rich. These men might decide to hold you for ransom rather than kill you. You know your brother would pay anything for your safe return. You wouldn't want that, would you?"

"Gracious no. Not at all." Aunt Clare, nodding vigorously at Penelope first, then turned her blue eyes upon the men. "On second thought, could you please go ahead and shoot me, too? If you ransomed me and took all of Bendford's money, well, I would just never hear the end of it."

"What would they care about your sensibilities?" Penelope shrugged and said with a feigned bitterness. "They would be famously wealthy and could take off to the colonies. Live like kings."

"Dearest." Aunt Clare looked hurt. She truly did. "You should not be throwing that at my head as you do. Have you but considered that you are just as rich as Bendford? And your father would drop a fortune for you, too."

"You mean it would be a double ransom?" Penelope appeared to consider. She peeked to see all the men staring, mouths agape but eyes starting to light. She tried for a surprised look. "Gracious, no. But it could be a triple ransom. For Miss Morris is a wealthy heiress as well."

Cecily stopped rattling the now still—tensely still—Andrew. "But I'm not flash gentry. I'm a cit's daughter, as everyone insists on reminding me. Why should I be killed with the rest of you?"

"Hush. They truly would like your father's money more then," Penelope said solemnly.

"But dearest . . ." Aunt Clare said. "They . . . these men, if they ransomed us would be . . . oh, my . . ."

"Do not fear, Aunt Clare." Penelope hoped the hook was well entrenched in their jaws. "They probably will kill us instead. After all, they would have to be mighty clever to keep us alive and safe. And look at Treeble. He is far too trigger-happy. He'd rather kill a chance at a fortune and spend the added time disposing of our bodies at that."

"True dear." Aunt Clare nodded. "Look what he did to poor Andrew."

"But I didn't like him," Treeble said. "I like money. I like it a lot."

"And he ain't in charge." Merston's chest puffed out. "I am."

Penelope shook her head. "It would take a mastermind to manage three abductions at once."

"Oh, no, dear. I did it," Aunt Clare said in a reasonable tone. "And it is clear I am no mastermind."

"Hmm, yes. We are all defenseless and under their control," Penelope said in consideration. "They could pull it off, perhaps."

Merston's brain was clearly working.

So was Treeble's. "We could kill yer and still gets the ransom."

"Oh, no." Aunt Clare looked at him with shock. "Bendford isn't the type to buy a pig in a poke. He wouldn't give you a fortune unless I was returned to him alive."

"As for my father, you might know of him. He is Jacob Lancer. He's a curmudgeon."

Merston nodded. "I've heard of him. Tight-fisted bloke."

"He only pays for goods that aren't damaged." Penelope nodded.

"My father is famous for his business sense," Cecily added. "He's as shrewd as he can stare, you know. And he's already hunting for us. If he found us all . . . dead, he would never pay. Not a ha'penny."

"We'll take them with us," Merston said quickly. "We'll take the booty to France and them with us. We'll have time to think this all through. But I ain't killing these gooses if they can lay them golden eggs. Now let's go!"

Nine

Matthew sat in his room, ensconced in a huge, comfortable wing-backed chair, a bumper of brandy in his hand. He wasn't comfortable, however. He stared at his drink more than he drank it, as if its amber depths might hold the answers.

He clenched his teeth. Penelope had been correct—he had acted the bounder. In truth, he had gone to see her in honest concern. He had seen how her open and excited face had slowly closed during dinner. He had seen how she would no longer look at him. And he had grown concerned, very concerned.

Faith, not to have her green eyes meeting his in open communication had driven him to distraction. Penelope had noticed the ladies' attentions more than he had, to be sure. He had merely dealt with them as politely as he could and still remain a proper host. Yet Matthew called his subconscious to account. Penelope had lifted the mirror up with a vengeance. He did act like a rake when they found themselves alone. He couldn't seem to stop himself from reaching for her or teasing her into stolen kisses.

Now, because of it, he had destroyed their friendship. *Do not take it to heart—I am quite able to take care of myself. I do not need you, I promise.* The words sank deeper into him. He should heed her advice. He should not take it to heart. Indeed, he had no right to take anything to heart in regard to Penelope.

He sighed and consciously attempted to relax his muscles. It was impossible. Everything felt . . . wrong, frightfully wrong. Granted, he had lost his second bride and the day had been chaotic, and he had just been turned off sharply by . . . a dear friend, but something else prodded him. Something else whispered of trouble. Faith, if he did not know better, he would swear he was experiencing something akin to one of Aunt Clare's "forebodings."

He gritted his teeth. What could it be? Springing up, he prowled about the room, seeking to divine what he felt. He froze then as he heard the slightest sound from outside his door. A mere whisper, to be sure, but it was enough to pull at his taut nerves.

That mere whisper turned into a gigantic thump and bump. Cursing, Matthew strode to the door, jerked it open, and plunged into the hall. He was prepared for anything.

The two feminine shrieks, therefore, did not faze him. Only when he recognized the girls did Matthew sigh, his tension draining away. "What are you two doing, pray tell?"

"Shh." Christina clutched a night lantern to her. "You will wake someone."

"I will?" Matthew whispered before he realized it. He shook his head in exasperation. "Step into my room directly, please."

"Matthew." Monica's voice held a particular plea to it. "Please, we have no time to talk."

"Why not?"

"We are going in search of Miss Cecily," Christine said. "We do not want Aunt Clare and Penelope to steal a march on us."

Matthew chuckled despite himself. "I believe you may rest easy upon that head. Penelope is retired, as is Aunt Clare, I am sure. Unlike you two, they have

more common sense than to go sneaking about in the
dead of night. Now step into my room, please."

He employed the proper tone to make the girls bus-
tle quickly into his chambers. Matthew glanced down
the hall to ensure that the commotion had not drawn
any attention, and then he followed the girls and
closed the door firmly. He turned to them, applying
his most stern look. "Now what game is this? You cannot possibly think to discover Miss Cecily in this manner."

"Why not?" Christine asked. "Just because we haven't found her yet, and just because the Squire and
his men didn't . . ."

"Andrew is right. Squire Wilson is a nodcock,"
Monica said with great haughtiness.

"I beg your pardon?" Matthew lifted his brow. "Regardless of what Andrew says, and regardless of Squire
Wilson's er . . . mental capacities, young ladies do not
go about calling those who are older, and in authority,
nodcocks. Understand?"

"Yes," Monica said, her voice lacking any form of
contrition. "But Miss Cecily may be hidden about still.
You know that is why Aunt Clare and Penelope came."

"And we want to win the bet." Christine nodded.

Matthew sighed. "Aunt Clare and Penelope only
made that tarradiddle up in order for Aunt Clare to
come here. Mother fell directly into her trap."

"Oh, no. Matthew, how can you say that?" Monica
gasped. "Aunt Clare wouldn't do something like that.
She is such a sweet lady."

"And it makes more sense for Cecily to be somewhere about our house," Christine said. "It was totty-
headed for old Harold Morris to go howling and
raging through Penelope's house."

Matthew gritted his teeth. "Just because Morris is a
hothead doesn't mean you need be one also. I understand you wish to win the bet, but use your heads. Why,
pray tell, would Miss Morris be hiding in our house?"

The girls' faces fell in unison.

Monica's brightened first. "Perhaps she has become lost? It is a very large house, you know. Why, we have discovered places we didn't even know existed before, and we have lived here all our lives."

"Imagine that," Matthew said dryly. "All of fifteen years at that."

"Perhaps we have a ghost," Christine proposed. She shivered. "It was the ghost of Severs Hall who abducted Cecily."

"That *is* crack-brained and you know it." Matthew grinned. "Confess it, you two girls want an excuse to play hide-and-seek."

Monica and Christina looked guilty.

Monica rallied. "Matthew, it could be true, you know. Why couldn't our house have a ghost? It is just as good as any other house in England and . . ."

As if on cue, a moan arose from within the chamber walls.

Monica froze. Christine's mouth dropped open. Matthew frowned.

Now a howl arose. Christine and Monica screamed.

Matthew put his hands to his hips and glared at them. "Enough. I thought you girls too old for pranks."

The two girls did not answer, only jumping to clutch at each other. He barely caught the lantern as Monica dropped it.

"What is it?" he asked as she wheezed and pointed a shaking finger at a point behind him.

Matthew whirled about. He raised one brow as a portion of his bedroom wall opened up. The picture of his late ancestor upon that wall swung madly.

"It is a ghost!" Christine squeaked.

"Blast and damn!" A familiar voice growled from the wall. Andrew stumbled through the enclosure, bloodied and tattered. The two girls naturally screamed again.

"Cut line, will you?" Andrew, pale as parchment,

swayed forward. His frown was dark. "I'm not a ghost yet, thank God. What the devil are you two brats doing here? You are supposed to be in bed."

"We-we were g-going to hunt for Cecily." Christina stammered. "Is—is that real b-blood?"

"Looks real, what?" Andrew grinned wryly. "How's that for a proper prank? Now toodle off to bed, won't you? I-I need to talk to Matthew."

"That is clear," Matthew said. "You girls leave. And no gabbing about this, mind you."

"You can't gammon us." Christine crossed her arms. "That is real blood. And you are just trying to get rid of us."

"How did you come through that wall?" Monica asked. "It's a secret passage, isn't it? We have a secret passage in our house. Famous!"

"Girls, put a damper on it." Matthew strode over to Andrew. He strove for a cool attitude. "Come and sit down. How bad are you hurt?"

"There's more blood than wound." Andrew quirked his lips. "All I can f-figure is the shot went clean through."

"What happened?"

"W-we don't have time for that." Sucking in a clear breath of pain, Andrew frowned. "Blast it girls, clear out, will you? This is a matter of life and death, and . . . and you've got to leave. And no tattling."

"Of course not. We won't cry rope on you." Christine walked over and plopped down upon the bed. "We wouldn't dream of it."

"We aren't snitches." Monica followed suit. "How did you know about the secret passage?"

"I caught Father slipping in through one of the passages from a late night of Picquet."

"Passages!" Monica exclaimed. "There are more?"

"He warned me never to use them and now I'm warning you two. It will lead you to trouble." Andrew's laugh was short. "Too much infernal trouble."

"Heed him, girls." Matthew watched Andrew intently. "Why were you using them, Andrew?"

"I did not want to drip blood down the hall. Knew that would send Mother into the boughs, what?" He turned back toward the passage. "Hang the ch-chatter. We've got to go, Matthew."

"No." Matthew knew his brother. "You'd best tell me where we are going and to what purpose. You often overlook the particulars."

"Can't tell you." Andrew grimaced. "Not in front of the girls."

"Sit down before you fall down."

"Very well." Andrew staggered over to the chair and plummeted into it. "If you insist."

"I do," Matthew said dryly. He strode over and picked up the forgotten brandy. "Now out with it. Never mind the girls. I will kill them later."

"Good." Andrew sighed. "To make it short and simple, I've been in league with smugglers and the bastards have taken off with Cecily, Penelope, and Aunt Clare."

"Smugglers!" Christina squeaked. "You have been smuggling?"

"Cecily?" Monica gasped. "You knew where Cecily was all this time?"

"Where?" Matthew asked curtly. "Where are they going?"

"I knew I could count on you. You're a cool customer." Andrew sighed. Then he glared at the girls. "Not like some goose-caps I could name."

"I intend to knock the daylights out of you, brother." Matthew stalked over to Andrew, who had the sense to rear back. He stuck out the bumper of brandy. "After we retrieve the ladies. Do you know where the smugglers are going?"

"They loaded the cargo and our ladies in the boats. They will meet up with the ship. And then . . . then they plan to take the ladies to Vasouy near Le Havre.

Penelope convinced the villains to hold them for ransom rather than kill them."

"That's my Penn for you," Matthew said softly. Thinking hard, he strode over to his armoire. He pulled out a satchel.

"What is that for? Never say we are going to ride for it?"

"Truly?" Monica and Christine jumped up and down on the bed. "Are you?"

"No. It has an ointment in it and bandages. We are not going to ride for London." Matthew's smile turned grim. "The *Lady Florence* is still moored in the harbor, isn't she?"

"Oh, yes!" Christina breathed.

"It is." Monica nodded.

Andrew blinked. "Gad's, I-I must be all about in my head. She sure is!"

Matthew smiled, this time with true pleasure. "It will feel good to have her under sail again. We can catch anyone if it is her deck beneath our feet."

"I don't know," Andrew groaned. "They have a goodly lead upon us. I-I couldn't do anything while they cleared the kegs from the cave since they were leaving me for dead."

"Cave!" Monica gasped.

"Dead?" Christine gulped.

Andrew cursed. "I would have stood and fought the blackguards, only Penelope had made it obvious that I was supposed to be dead. And Cecily er . . . wouldn't give me a chance to rise but forced me to stay down."

"Good for her. I am glad someone has some intelligence," Matthew said dryly. "Too bad none of it is within our family."

"Well. I wanted to speak to you about that . . ." Andrew said, flushing.

"But not now," Matthew said sternly. He stalked toward the tunnel. "You girls return to your rooms."

"We can't, silly." Christine sprung from the bed, her eyes sparkling. "Can we, Monica?"

"That's right." Monica stood, but it was clear she was confused.

"I've had more than enough." Matthew roared. "Leave us."

"Sorry, Captain." Christine held her ground. "You shouldn't shout at your crew like that, you know?"

"Oh God, no," Andrew groaned. "Don't even think it."

Matthew stared at his siblings long and hard. Both girls had learned sailing at their father's knee. Robert Severs was an appalling card player, but he could sail any craft created. Nor had he withheld his knowledge from his family, females or males alike. The *Lady Florence* had been named after Matthew's mother as a jest. She alone in the family vowed she would not be a deckhand to Robert. It was not only dreadfully unfeminine, she declared, but far too taxing.

Matthew nodded. He really had no choice and the girls knew it. He'd not let anyone take Penelope away and for that he needed a crew. Fast. "Very well."

"Thank you." Christina clapped her hands together. "Thank you."

"What?" Andrew dragged himself from the chair. "Are you cracked in the head?"

"No," Matthew said curtly. "I need a crew that won't drip blood all over the decks. And since you are apparently involved with the smugglers, we must keep it within the family."

Andrew stared at him and laughed. He shook his head. "Very well, if it's to be a family do, let us have at it!"

"Can we have pistols, too?" Monica exclaimed. "Can we?"

"No," Matthew said sternly. "You are to sail and not be seen. Do you hear me?"

Andrew grinned. "As I said. It is to be a family do."

Matthew returned a wicked smile. "Girls, you may attend to Andrew's bandaging once we have set sail."

"I never imagined I, myself, would someday be abducted." Aunt Clare, crowded next to Penelope and Cecily, looked bemused and actually rather excited. With their hands tied behind their backs, the ladies leaned against each other heavily for support in the rocking boat. They were the main cargo in the craft, accompanied by Merston and Treeble. The other men followed in another boat filled with the original haul of kegs.

"Neither did I." Cecily nodded. "I admit, I liked Andrew's abduction far better."

"Then it was he who stole you away?' Penelope asked, her heart pounding. Absurd—she was being abducted by smugglers and all she could think about was what might be the relationship between Cecily and Andrew, and Cecily and Matthew.

"Yes. I-I fell in love with him the very moment I saw him," Cecily said. "And . . . and he the same."

"What are you three hens cackling about?" Merston asked from his bench of the boat. "Trying to plan an escape?"

"Yeh. Shut your chaffers"—Treeble called as he rowed—"or I'll feed you to the fishes."

"My poor Andrew!" Cecily promptly set up an obligatory wail. "He is dead!"

"Oh, God!" Merston actually did raise his eyes to the heavens, but not very respectfully. "I should have known."

"Can I kill her?" Treeble asked. "Please."

"She's worth a fortune to us, ye bloody idiot!"

"Wish she were a more quiet fortune," Treeble growled. "We should have gagged them. Why didn't we gag them?"

" 'Cause we didn't think of it and we have wasted

too much time," Merston said. "We don't want ter miss the ship. Now stubble it, yourself."

Penelope gulped on a laugh and turned it into a wail of her own. "I am so frightened." Indeed she was, but there was no use letting it overwhelm her. She lowered her voice. "Why did you accept Matthew's proposal?"

"Papa has suffered a downturn of fortune. He—he lost one of his most prosperous ships at sea last month. And he has always desired a title for me. I-I thought I could do what he wished. I wanted to be dutiful, truly."

"I see." Penelope's heart burned with pain. Poor Matthew. Once again he had lost a fiancée to another, and this time it was his brother. Penelope sternly reminded herself that it was Matthew's own fault. He wanted a marriage without love and he could not expect faithfulness from ladies who did not give a rush about him.

"I truly did. Yet when Matthew and I kissed . . ."

"What?" Jealousy ripped through Penelope. She really didn't want to hear more, yet she couldn't stop herself it seemed. "Forgive me. Of course you kissed. But . . . do go on?"

Cecily glanced over to Merston and Treeble. She let out a loud cry. Then she continued. "When we kissed, I felt nothing. Absolutely nothing."

Penelope wailed, too, this time with fervor. If only that was the case when she kissed Matthew. "Then what did you do?"

"*I* did not do anything." A proud smile crossed Cecily's face. Merston glared at her in suspicion and she schooled her face back into a frown. "Andrew did. He came to my room last night and vowed he was going to abduct me. He said he was sorry, he knew I was Matthew's fiancée, but he could not live without me and that was that. Furthermore, he said that Matthew had confessed to kissing me and that Andrew wasn't going to permit it again. It was too much for him to swallow his spleen. Enough was enough."

Penelope nodded. "Andrew was driven by jealousy."

"No." Cecily giggled. "Matthew had told Andrew that when we kissed it was all right, and nothing more. Andrew said that cleared his conscience about abducting me. His family tree is famous for passion and piracy, you know, and he wasn't going to let it go into a decline with Matthew and me." She flushed. "When Andrew and I kiss it is everything marvelous."

"Gracious," Aunt Clare exclaimed. "I am so very proud of Andrew."

"I cannot wait until he comes and rescues me." Cecily said it with all the confidence in the world.

Penelope sighed. How wonderful it must be to feel that way. Matthew would not come to rescue her. Even if he knew of her troubles, she had told him that she did not need him. And, of course, he did not love her and that made a difference, too.

"Blimey!" Merston lifted a hand to his eyes, peering across the mist-laden water. "Treeble, does that look like a boat to yer?"

"Can't be," Treeble snorted and kept rowing. "Not if it's coming out of Deadman's Wreath. Nobody living is fool enough to sail through them."

"Oh, my poor Andrew!" Cecily set up a wail. "He is dead! Dead! Dead!"

Penelope squinted to see through the dark and fog. It looked like a sail, a sail of a ship coming at a fast clip. Could it possibly be? Heart pounding, Penelope added her own shouts and cries.

"Oh. Yes." Aunt Clare's mouth pursed. She smiled. "My poor Percy. Where is my poor Percy?"

"Bloody hell!" Merston shouted. "You ladies pipe down. You'll have the entire ocean down upon us. We're trying to smuggle here, don't yer know?"

"But, you are kidnappers now," Penelope shouted over the two ladies' howls. She vowed that the white blur was coming directly at them. "You'll have a greater profit, I assure you."

"Percy!" Aunt Clare yowled. "Will I ever see my Percy?"

"Who the hell is Percy?" Merston said, diverted a moment. "Don't tell me yer gots a lover, too?"

"Percy is her cat," Penelope said.

"Let me kill them, please," Treeble all but whined. "I don't like this abduction business. I'm sorry I ever laid my glims on them. I can't abide crying females."

"Shut up and row," Merston ordered. "We'll be reaching the ship soon."

Cecily and Aunt Clare wailed at that. The men in the boats behind, shouting, pointed frantically. Cecily rocked the boat by flinging herself into Aunt Clare's arms.

"That's it. I don't give a damn about a fortune." Treeble dropped his oar and stood to pull the pistol from his waist. "I am killing them."

"You fool!" Merston's mouth dropped open. He pointed himself. "God! A ghost ship!"

"Naw! It can't be." Treeble, however, stopped to stare at the ship bearing down upon them. Not a soul could be seen upon its deck.

"Treeble!" Andrew's voice called as the ship slowed and swung about. "You bloody murderer!"

"God, it is!" Treeble trembled. He jerked his pistol up and shot.

"You can't shoot at ghosts, you confounded fool," Merston shouted.

A shot came reverberating back. It tore the pistol out of Treeble's hand and sent it splashing into the brink.

His mouth dropped open. "Ghosts ain't supposed to sh-shoot back!"

"They ain't ghosts!" Merston grabbed for his own pistol.

"Best abandon ship, chaps! Or we'll shoot you like

wafers," Andrew's voice advised with good cheer. A bullet zinged past Treeble's ear. For a man who was quick to shoot people, when the pistol was in the other hand, Treeble was not so courageous. He dove into the water.

"Take cover, ladies!" Andrew could now be seen on the deck. He did not appear a ghost, rather more like a half mummy, swaddled in a multitude of bandages.

Penelope, Aunt Clare, and Cecily obeyed promptly, since Merston fired his pistol at that moment and a volley of new shots were added from the other boat. Penelope would never have imagined that she would gladly press her lips to salt-brined wood, but that she did. She gulped for breath. Cecily and Aunt Clare were piled atop her.

"Damn and blast!" Merston cried as a shot clipped his shoulder. Where it came from was difficult to determine, for the wildest shots were coming from his very own crew in the other boat. "Cease fire, men!"

The answering volley clearly did not calm his fears. He did not bother to stand, but slithered into the water, going the way of Treeble. His curses were varied and many as he splashed away from them toward the other boat.

Penelope did not lift her head, however, to watch Merston's departure. Only when the boat lurched mightily did she do so. Then she sighed in relief. Andrew, employing but one arm, had lowered himself into the rowboat. He still clutched a rope ladder.

"Andrew!" Cecily clambered up. A shot whined past them. Cecily tumbled back down, jarring Aunt Clare and Penelope. "Oh, my. Do forgive me."

"Cecily. My love." Andrew knelt down.

"Andrew!" Cecily climbed to him again.

They kissed wildly.

"Andrew, we are tied," Penelope gritted out. Faith, she disliked being a spoilsport, but indeed, this was obviously not the time for kissing. The two were utterly lost to common sense, not to speak of convention.

"Yes, children. You may kiss when we are safe." Even Aunt Clare agreed, and normally a more romantic lady could not be found.

"Oh, yes." Cecily drew back, gasping. "Oh, my."

"Forgive me, ladies." Andrew laughed. He reached to untie the ropes about Cecily's wrists. He then untied Aunt Clare's and finally Penelope's. When that was done Andrew cupped his hands and yelled, "We're coming up!"

A new round of fire directed at the other boat resounded. Under its fierce protection, Andrew assisted Aunt Clare up the ladder. Penelope, from her lowered vantage point, gasped as she saw that it was Monica reaching down to assist her on board.

"Now you, my love!" Andrew said to Cecily, his eyes ablaze.

"I knew you would rescue me," Cecily returned. "I love you."

Penelope bit her lip. She hoped they were not about to kiss again. She sighed in relief when Andrew but placed her hands firmly upon the ladder and watched her climb.

"Come, Penelope." Andrew grinned then and offered his hand. "If you are still breathing."

Penelope laughed and stood. It seemed as if the firing had ceased for the nonce. No doubt, reloading from all sides was a necessity. She made haste to the ladder and up it, determined to take advantage of that lull. She could hear Andrew chuckle as he followed behind her.

"Welcome to the *Lady Florence*." Monica grinned as Penelope felt sturdy planks beneath her feet.

"Penn!" Matthew's voice called out. "Are you all right?"

"Matthew?" Penelope peered about. Matthew stood rather obscured by a pole, one pistol in his hand. The rest of an absolute armament lay at his feet. It was he who was shooting so adroitly. "Matthew!"

She did not think, she only acted. She bolted across the deck, throwing herself into Matthew's arms. "You did rescue me!"

"Of course." Matthew's gaze turned fierce. He dropped the pistol and hauled her close. Penelope kissed him. Or he kissed her. It did not matter. Only their wild meeting of body, lips, and spirit did. Life was everything at that moment. They were everything at that moment.

Then a shot rang out. Unfortunately, that did require attention.

Matthew looked up. "Confound it."

"Oh, dear," Penelope said, blushing. "I—"

"Get down!" Matthew cried.

Penelope dove to the deck very obediently as the next shot whined close. Matthew retrieved a pistol and returned the fire. Once again, Penelope's lips were pressed against wood. This time she mouthed a prayer that Matthew would not be killed because of her rash actions. Faith, she had thought Cecily and Andrew insouciant. She had been worse!

It sounded as if a cannonade were suddenly added to the fire. Furthermore, it came from a different direction.

"Blast! It's their ship," Andrew shouted.

Matthew grinned and his eyes flashed. "We shall go through Deadman's Wreath again. Let them follow if they like."

Penelope glanced up. Matthew's gaze was alight with amusement, actual amusement, as he looked out over the water and then turned to cast an order and move to assist Monica. A sense of shock coursed through her. She was forever grateful that he had come to rescue her, yet she couldn't doubt that the challenge itself had been rewarding to Matthew. A slight smile curved Penelope's lip as she watched him. His surety of footing on deck was as graceful as any Exquisite dancing the Galliarde at Almacks. He might not know it, but the blood of his ancestors showed most magnificently at the moment.

Penelope lay quietly as she heard the calls between Matthew and Andrew, Monica and Christine, their language of spreaders and jibs, battens and tacks foreign. Penelope truly did not care. What mattered was the speed with which their ship departed. The sound of shots grew more and more distant.

Deeming it safe, Penelope crawled to her knees. She immediately sucked in the salty air in a wheeze. Safe? They were speeding toward a circle of huge, jagged rocks. It was no wonder that Merston had thought only ghosts could come from out of them.

Penelope trembled with fear, and, in truth, awe of the majestic and cruel sight. She spied Aunt Clare sitting sprawled a distance away. Cecily sat close beside her. Penelope crawled across the deck to join them. She wished to be close to someone if the ship were to hit the rocks.

"Hello, dear." Aunt Clare smiled. Her blue eyes reflected only the awe of it. "Are they not wondrous?"

"Yes, Aunt Clare." Penelope's tone was dry. "Without a doubt."

"I wish Matthew and Andrew had sailed my father's ship," Cecily murmured. "It would never have gone down and we wouldn't be in such a coil."

Nothing more was said, the ladies sitting in hushed communion as the ship glided between the craggy laurels of Deadman's Wreath. At one juncture, if any of the ladies wished to be so bold, they could have walked to the edge of the boat, leaned over, and touched the monstrous stone.

Passing the last rock, the *Lady Florence* sailed into a gentle harbor, beautiful for its clear, open waters.

"They did it," Cecily breathed.

"We did it!" Monica's voice echoed. "We did it!"

"That we did!" Andrew laughed. "Deadman's Wreath is child's play. For Severs offspring, that is!"

He lifted a hand to his mouth and shouted to the open waters. "Hallo there? Didn't choose to follow us, what?"

"Andrew." Cecily, laughing, sprang up. She rushed to him.

He welcomed her into his arms, though he paled and staggered. "Ooff."

"I am so sorry," Cecily breathed.

"No, no." Andrew grinned. "It is all my pleasure." He kissed Cecily then.

"Yes, now is the time." Aunt Clare smiled benevolently. "That is all right." Andrew and Cecily's kiss might have been drawn out, except Monica and Christine dashed up, laughing.

"Look at the lovebirds . . ."

"Oh dear, I forgot." Aunt Clare hastened forward, flapping her hands. "Andrew and Cecily, stop. Not in front of the children!"

"Indeed." Matthew strolled up to the group. He cast them a fierce frown as Andrew and Cecily sprang apart. "That isn't exactly proper behavior for my fiancée and brother, I believe."

"Neither was you kissing Penelope," Monica giggled.

Penelope flushed bright red. Matthew ignored the comment completely. "I know this should be a matter of pistols at dawn, but I believe we've exhausted all the ammunition."

"I-I need to talk to you about that, Matthew," Andrew said gravely.

"No, you don't, you clunch." A slow smile crossed Matthew's lips. He cast a gentle look to Cecily. "I do assume my scapegrace brother has at least been decent enough to offer you marriage?"

The fear left Cecily's gaze and her eyes lit like stars. "I . . . yes, but we do not know h-how to go about it. Father has his heart set upon my marriage to you. He loves me dearly, but he can be very . . . obstinate about his wishes."

"I understand." Amusement flared in Matthew's gaze. "However, I do know the direction to a certain blacksmith shop in Gretna Green for you."

"Do you mean we should elope?" Andrew asked. "But that is improper, very improper."

"Indeed it is," Matthew said calmly. "But we are not exactly the proper family. And at this moment, I thank God for it. Else our ladies would be somewhere in France by morning." He winked at Christine and Monica. "And we would have been shorted a brave crew."

"True." Andrew frowned, looking determined. "But I want it to be aboveboard for Cecily."

"Andrew, I would not care about the gossips," Cecily said. "Truly."

"But I intend to reform." An embarrassed look crossed Andrew's angelic features. One, admittedly, that was uncommon to him. "I was thinking that in the cave, you know? I sort of made a promise that I would reform if I ever got you back safe. And eloping ain't proper."

"I am glad to hear you are going to reform," Matthew said. "However, the simple truth is that it would be best for you to leave this area for the nonce. There might be repercussions from your free-trader friends, though I doubt it. As for gaining her father's consent, it might take far too long. It does not appear to me that you two will survive an extended engagement."

"No, b'gad, but I wouldn't." Andrew's look of horror was comical.

"Oh, no indeed." Cecily peeked at Andrew. "Could we go, please?"

"Very well, yes." Andrew grinned. "I'll reform after Gretna Green."

Monica clapped her hands. "Famous. We will have Cecily as a sister after all."

"How lovely," Aunt Clare sighed. "And so very unexpected."

"Yes." Matthew frowned. "And I applaud your change of occupations."

"It isn't too difficult." Andrew grinned wryly. "I'm not as good at smuggling as I thought I'd be. Don't know how our grandfathers did it. I don't seem to make a farthing at it. It always goes into moving contraband that never pays out. Guess smuggling just isn't what it was. And I own I disliked Merston and Treeble as much as they did me." He grinned and looked at Cecily. "The only thing I've ever successfully smuggled away is Cecily."

"Good. As long as you keep it that way."

"But what about you, Matthew?" Monica asked, her eyes brimming with impish merriment. "You are going to need another fiancée, and we don't want Sherrice or Violet."

"We will discuss that later," Matthew said in a firm tone. "Now, man your posts, girls."

"I think if you kissed Penelope, that you should offer for her," Christine observed. "Elsewise you would be a . . ."

"A rake?" Matthew asked. His brow lifted and he cast a teasing look to Penelope. "So I have already been informed."

"Er . . . yes." Penelope wished to sink. Then she drew in a deep breath. "But . . . he . . . well, he didn't kiss me. I-I kissed him and . . . and it was out of gratitude for saving me." Relief overwhelmed Penelope. That surely was a reasonable excuse. "That makes it a very different thing."

Christine tried to look innocent. "You aren't going to kiss me like *that* in gratitude, are you?"

Penelope smiled, despite herself. "No, of course not."

"And you better not kiss Andrew with *that* amount of *gratitude*," Cecily said. "I fear I would be very jealous."

"Enough!" Matthew held up his hand. "Penelope kissed me from gratitude . . ."

"And you kissed her back with gratitude . . ." Christine giggled.

"Something like that," Matthew said in a smooth tone. "But no more roasting us. Tonight is out of the ordinary and surely that should be explanation enough for Penn's and my, er . . . gratitude. Now, we have much to do. We must send our brother and his future bride upon their way. And all of this must be done before dawn so that we are back in our beds before the household awakes."

The girls exclaimed and hastened back to their sheets, or knots, or ropes, from what Penelope could divine.

Andrew drew Cecily aside. They kissed but a moment, and then fell to whispering, their eager and loving eyes trained only upon each other. Penelope turned her gaze from them. It was a private moment. Or was it that her heart turned away with its own yearning? How lovely it would be to whisper to your loved one about your future life together.

Aunt Clare sighed and sat down upon the deck. "I have never been sailing before. I quite enjoy it." She stared out over the sea. Her face took on a very stunned look. "Gracious. I *am* a birdwit. Why, why did I spend so many years without trying . . ." Her voice trailed off, and her gaze changed to one where dreams danced in her eyes.

Penelope left Aunt Clare quietly. She moved to the side of the ship and drew in a deep breath of the sea. It *was* an uncommon night. After such danger, to look out over a calm harbor did something to a soul. It made one think how short life was, and it made one think how long dreams were.

"I thank you for coming to my rescue," Matthew's voice murmured from behind.

Penelope turned in astonishment. "What do you mean?"

"I noted you claimed the responsibility for our kiss." Humor threaded his voice. "That it was a kiss of gratitude was a very good notion."

"Thank you." Penelope flushed. "Though . . . I also wish to thank you for coming to my rescue."

"Always at your service, my lady." He offered a wry bow. As he straightened, a quizzing light entered his gaze. "Then I was not . . . too overbearing in my assistance?"

"Of course not," Penelope exclaimed.

"Good." Matthew's voice lowered. "It is nice to know I am needed after all."

"Oh, my." Penelope looked at him in embarrassment. It seemed as if she had spoken those words years ago. "I . . . ah . . ."

"No, Penn . . ." Matthew laughed, though his eyes darkened, more midnight blue than the waters about them. "Do not look so endearingly guilty. And whatever you do, do not apologize."

"But I should. I was . . ."

"No, for it was I who was grateful for your kiss. I . . ." He halted. He proceeded in a far different, neutral tone. "Let me explain it this way. If you dare to apologize I will be villain enough to collect payment upon your gratitude. And then we will be in the suds with the girls. They are too young to see the head of the household acting like a positive wolf, don't you think?"

A warmth, sweet and seductive, glowed through Penelope. She swallowed hard. "Indeed, yes. W-we should set an example. I mean, better than we have er . . . before."

"I will take my leave of you therefore," Matthew said, his voice low and husky. It sent shivers down Penelope's spine. His eyes lit, twinkling in place of the night's absent stars. "I am sure those other dashing pirates were never addlepated enough to bring their siblings along upon their adventures, or they'd not be doing much dashing. Next time I shall do better, I promise."

A gurgle of amusement escaped Penelope. "Matthew! Do not think I will offer myself up for another abduction in order that you may *do better.*"

"You do have a point." An emotion passed through Matthew's eyes, too swift for Penelope to define. Solemnly, he took her hand in his large one. "Only know this, my Penn, I shall always be glad to be at your service, whatever your need be. I know you told me not to do so earlier, but I cannot help myself. When matters concern you . . . I take it to heart." His grip tightened. "Deeply to heart."

"Do you?" Penn's voice came out so very obviously wistful.

"Yes, I do." Matthew, that emotion now lurking in the back of his eyes, stepped closer. He would kiss her, Penelope thought with shocking delight. Only he paused and then stepped away, expelling a rasping breath. "No. I am sure we have had enough drama this night."

Penn couldn't hide her heart within her eyes. "Have we?"

He smiled tightly. He bowed once more and Penn missed his expression. Then he pressed her hand to his lips with a courtier's grace. Matthew upon his ship was a different Matthew, to be sure. "Most definitely, yes. You, my fearless Penn, might cry for more. But I cry *pax.* I daresay my heart would go off in an apoplexy if it were to experience any more excitement."

Penelope laughed at the same time she blushed. "I would not have that, to be sure. It would be too shabby of me to send you into a decline after your dashing rescue of me."

He rose, his eyes a mixture of deep pools of mist and shadow and promise. Penelope bit back a gasp. For that illusive emotion in his eyes was clear now. It was surely love. "Only try and keep the pace slow for me, shall you, Penn?"

The most feminine smile crossed Penelope's lips. She had never felt such emotion before, or smiled so before. "I shall attempt to, Matthew. But this Penelope has finished all her weaving, I fear, and intends never to unravel her works anymore. In point of fact, I am looking about for a better occupation."

"Beware, vixen," Matthew chuckled. Grinning, his eyes feigning threat, he then turned and left her.

Penelope looked back out to the seas. Yes, tonight was an uncommon night, and dreams did not seem so long and far away after all.

Ten

Matthew didn't pace across the library floor this time. Neither did he feel tense or nervous. He sat in the large chair, staring at the ring that he was about to offer to a woman once more. He had made the right decision, of course. Honor demanded it of him.

God help him! His worst nightmare had occurred. He had fallen in love with a lady when a marriage of convenience would be the only honorable course for him. Yet that night upon the *Lady Florence*, he had almost thought to cast aside honor. When Penelope had flown to him on deck and had kissed him with all her being it had turned a wheel deep within him. Part of the response was the result that she felt safe after those creatures dared to think they could harm her. But the greater part was because she acknowledged she did need him and he had realized that he wanted that above all else, for he needed her, too.

At least good sense had stopped him from proceeding any further that night, though it had taken his strongest will not to speak of love and passion to his Penn as she gazed up at him with her heart in her eyes. Nor had it been easy to demand that she and Aunt Clare leave for the Lancer Estates in the morning. He had offered some weak excuse that he did not wish them under his roof until he had combed the passages within the house and secured them.

Three days had passed since then and Matthew had made the only decision he felt open to him. He could not marry Penelope. He'd already enumerated within his mind the forty-five reasons he could not wed her. Faith, he had dreamed them as well, every night.

Nor had this morning brought anything but the forty-sixth reason why he could not marry Penelope. Knowing that Andrew and Cecily were far enough into their journey to Gretna Green to be safe from deterrence, he had taken pity upon Sir Harold Morris and confessed to him. His hand was forced. The man had been about to go to the Bow Street Runners.

Therefore, it was a pleasant surprise to discover how well Sir Harold had received the news. He clearly loved his daughter. To discover she was safe had been a mellowing factor. He had responded with heartwarming relief. As for his little girl sinking herself below reproach by making a dash to the border, it had not disturbed him one whit. He even went so far as to observe since both families were at low ebb that a marriage over the anvil was far more economical than a large wedding would have been. He regretted that his little gel hadn't snagged a title, yet she still had married into a noble family.

Harold Morris was a man to cut his losses when necessary and not look back at that. He eagerly announced the marriage of Cecily and Andrew to all and sundry, calling her a sly minx and whatnot, but showing himself to be a very proud father. He let the other parents know without a doubt that Cecily had indeed successfully married into the Severs family—something no other lady in the party had managed to do.

That was when the forty-sixth reason Matthew could not marry Penelope cropped up. Lady Sherrice and Lady Stapleton, acting as liaison for the silent Violet, had both been open in their demands to know which forbearing lady would now receive Matthew's proposal.

This time, Matthew did not attempt a vote between his mother and the two girls. He did not care to hear their arguments or complaints. He knew Lady Sherrice to be somewhat . . . shrewish, but the thought of living with shy Violet, with her large-eyed regard upon him every day, was far more abhorrent. Therefore he had merely informed his family of his decision.

A tap sounded at the door. Matthew shook himself from his reverie. Returning the ring to his vest pocket, he stood. "Enter."

The door opened and Lady Severs bustled into the room. "Hello, dearest. I came to see how you fare. It has become quit a tradition, has it not?"

"For shame, Mother." Matthew forced a laugh. "Do not even jest about it. I shall be sunk if I have one more lady flee from me."

"I highly doubt you will suffer that difficulty with Lady Sherrice Norton." Florence Severs's tone was dry as she reached up and twitched at the folds of his cravat. "Rather you'd best watch that she does not bind and gag you and carry *you* off instead."

Matthew flushed. "I know that you would prefer Lady Violet . . ."

"No." Lady Severs's eyes darkened. "I-I think her a very soothing and well brought up young lady, but . . ."

"But what?" Matthew asked softly.

Lady Severs sighed. "The truth is that I have reconsidered. All I wish for you is to be happy, and . . . and hang the money."

"Mother!" Matthew was caught between astonishment and amusement. "Such a thing to say."

"I know." Lady Severs flushed. "Such slang is very unfeminine, but I-I feel that way. There simply must be another way to turn our fortunes about and we shall find it. I married your father for love, dear, and I have never, never regretted it. And I am grateful and proud of all his children. I do not believe I could have been as fond of children born to another man as I am of you all."

"Thank you, Mother." Matthew smiled despite himself.

"You wish to laugh, but it is true, dear. I look at you and I still see Robert, both his best and worst qualities, and I cannot help but love you for them." She sniffed. "What I wish to say is that I am afraid that I let my worries for my family's future sway me, and . . . and you sounded so very positive about this endeavor."

"Mother . . ." Matthew shook his head.

"And now that Andrew has married for love, I feel it frightfully unfair if you are forced to marry without it."

"I am the head of the household, Mother."

"Yes, dear. But Andrew has the right of it. A Severs should love deeply, and . . ."

A knock at the door interrupted them.

"That will be the two girls, I make no doubt," Matthew said with wry amusement and no small relief. Lady Severs was shaving too close to the bone. "Enter."

The door opened. It was Sir Harold, however, who entered, his round face lit with pleasure. "Ha! I caught you before you popped the question."

"So you did." Matthew strove for patience. "I make no doubt that Lady Sherrice shall be here at any moment, though. How may I help you?"

"Just wanted to let you know that the Norton fortune is not puffed off. I had my associate investigate that. Which I will confess, now, you should have done with the lot of us before you invited us here, heh? Fortunately, you have me now to look out for those matters. Gentlemen don't ever think about such trifles, which they shouldn't. They are noble, what?" Such was Sir Harold's nature, that he had taken his membership in the Severs family to its full measure. He rubbed his hands together. "But the Norton fortune should make the family estate flush again, once you marry the gel. I must admit, I didn't like her nohow when I thought she was competition to my Cecily, but now I think she will be just the ticket . . ."

Yet another rap upon the door sounded.

Matthew studied Sir Harold as he called, "Come in, Christine and Monica."

The door opened and the girls entered, their eyes large with excitement.

Sir Harold raised his brows. "How did you do that, me boy?"

"I have *forebodings,*" Matthew said gravely. Indeed, it was no lie. He could feel it. This was surely going to be his worst proposal to date. "Quickly, girls, what do you want? Lady Sherrice shall soon arrive."

The two girls promptly took up seats upon the sofa, appearing to be in no hurry.

"We want to be positive that you wish to marry Sherrice Norton," Monica said.

"Yes." Christine nodded, her tone reproachful. "You did not ask us our opinion."

"That is because I already know it," Matthew returned.

"Of course he wants to marry Lady Sherrice," Sir Harold exclaimed. "Her fortune is real, all right and tight. Why wouldn't he want to marry her?"

"We think Matthew should propose to another lady," Monica said, a sly look crossing her face.

"Yes," Christine nodded vigorously. "We do."

Sir Harold's eyes narrowed in suspicion. "Does she have the ready?"

"Yes, she does." Christine nodded.

"She's an heiress, too. Her father's a regular Midas," Monica said.

Sir Harold's brows rose. "Blast, Matthew, how do you find them?"

Matthew stiffened, offering a warning glare to the

girls. "I believe everyone better leave now. Lady Sherrice will be here at any second."

"But wait, who are the girls speaking about?" Lady Severs asked. "Do I know her?"

"We do not have time to discuss the matter. I have made my decision and that is what matters." Matthew waved at the entourage. "Now, leave."

"What is the girl's income?" Sir Harold persisted of the girls. "The Norton chit's is very warm, you know?"

"So is P . . ." Monica began.

"Out!" Matthew roared before he could stop himself. His family and prospective family alike jumped. He drew in his breath. "I'll not have you talking about . . ." He clenched his teeth. "Leave, please."

"Yes, dear," Lady Severs said, softly. "But dearest, if you . . ."

"Do go, Mother." Matthew gently took her by the elbow. "Lady Sherrice will soon be here."

"But . . ." Monica sprang up. "I . . ."

"Morris, please assist the girls," Matthew said curtly.

"Very well." Sir Harold, looking distracted, walked over to the two girls and grabbed up their hands. "Perhaps you shouldn't be so hasty. If you have another pigeon, one who ain't as top lofty . . ."

"Oh, she isn't," Christine said, as Sir Harold pulled her along. "She . . ."

"I am proposing to Lady Sherrice and that is final. End of discussion!" Matthew cut the order quickly. He closed his ears to the babble as he politely pushed his mother out the door, and then the girls and Harold Morris. He slammed it shut. Then he jerked it open. They were still milling about. "Be quiet and please disperse. The only one I want knocking upon this door next time is Sherrice Norton. Do I make myself clear?"

The girls pulled long faces. Lady Severs pursed her lips in a frown. Sir Harold's chest puffed out in offense. Matthew ruthlessly closed the door upon them. Stalking over, he threw himself into a chair.

"We shall await you in the parlor, son." Lady Severs's voice drifted through to him. "After you propose, of course."

"Of course!" Matthew said, with bitterness.

He settled back into the chair, unclenching his fists. Leave it to his family to set his back up just before a proposal. He drew in a steadying breath. "Collect yourself, old man."

He glanced at the ornamental clock. Thankfully, Lady Sherrice was late for their appointment.

Another minute ticked by. Then ten minutes. Then twenty.

Within that silent waiting time, Matthew collected himself so very well that his heart nearly failed him. It was his imagination that was his undoing. He envisioned the upcoming proposal to Lady Sherrice. He envisioned kissing her. He envisioned living with her. He envisioned their children: three more little shrewish replicas of their mother added to the earth, and two snotty little lads who would smoke cheroots at the age of six.

Chasing those abominable visions away came bright ones of Penelope. They were merciful indeed, sweet as rain to the parched ground. They excited Matthew's mind, warmed his heart, and ran deep within his soul. Faith, he'd be happy to have ten little green-eyed Penelopes sitting at his feet at night. As for the boys, he could see them looking like him, but possessing more of Penelope's patience and kindness.

My God! His mother was right. Hang the money! Hang his honor, if that was what it was. Hang the forty-six reasons why he mustn't marry Penelope. They could not match up to the one good reason why he should marry her. He loved her desperately. He wouldn't be able to live without her.

Gad's, but what a dangerous misstep he had almost taken. He glanced at the clock as it continued to mark ten more minutes. It also marked a complete change within Matthew's heart. He stood slowly.

A knock sounded upon the door. Matthew swallowed hard. "Enter."

The door opened. Lady Norton entered. Her face was hesitant and eager at the same time. That was until she scanned the room.

Lady Norton gasped. "Where is Sherrice?"

"She is not here." Matthew frowned.

Lady Norton's bosom expanded in indignity. "I cannot believe it. I told Sherrice to come directly to me after you proposed to her."

"Lady Sherrice has not arrived yet to receive my proposal," Matthew said cautiously.

"What?" Lady Norton exclaimed. "But . . . but she was to meet you almost an hour ago."

"She has not. I have been waiting. I assumed she was merely late," Matthew said it as honestly as he could. He could not very well admit that he had been waiting in hopes that Lady Sherrice had thrown him over.

"Oh, my God!" Lady Norton's plump hand thumped her chest. "Where is she?"

"Please, Lady Norton. Do—do not jump to conclusions."

"Not jump to conclusions!" Lady Norton listed sideways. "How can I not? Sherrice was not in her room when she was supposed to be dressing. Now . . . now she is not here."

"Perhaps she has decided to reject my proposal."

"No, she wished for it above everything else." Lady Norton flung up her hands. "My baby girl has been abducted."

"Why should you think that?" Matthew tried for calm.

"Because every woman you propose to disappears. That is why! Oh! My poor baby!" Lady Norton immediately crumpled to the ground.

Matthew stared at her. From past experience, he knew better than to think he would be able to revive her without assistance. He went to the sofa and, picking up one of its lace pillows, went to place it beneath her head. He then stepped past her and found his way to the parlor. He drew everyone's eye as he entered.

"Well, Matthew?" Lady Severs asked. "Did you propose?"

"Yes, son, did you?" Harold Morris asked.

Matthew looked as grave as he could. "Lady Norton has fainted and requires smelling salts."

"Has she?" Lady Severs rose. "Does that mean you didn't . . ."

"We must also form a search party. It seems Lady Sherrice is missing."

"What, again?" Sir Harold asked.

Matthew, however, did not respond. The joy in his mother's face and the pleasure in the girls' expression almost unmanned him. He turned away quickly, before he broke into a foolish grin himself.

"What a lovely baby horse," Aunt Clare sighed as they left the stall of the newest foal to the Lancer stables in the care of Stewart, their head groom.

"Yes, isn't he?" Penn smiled in abstraction as they walked through the large stables to the door. Three days had passed and they had not seen Matthew as of yet. What was transpiring at his house? He should have told Harold Morris of Cecily and Andrew's elopement by now.

She couldn't help but wonder what he intended to do in regard to marriage. She knew she loved Matthew irrevocably. She also thought that he loved her. She constantly reminded herself of that look in his eyes that night upon the sailboat. That night she was sure it had been love. Yet over the three days she had begun to fear. It might have been nothing, and she had only

read it as love for she so desperately wanted it to be
so. She knew her heart would break if he proposed to
another.

"Living in the country is very different than in the
city," Aunt Clare observed. "It is so . . . peaceful."

"Yes. Isn't it?" Penn laughed. In truth, she was showing Aunt Clare anything she could that was outside of
the manor house. Aunt Susan still remained in resi-
dence, marshalling the cleansing recruits for the kingdom of God. She looked about the stables. "Is there
anything else you would like to see? The chickens, perhaps?"

"Chickens?' Aunt Clare blinked. Sir Percy meowed.

"Dear me, no." Penn glanced down at the cat beside
Aunt Clare. "I quite forgot you. Forgive me if I do not
trust you with my birds."

"Meow!"

Penn laughed. The sounds of approaching hooves
from without stopped her.

"Hello, Stewart!" Matthew's voice called out. He
strolled into the stable, leading his horse, Wind
Dancer. He halted as he saw her and Aunt Clare. His
blue eyes flared with undeniable pleasure and approval. "There you two deceiving women are."

"I beg pardon?" Penn's brows shot up. His words
did not match his gaze. Nor were they the type a
woman dreams of as a greeting from a man she hopes
loves her.

"Gracious, Matthew." Aunt Clare's brows went
down. "Why ever do you say that?"

"Do not mistake it, Aunt Clare." Matthew strode
over and actually kissed the little lady upon the cheek.
"I am in alts that you took Lady Sherrice. So much so
that I cannot even dissemble."

"T-took Sherrice?" Aunt Clare gasped. She looked
at Penelope, her own blue eyes welling with sympathy.
"Oh dear. Oh dear. You did not . . . ?"

"No." Matthew laughed. *"You* did, and you might as

well own it. It has been your best act of charity to date."

Penelope's stomach turned as she watched Matthew. She lowered her gaze from Aunt Clare's knowing one. Her heart cracked in two at that very moment. "You proposed to Sherrice Norton?"

"No, I did not." Matthew, the cruel creature, grinned. "Aunt Clare spirited her away before I could commit such a folly."

"Well, that is good, to be sure." Aunt Clare sighed. "Though now we must wonder who has taken her."

"You do not need to pretend." Matthew reached into his vest pocket and drew out a scrap of lace handkerchief. "You forgot this in her bedchamber, Auntie."

"Oh dear." Aunt Clare blinked. "I wondered where that had gone to. I forgot it at your house, I knew. But I am sorry, Matthew, I did not steal Lady Sherrice away."

"I shall not brangle with you, Aunt Clare. I know you shall return Lady Sherrice when I do what I should have done long before this." His eyes glowed as he looked at Penelope. At any other time, the mixture of desire and mischief within them would have set Penelope's heart aflutter. At this moment it burned that wounded organ as if he'd dumped hot coals upon it. "And so I shall, if you will but permit me to speak to Penelope in private."

"I see no reason for us to do so," Penelope said stiffly. If he intended to discuss his next course of action with his *good friend* Penn he was shockingly abroad. Worse, if he dared to think he could steal a kiss from her before he once again went to propose to another, she would box his ears—see if she did not!

"Oh dear, Matthew, please, I do not want you to do what . . . what I think you are going to do." Aunt Clare stepped toward him and placed a hand to his arm. "Not at this moment. It . . . it would not be wise. It . . . indeed, it would be quite an inopportune moment."

"What?" Matthew did not take his gaze from Penelope. She wished he would. The emotions tearing through her were too private for inspection. Matthew had actually wanted to marry Lady Sherrice. He had proposed to yet another woman, or he would have if it had been possible. She had been a complete ninnyhammer. It was not love she had seen in his eyes before. Her broken heart admitted bitter defeat.

"Matthew, dear, why do we not leave Penelope for a moment?" Aunt Clare tugged at him. His horse, whose reins he held, snorted and skittered back the other way. "I-I have a matter I wish to discuss with you. Truly I do."

"No." Matthew's smile turned warm, his eyes warmer even yet. "I cannot wait another moment, Aunt. You have succeeded. Penelope has succeeded, and I am prepared."

"Er . . . Matthew, dear . . ." Aunt Clare said.

"Succeeded?" Penelope narrowed her gaze. "Succeeded in what?"

"No, no." Matthew laughed. "Do let us go up to the house. I refuse to propose in these lowly environs."

"Propose!" Penelope's mouth dropped open.

"Oh, my stars," Aunt Clare moaned. "You just did, Matthew."

Matthew lifted a brow at her. Then the beast laughed. "So I did. But not properly, to be sure." He turned and said with the most teasing voice, "Come, Penn. Do let us go to the parlor. I vow, I will do it up to the hilt."

"No." Penelope crossed her arms. "I am not going anywhere with you, nor are you going to 'do it up.' Or me up, for that matter!"

"What?" Astonishment washed Matthew's face.

Penn clenched her teeth. The man was insufferable. "You may climb back on your high horse and leave, sirrah."

"Oh dear. Hmm, yes," Aunt Clare stammered. "I

suppose I can leave you now since the fat is in the fire." Aunt Clare patted Matthew's sleeve with solace. "You've changed in midstream, dearest, which is not an easy thing. Now you must prove yourself. Do so, dear, please do."

"I do not understand." Bewilderment crossed his face.

"You will in a second. However, I shall leave you now." Aunt Clare picked up her skirts. "Come, Sir Percy, the children need privacy."

Penelope waited only long enough for the two to leave the stables. She turned steely eyes upon Matthew. At least, she hoped they were steely, rather than clouded with tears. "I said you may leave, Matthew. And since you do not understand, I will explain it to you. You may consider me desperate . . ."

"Penn, I do not consider you that at all."

"But I am not that desperate!"

"I did not think you were."

"You must surely have," Penelope said in a strained voice. "Else you would not come here to propose to me directly after admitting that you would have proposed to Lady Sherrice this morning."

Matthew paled. "God. I-I did not mean for it to appear that way. Only . . ." He stepped up to her, his gaze sincere. "Faith, I am a clodpole. But Penn, I have discovered that nothing matters but that I love you."

"Love me?" Penelope shook her head. "Amazing. *Now* you love me. Of course, this discovery happened only after you discovered Lady Sherrice was gone. What is it, Matthew? Do you not wish to take any more chances but wish to go for a sure bet, as you know I am?" She flushed. "Or think I am."

"No, Penn. I didn't think that!"

Penelope drew in her breath, saying her worse fear. "Or are your bills that pressing that you will resort to me?"

"Resort to you?" His brows snapped down. "That is poppycock!"

"I was your fourth choice, was I not? Sherrice has decamped and here you are at my door. Or my stables, that is, thinking that I will accept you in pitiful gratitude. I suppose I am to be flattered that you chose me before Lady Violet."

"Penn. It isn't like that." Matthew stepped forward. Only his horse neighed at the moment, and tugged on the reins. "Blast it, Wind Dancer."

"Just what added quality do I have over poor Lady Violet?"

"What indeed." Matthew stepped closer. Wind Dancer snorted. "Be still!"

"I will not be still!" Penelope snapped.

"I meant the horse and you know it."

She did, but Penelope wasn't giving quarter. "I do not."

"Blast it." Matthew looked about, his gaze harried. "Where the devil is Stewart?"

"He is in the back of the stables. Why? Would you like to propose to him now that I have turned you down?"

"No, confound it!" Matthew's face darkened. He dropped Wind Dancer's reins and let the horse amble off to a mound of hay. Stepping forward, he gripped Penelope's shoulders. "Will you listen, please? No matter what it looks like, the fact is that I love you. It only took me this long to realize that I loved you so much that . . ." His lips twitched. "That everything else can go hang."

"Indeed?" Penelope asked, her tones unappeased. Her heart, however, listened with ever-budding hope.

Matthew's gaze was piercing. "You must not think it is the money, Penelope."

"Why not?" Her heart chilled again. If only he had remained upon the path of his reassurances of his love, she would have succumbed. Instead, he had immediately swerved to finances.

"If that concerns you so much I will . . . speak to your father and we will make it so that all your money will remain yours." He released her shoulders and delved into his waistcoat pocket. He quickly withdrew a box. He opened it and knelt most properly. His hesitant smile twisted wryly. "Please, Penn, I have made a mull of it. But . . . I am down upon my knees to you, in a stable at that. Indeed, no telling what is below my knee at this moment. Does that not prove something? Please marry me."

Penn silently took the box and ring. She gazed at it. It was beautiful.

"I'm not marrying you for your money, Penn. Truly, I am not."

The beauty of the ring dimmed immediately at his mention of currency. Matthew had been far more right than she. In the beginning he vowed he could not marry a woman who loved him when he was but after money. It was a hard lesson that Penelope learned at that moment. If she could not have love for love, she would accept no other tender.

"No. I will not marry you." Penelope whirled away and dashed toward the stable door. Only then did she remember the ring in her convulsed grip. She came to a stand and turned. "Forgive me. You will need this for your next enterprise. Lady Violet shall adore it!"

Snapping the box shut, she threw it at Matthew. She heard a gasp. Stewart had approached from the back of the stables. He stood stunned, mouth agape. She flushed even as she saw Matthew's face turn thunderous with anger. "Stewart. Please assist Lord Severs with his horse. He is having difficulties with leaving us, it appears."

"No, I am having difficulty proving . . ." Matthew halted. An unutterable sadness entered his eyes. "Why should you believe me? I myself did not until now. I should have known it was too late."

Unable to answer, Penelope lifted her skirts and ran from the stables, tears blurring her every step.

Eleven

"Matthew, may we speak to you?" Christine's voice whispered through the bedroom door, accompanied by a slight tapping.

Matthew expelled a long sigh. The entire evening had been torture. He thought he was at last free of scrutiny. He should have known that would be an impossibility with his family. As could be expected, his sisters had been feigning obedience when he had told them he would not speak of what transpired when he visited Penelope. Not that they had known he intended to propose to her. "It is late. What is it you need?"

"It is very private." Monica's voice grew louder. "We cannot speak of it here through the door."

Matthew shook his head as he seated himself in his favorite chair, preparing himself for the onslaught. "Very well. You may enter."

Christine and Monica entered. Matthew studied them, his surprise growing. Gone from their faces were the infamous looks of "inquisition" that he had expected. Their "guilty of the lowest deed" look was present instead. "Very well, what have you two done?"

Christina almost sighed in relief. "We thought you would never ask us."

"Yes." Monica's tone was morose. "Usually you always spy our rigs."

"We were glad at first you hadn't noticed . . ." Christine continued.

"But now, well . . ." Monica hesitated.

"Our guilt is . . . is something frightful," Christine finished.

Matthew smiled. "Sit down and confess to Father Matthew."

Both obediently moved to take up chairs.

Monica twisted her hands. "Please do not fly into the boughs . . ."

"I will try not to do so," Matthew said levelly.

"We . . . we did mean it for the best . . . Only, well . . ." Monica shook her head. "Aunt Clare is a far better woman than we are."

"Indeed?" Matthew asked. He wouldn't dare mention the age variance.

"How she could have kept her resolve for so very long is wondrous." Christine, her eyes large, emitted a glum sigh. "We could only withstand it for one day."

"Wait!" Matthew lifted his hand. He tried for a stern look. "I believe I see where this is leading. You helped Aunt Clare abduct Lady Sherrice, did you not?"

"No." Christina shook her head. "We didn't."

"And it was very bad of us to make it look like she did it." Monica gulped. "When we were the ones who stole Lady Sherrice."

Matthew stared. "No. Impossible!"

"We did." Monica flushed a deep red.

"We are sorry," Christine said. "But we don't like Sherrice Norton. We didn't want you to marry her. She is very . . . very nasty-tempered, Matthew. She can also curse like no lady ought."

"And she always has her nose stuck in the air," Monica muttered. "We thought that if Aunt Clare cared enough about her niece to steal the bad bridegrooms . . ."

"Thank you," Matthew said dryly.

"Oh, no. I did not mean you," Monica said quickly.

Then her eyes crossed in perplexity. "Only, I guess Aunt Clare knew you would be bad for Lady Julia . . ."

"Just like we thought Lady Sherrice would be bad for you." Christine twitched with anxiety. "Are you terribly angry with us?"

"No," Matthew said slowly, collecting his stunned wits.

"Disappointed with us?" Christina supplied with resignation.

Matthew firmed his twitching lips and forced a frown. "It is lowering, you must understand, to realize that it is my very own family who has pilfered most of my brides from me."

"We are sorry," Christine said. "Truly we are."

"We won't do it again, we promise." Monica nodded.

Christine clearly choked upon her next words. "If you want to marry Lady Sherrice, we will let you."

Matthew choked himself. "No! I mean, that is very kind of you to offer, but no."

"What?" Christine asked, her eyes shuttering wide.

"I said no, thank you," Matthew said, sobering. He had let Penelope turn him away this afternoon. Indeed, he had left, fully prepared to accept his well-deserved defeat. He would be a proper gentleman about it. Those forty-six reasons had asserted themselves. As well as the forty-seventh, that it was clear Penelope would never trust him within their marriage. His fear of that had been directly upon the mark.

Yet, suddenly those forty-seven reasons were easy to brush away. That his two sisters had taken the pains to steal Lady Sherrice from him made a strong application to him to take action. If they were going to make a push to keep him from marrying the wrong woman, it behooved him to make a push to marry the right woman. Furthermore, Penelope was no ordinary woman, and he loved her past anything he could imagine. With those two important components taken into account, surely they could overcome forty-seven bad reasons. Faith, they could overcome hundreds of bad reasons, if need be.

Matthew slowly smiled at his two sisters, who watched him with eyes full of apprehension. "You girls were right. I do not wish to marry Lady Sherrice. I do not wish to marry her one jot."

"Really?" Monica broke into a great grin.

"Yes. Really." Matthew rose. Walking over, he kissed each of his sisters upon her forehead. "We must accept it, darlings. Piracy flows within our blood."

"What do you mean?" Monica asked, wide-eyed.

Matthew smiled. "Where did you hide Lady Sherrice, by the by?"

"In the tower room," Monica confessed.

Matthew raised his brows. "I did not know we possessed one."

"We discovered it when we were looking for Cecily," Christine said.

"We found this tower at the end of Tudor Courtyard just past that round, rococo conservatory. The one with all that iron scrollwork in giant scallops. The one you always say looks like frosting on a cake," Monica piped in.

Not to be outdone, Christine grabbed the conversation from there. "At the end of the conservatory behind the huge, shell-shaped fountain is a stone alcove that opens to this stone path with high stone walls on each side. They're covered over now with ivy vines and you almost can't tell there was a promenade there at one time. The tower is at the end of that. But you just can't see it because of that ugly conservatory."

"Though why we keep that ugly old thing is beyond me. You yourself said it didn't fit with the Tudor garden court beside it. You said it was like standing the Marquis de Sade alongside Mary Tudor and asking them to shake hands," Monica said.

"Further proof why you shouldn't listen to everything I say," Matthew murmured. "Very well, since you have taken on the cataloging of every folly ever added by our misdirected Severs ancestors, please use it to advantage and keep Lady Sherrice hidden."

"What?" Christina exclaimed.

"Only until I have time to steal my own bride, you understand. Then you will have to let her go."

"Your own . . . ?"

Matthew smiled wryly. "I offered for Penelope this afternoon and she threw the ring back in my teeth."

"She did?" Monica gasped.

Matthew grimaced. "I rather muffed the proposal, I am afraid."

"You couldn't have!" Christine said stoutly.

"Thank you for the vote of confidence, but I did. She believes I do not love her. I fear it will take strong tactics to persuade her otherwise. Else I will have to wait a decade for her to forgive me and a decade is too long."

"Indeed, we will be quite old by that time. So will you. You must abduct her," Monica said with decision.

"Yes." Christine nodded. "Please do not wait a decade."

"Unconscionable, each and every one of us." Matthew shook his head sadly, though his mind already schemed. Like it or not, Penelope would have no other pirate in her life but him. A-buccaneering he would go.

Matthew slipped down the hall toward Penelope's bedchamber. He smiled with wry humor. A short time past, he could not have believed what love would drive a man to do. Here he was, dressed completely in black. He had even made certain of his flashing black cape. Faith, all he needed for the outfit was a black eye patch on a band. But tonight it was important he see where he was going and there was no room for it in his pocket, where he carried the ring that had been flung back at him.

That was all he carried except for a night lantern. He possessed no ropes or gags. Pirate he may be, but if he could not abduct Penelope without such things, he would concede defeat. His smile tipped up even further. Perhaps it was not the blood of his early buccaneer ancestors that ran through him as strongly as did that of his own father. He would gamble upon convincing Penelope to go with him without restraints. His carriage awaited them downstairs.

He halted before the door to Penelope's chamber. Life had its own devices. He had Harold Morris to thank for his knowledge of Lancer Manor. Extinguishing the lantern, he set it down. He then clicked the door open and slipped into the room. Gratefully, beams of moonlight illuminated it. He traversed the room, pleased at his silent entrance. That was, until he tripped over some unseen obstacle. The noise of him stumbling sounded obscenely loud. He paused, tensely waiting. Penelope did not stir.

Grateful for that, Matthew managed to cross the floor without further hazards. He reached the bed still undetected.

Then he halted, chagrin filling him. He had succeeded to her bed undetected because she was not in the bed!

"Penelope?" An unreasonable chill coursed through Matthew. He reached to quickly find a toppled candle upon the bed table and light it. The chill invaded his bones. Penelope's bed sheets where tangled in an obvious sign of a struggle. He peered sharply about the room. An ottoman was overturned, as well as a chair.

"God!" Matthew forced himself to a calm. Someone had been here before him with the same notion of abducting Penelope. A meager hope flared up then. Aunt Clare could be involved with this. He couldn't see why she would be, but he'd be glad if she were.

A fear entered him. He suddenly knew why Aunt Clare had removed Penelope from his path. She *had* said that she did not believe Matthew and Penelope belonged together and when Aunt Clare believed such a thing, people went missing. Who knew this better than him? And, this afternoon she had asked him to prove himself. He hadn't taken it as a challenge then, but that might very well be what it was. "Blast it!"

He snatched up the candle and strode out of the room. He marched down the hall with more haste than stealth. He found the door to Aunt Clare's room and rapped upon it.

"Aunt Clare?" He heard no response. He rapped again. "Aunt Clare. Please, open up."

This time he heard a cat meow. It must be Sir Percy. Then he heard noises. Finally the door opened. Aunt Clare, blinking like an owl from beneath the largest lace cap, peered out. "Matthew? Gracious. What are you doing here, dearest?"

"Where is Penelope?"

Her eyes widened. "My, how absolutely heroic you look. You can set a lady's heart aflutter."

"I had hoped to do so. Now, where is Penelope?"

"Penelope?" Aunt Clare stared at him in befuddlement. "Why, by now she should be in her room asleep. Unless you overset her too much. Then I would imagine she is lying awake and gazing at the ceiling. At least, that is what I would do . . ."

"Aunt Clare! Please, pay attention to me, it is important."

"Oh, yes. Forgive me." Aunt Clare rubbed her eyes. "I was sleeping, you see. And I never wake up quickly. Some can awake and immediately be prepared and ready to . . . well, to actually think. Now I, even when I . . ."

"Aunt Clare!" Matthew tried again. "Where is Penelope?"

She frowned and sighed. "Dear, I can tell you are

trying to trick me in some manner. My answer is that she is in bed and asleep." She frowned. "And now that I think on it, so should you be in bed, asleep. In your own house that is. This is the country, you know, dear, and they retire much earlier." Her gaze filled with sympathy. "Ah, you are feeling upset about your proposal today. I understand. What you need is a good cup of tea."

"No," Matthew seethed through his teeth. "I do not need tea. I need Penelope."

"Gracious." Aunt Clare stood dazed a moment. Then she nodded. "I admit that I think you need Penelope as well, but as Garth would say, you bungled your chances. Now the only thing to do is . . . er, retreat and plan a new strategy. You remember how you always advised me of that when you and the boys were helping me?"

"I already have a new strategy."

"Do you, dear? How lovely." She blinked. "What is it?"

"I intend to try again."

Her eyes widened. "Ah, you are here to propose and wish for me to chaperone?"

"No." Matthew's heart sank. He could no longer hope that Aunt Clare was involved with Penelope's disappearance. "I came to abduct Penelope. . . ."

"Truly? How wonderful. That is a very good scheme. I am sure Penelope will love to be abducted by you." Aunt Clare halted and frowned in puzzlement. "But why are you tarrying here with me?"

"Because she has already *been* abducted." Matthew clenched his fists. "I thought you might have done something with her."

"What? Matthew, dear, how long will it take before you believe in people and believe in love?"

"I believe Aunt Clare. I believe . . ."

"You have ignored . . ." She blinked. "What?"

"I said I believe," Matthew said. "I do, Aunt Clare."

"Oh, I am so glad to hear that." She frowned. "But then why did you . . ."

Matthew flushed. "I thought you did not want me to marry Penelope. In light of my asinine behavior I could very well understand why you would think me unworthy of her. Which I am, but I am going to marry her regardless. That is, if I can find her, I will. Who could have abducted her?"

"Oh dear," Aunt Clare gasped. "I am waking up and . . . oh dear, it is my foreboding of danger. The one I had when I first arrived. It is coming true tonight and I almost slept through it. Thank heaven you woke me."

"Do not talk nonsense." Matthew clenched his teeth, ignoring the alarms ringing in his own ears. He whirled back toward Penelope's room.

"Where are you going?" Aunt Clare slipped out and followed behind him.

"We must search her room." Matthew cast a glance over his shoulder. He bit back a curse. Aunt Clare had left the door open and her kitties were darting past him as an unwanted advance guard.

They entered Penelope's room once more. Matthew held up the candle to study it with meticulous care.

Aunt Clare sniffed deeply. "Never say you sat down for a cigar before you came to see me, Matthew?"

"Of course I didn't." Frowning, Matthew tested the air. "Faith, why didn't I notice that? It does smell of cigar smoke." He strode toward the bed, but froze before reaching it. His gaze narrowing, he bent and picked up a crushed flower from the carpet. He held it up to study it. "Theodore."

"Theodore?" Aunt Clare gasped. "Oh no, dear, you must be wrong. He is such a nice man. He wouldn't abduct Penelope."

"Who else smokes cheroots and wears impossible boutonnieres?" Matthew crushed the already mutilated blossom, stalking toward the door.

"Where are you going?" Aunt Clare drifted behind.

"I am going after Theodore, of course."

"Matthew, I am sure you are wrong. You are only looking at the facts."

Matthew snorted. "Yes, and they are damning."

"But we haven't considered the signs," Aunt Clare dithered. "We shouldn't overlook them."

"Signs?" Anger rose in Matthew. Wait until he came up with Theodore. He'd floor the fellow. "What are they?"

"Oh . . . never mind, dear. You attend to the facts, for I have never done well with them. I shall see if there are any signs," Aunt Clare sighed. "I simply cannot believe that that nice Theodore could have abducted Penelope. Whatever could he want with her?"

"Why are you doing this?" Penelope clenched her bound hands as she stared across the carriage at her uncle. He sported a large bruise over his right eye and three scratches down his cheek. She could not help her sense of satisfaction. Theodore had not bound and gagged her without retribution.

Though she still owed him for wrapping her up in a large cape and informing Jeremiah, his coachman, whom Penelope had known for ages, that Penelope had become quite foxed—indeed, jug-bitten—and not to heed her condition.

"Because, puss, I cannot permit you to marry Matthew." Theodore blew out a cloud of smoke.

"What?" Penelope stifled her astonishment, and a cough from a chain of cheroots in an enclosed carriage.

"Or anyone else, for that matter." Theodore shook his head. "Though you should thank me, you know? Marriage can be the very devil."

"I always thought you happy with Aunt Susan."

"I am. Happy as a grig." Theodore nodded. "And I want to keep it that way."

"I still do not understand. What would my marriage have to do with *your* marriage?"

Theodore sighed. "This isn't the thing I wish to confess to my niece, but better you know than Susan. I am not as strictly moral as your dear Aunt is, Penelope."

"You are not?"

Theodore nodded. "Truth is, I enjoy gambling."

Penelope's mouth fell ajar. "Uncle, I never knew!"

"And I am very fond of the demon spirits, from expensive wine to penny Blue Ruin." Theodore ruminated a moment. "But best of all are those naughty, naughty ladies. I never can resist them, alas."

"Uncle!" Penelope did gasp.

Theodore lifted a lazy brow. "Shocked you, have I not?"

"You can surely say that." Penelope shook her head to clear it. She stared at Theodore. Amiable, good natured Theodore possessed all those vices.

"Whisht, I've knocked you all to flinders, I can tell. Now just imagine what your Aunt Susan would do if she learned of my penchants." He sighed. "The sad truth is, Penelope, that gambling and drinking and inducing those lovely Barques of Frailty to give a man like me the nod requires the ready."

"I would imagine," Penelope said sternly. Then the curious thought crossed her mind. "Heavens, if Aunt Susan does not know all this, however do you manage to induce her to fund your . . . frolics? Does she not know what she is shelling out upon them?"

"She isn't paying out on them." Theodore smiled jovially. "You, sweet niece, are standing buff for me."

"What?"

"With interest, of course. Never fear that. Your father is such a curmudgeon that he'd never lend me money. I mean his own money, that is. But he has been lending me out of your inheritance quite readily." He winked. "He likes the notion of the interest, don't you know? Has the heart of a cent-per-cent, he does."

Penelope blew out a breath. "You haven't even paid him upon the principal, I will lay odds."

"There you have it. These years have been good to me." Theodore shook his head. "But I would hate an accounting to be taken. I am not bacon-brained enough to think that a future husband of yours would not demand it. Even if he were to hold my vowels now without complaint, I doubt he would assist me in the future. Only your father understands the ticklish situation in which I live. Susan would toss me out on my ear if she ever heard a whisper of this."

"I suppose you could not reform and give up your expensive vices that are draining my pockets?"

"And live with your Aunt Susan without any escape?" Never had she seen Uncle Theodore under the sway of such strong emotion. Indeed, the appellation upon his features was marked. His large body shook. "Gad's, no. A man must have his diversions, puss."

"And therefore I must remain a spinster?"

"If only Matthew had not returned, and unmarried to boot. What is the true sin is that the chap could have had any woman at any time," Theodore sighed. "Guess there is no sense in repining, what? I knew I was in the basket when your father told me Severs had come sniffing back around and that you and that crazy Aunt Clare were set upon helping him."

Penelope swallowed hard. "But you aren't in the basket yet. And you have put yourself out in this abduction for nothing. I am not going to wed Matthew."

"You say that now." Theodore offered her a knowing grin. "He muffed it proper in the stables. Heard all about it from the servants. What a stroke of luck for me. It prodded me to take action before it was too late, Gad's but it did. He would talk you around soon enough if time were permitted. And that I cannot have."

"He will not. You and he are both under the wrong impression." Penelope looked away. "I refuse to marry any man who does not love me."

"Gadzooks, Penelope." Theodore rumbled a laugh. "Who are you trying to gammon? Matthew loves you. He always has. And you love him. I wouldn't have been forced to stir up that feud when you were fifteen otherwise. It was clear as a pikestaff that you would make a match of it if I did not act. Your father liked Severs too damn much. He let him sit in your pocket when he'd not tolerate any other fellow. No, eventually he would have caved in and given his permission. He needed the feud to make him change his mind."

Penelope stiffened. "Are you saying that the late Lord Severs did not cheat father?"

"Of course he did not. Robert Severs cherished gambling, but he never cheated. Stands to reason. He wouldn't have been under the hammer if he'd known how to cheat, now would he? No, he was a play and pay man all the way." Theodore drew from his cigar. "I knew the one thing surely to set your father's back up against Matthew was for him to feel as if he had been hoodwinked by his family. Jacob is a stickler about business."

The rage welling in Penelope almost overwhelmed her. What pain Theodore had caused. For her. For Matthew. Most surely, for Matthew who doubted his father's honor and because of that, his own. It was fortunate she did not possess a pistol at that moment, for she would have gladly placed a bullet in him.

"It did the trick nicely. But now here is the problem cropping up again. And I can't start another feud. Or tangle you two up with lies." Theodore sighed. "Matthew's older, and so are you. Nor will he accept your refusal, not for long. But if you are nowhere to be found, he will have to do so, what? His finances will force him to marry before you can ever make it to America—and back, if you so choose." He puffed on his cheroot in consideration. "Or Australia. Do you have a preference?"

"I do not think I would care for either," Penelope said coldly. Yes, Theodore deserved shooting, straight through his conniving heart. Suddenly, Penelope stilled.

"Well, we have time before I must make the decision." Theodore settled back. "I am sorry I have not planned this fully for you. Severs's proposal bowled me over. Glad you turned him down and gave me my chance."

"Indeed." Penelope glanced briefly to the right. Indeed, Theodore had not planned fully.

"This is my first abduction, you know?"

"I am glad to hear that." Penelope coughed. She was not about to go to America or Australia. It would be too galling after hearing Theodore's confessions. She coughed again, more fulsomely. "Oh dear. I fear I am going to be sick, Uncle."

"What?" Theodore's brows rose. "Whatever for?"

"The smoke, I think. It is too close in here. Could you please extinguish your cigar? Else I . . . I shall cast up my accounts right here in the carriage."

"Gad's." Theodore jumped to toss the cheroot out the window.

Penelope jumped in the other direction to where tucked into a leather sling to the side of the seat was a brace of pistols. She drew one from its proper place, holding it between her bound hands. When Theodore turned back, she leveled the barrel upon him.

"What?" Theodore blinked. Then he shook his head with a sigh. "Zeus, do not play with that. Someone could get hurt."

"Especially you. Now, stop this carriage. We are turning back."

Theodore frowned. "What a hum. I know you better than to think you would shoot me."

"I don't know." Penelope struggled with that strong desire. "I believe it would be my pleasure."

"You are miffed. But I am telling you, marriage isn't all it is touted to be. Even if you love the man. Look at it this way—you will travel and see things you never have before."

"Give the order to your coachman to stop the carriage."

"No." Theodore said it calmly.

"Very well." Penelope cocked the pistol. She then calmly pulled the trigger and released its charge directly into the satin squab, two inches to the right of Theodore. She bit her tongue in astonishment. The noise was deafening and the backfiring of the pistol nearly broke her wrists.

"Gad'shounds!" Theodore squeaked as the carriage came to a jerking halt. "You do mean it!"

"I demand . . ." Penelope didn't get any further. Theodore bolted toward the door and tumbled from the carriage. He set off at a pounding run. Penelope grabbed up the remaining pistol.

She climbed from the carriage more slowly, pistol in hand. She couldn't help herself; she shot high into the air, just to see Theodore yelp. She then looked to Theodore's coachman, the one who was under the impression that she was foxed. "Jeremiah, I am not foxed, but I am very wroth. Will you take me where I wish to go?"

Jeremiah's mouth was a yawning cavern of astonishment. Glancing in fright at the quickly disappearing Theodore, he nodded. "Indeed, Miss Penelope. I-I am yours to command."

"Excellent. I wish for you to take me to Lord Severs's estate. There is a country lane close to here that will take us there directly."

Penelope enjoyed giving Jeremiah exact directions

and then, after he untied her, she climbed back into the carriage. She sighed as it proceeded. She wasn't going to America or Australia. She was going to Matthew. She would be safe within his arms soon.

She would tell him that his father was no cheat, as surely he was not. She would then do all in her power to prompt him to repeat his proposal. And this time she would say yes without hesitation. Nothing would dare stand in her way. Nothing!

Matthew spurred Wind Dancer onward. With the moonlight illuminating the road ahead of him, he was making good time. That and the fact that Theodore had used Jacob Lancer's well-sprung carriage instead of his own led Matthew to have faith that he should be able to catch the carriage soon. That is, if the villain employed this main road. Stewart had been under the impression that was the direction in which the carriage had gone. He refused to think about what it would mean if Stewart had been wrong.

"Whoa!" Matthew sawed on the reins, confusing his horse. He himself was confused. He might be hallucinating, but he vowed he saw Uncle Theodore trudging toward him down the road.

Enlightenment struck. Apparently his dear Penelope hadn't taken to her abduction with docility. Grinning evilly, Matthew trotted his horse up to the puffing, gasping man bathed in sweat. "Hello, Uncle Theodore. Where did you misplace Penelope?"

Theodore mopped his brow. "Don't know, my boy. She took the carriage and my coachman and drove off."

"I see." Matthew prepared to dismount. Faith, but it would feel wonderful to drive a fist into the villain. This was a milling he would enjoy to the hilt.

"No reason to do that, son." Theodore lifted his hand.

"Oh, I think there is. Plenty of reason, in fact."

"Not if you are thinking to trounce me," Theodore said glumly. "Penelope already did that, I vow. She even shot at me, s'death."

"But didn't kill you. A shame."

"I was afraid she was going to do so for a moment." Theodore shivered. "Saw it in her eyes. She was fighting it, thank God, but it was a near thing. I didn't know the chit had so much in her."

"Yes." Matthew smiled. "Aunt Clare warned me she has a passionate nature. Which she does, I am glad to say."

"You can say that because she loves you," Theodore's tone was aggrieved. "She don't love me now."

"Was that when she discovered you were stealing from her inheritance?"

" 'Pon rep," Theodore said and raised a brow. "How did you know?"

"I saw your mountain of vowels and bills by chance. Faith, it was almost more than that armoire drawer could hold. I had wondered how you meant to pay for them." Matthew shrugged. "When I realized you had abducted Penelope I put paid to them, so to speak."

"It had been a good arrangement, my boy."

"Not for Penelope. No wonder she wanted to shoot you."

"No, no. She was rather understanding about that." Theodore studied Matthew a moment. He sighed. "Confound it, might as well tell you now. Before I do, though, I want to tell you that Penelope took off in the direction of your house. I don't doubt she will be waiting there for you."

"Will she?" Matthew grinned.

"I'm telling you this now." Theodore nodded. " 'Cause you are going to discover it anyway from Penelope. I was the one who created the feud between the families. It was all a hum. Your father never cheated Jacob."

Matthew could not move as the words went straight to his heart. An absolution washed over him. Then pain. He had never believed his father when he had sworn to his innocence. "Why? Why did you do it?"

"Penelope loved you. You loved her. You were still sowing your wild oats and hadn't a clue, but I knew if you two were allowed another year for Penelope to become a woman in your eyes, I'd be in the basket."

"I am going to kill you," Matthew said levelly.

"No, no. Think on it. If you are going to marry into our family, you aren't starting out with the best step forward. And . . . why spend your time here killing me when you could be going after Penelope. Besides, Penelope didn't kill me because she knows that her Aunt Susan is going to do it for both of you when this comes to light."

"Which it will, that I promise you."

"Expected it." Theodore nodded. He waved his hand. "Now go and get Penelope. Try and do better than what you did in the stables, mind. You bungled that, boy."

"I know."

He sighed. " 'Course, I muffed this abduction worse than you did your proposal."

Matthew actually found it within himself to laugh. Perhaps because he knew Theodore's retribution at the pious Susan's hand would be far more painful than anything he could mete out. Therefore, he left Theodore in the dust of Wind Dancer's hooves. Incorrigible the man might be, but he had the right of it. Nothing was worth keeping him from Penelope's side. Nothing!

Twelve

Penelope felt the pressure of the sword at her back. She clenched her teeth. "You know, you truly do not need to do this. I have refused Matthew. He does not love me."

"I know better than that." Lady Violet jabbed Penelope even harder and emitted a peal of laughter. It rang with a maniacal quality, in Penelope's opinion.

Of course it did. It was all too insane. For the second time that night she was being abducted. By quiet, cannot-say-boo-to-a-mouse Violet, at that. Now they were winding down ominous stone stairs; sinister shadows flickered in the torch light which Lady Violet carried. "Er, Lady Violet, where are we going?"

"To the dungeons."

"Dungeons?" Penelope gasped. "I didn't know there were dungeons in Severs Hall."

"Nobody does. I discovered them when we were looking for that odious Cecily Morris. They will never find you down here." Lady Violet's voice was smug. "It was to my good fortune that I was the one to open the door to you tonight. How improper of you to be knocking upon it at this late of hour. Did your governess never tell you that no good thing happens to young misses who pay late night calls to a gentleman's house uninvited?"

Penelope's heart sank. How had she fallen into such a coil? Granted, she had thought it odd when Lady Violet had greeted her at the door rather than the butler. Yet, she had been so very glad to be admitted quietly rather than being forced to knock loud enough to awaken the entire household. That Lady Violet had been passing by the door on her way to the library for a book to read had been rather neat. Penelope had not considered it at all unusual. After all, Lady Violet was a mystery and if she haunted libraries late at night Penelope did not feel it her place to question.

If only she had. Rather she had turned her back on the girl, wasting her time in debate upon how to proceed in finding Matthew—whether she still required a butler, or if she should merely go in search of him.

That debate was settled when Lady Violet had dragged out an ancient sword and flourished it upon her. Penelope could not believe it, except that the point of that sword still felt far too real. "Lady Violet, do you not wish to reconsider this?"

"No!" Lady Violet sounded so fierce that Penelope leapt forward rather than trusting her back to the sword. As a result, she stumbled into a large, lofty enclosure.

"Oh my." Chills ran down Penelope's spine from what was revealed in the circle of the torch's light. She spun about. "Truly, Lady Violet, let us talk about this."

"No! Matthew is mine!" Lady Violet slashed with the sword.

"Very well." Penelope jumped back. "I-I understand."

"You do not!" Lady Violet's eyes glittered. "I have loved Matthew all these years."

"You are wrong," Penelope said more gently. "That I understand completely."

"I was stunned when he invited me to his house party. Everyone knew what its purpose was. I had to beg my parents to accept. They did not think it necessary I waste myself upon him, but I had my way. Even though I did not have much hope he would choose me," Lady Violet's voice threaded to a whisper. Tears filled her eyes. They swiftly disappeared. "Except, after each of the other girls disappeared I began to gain hope. When Sherrice Norton disappeared, I knew. I knew then that Matthew would be mine. But then he proposed to you and I realized you stood in my way. I declare, it is too much to tolerate."

Penelope shook her head. "But Lady Violet, I have rejected Matthew."

"I am no fool. He would win you." She sidled over and lit another torch. It flared to life. Her eyes gleamed within the added glow. "He came for you tonight, do you know?"

"What?" Penelope frowned, determined not to scrutinize her surroundings too closely. Her courage did not need the extra weight of depression upon it for the nonce. "I do not understand."

"I had gone to abduct you tonight," Lady Violet said it calmly as she held the sword at Penelope with one hand and placed her torch into a holder with the other. She acted as if she were merely adjusting a wick while discussing a social event.

"You had?" Penelope blinked. "Faith, but I am popular."

"Only someone had beaten me there. I could tell by the room that you had not gone willingly."

"I did not. Uncle Theodore received a shiner for it. But . . . do tell me about Matthew."

"I had sat down to blow a cloud and consider . . ."

"You also smoke cigars!"

"Yes. What of it?"

"Oh nothing, nothing at all." Gracious, but Violet Stapleton was full of surprises. Unfortunately, none of them were pleasant.

Lady Violet smiled as if she knew what Penelope thought. "It pays to be quiet and submissive. No one ever really believes ill of you. A girl can do so much more than when she is watched."

"Er, yes." Penelope didn't want to consider that at the moment. She herself could not believe Lady Violet was doing this to her. Why, then, would anybody else? "Do proceed. You sat down to smoke?"

"I heard someone at the door. Of course, I hid." Lady Violet glared at Penelope with hate-filled eyes. "It was Matthew. He slipped into your room. He was dressed in black."

"Truly?" Penelope asked eagerly. "Did he have a cape on?"

"Yes. He looked wonderful."

Penelope smiled. "Did he?"

"I did feel he lacked a black satin eye patch. He would have been perfect. But no, he was coming to abduct you. Probably to carry you off to Gretna."

"Drat! And I missed it!" Penelope frowned darkly. "I should have killed Uncle Theodore!"

"Too late now." Lady Violet smiled. She nodded toward the wall. "This will be your last abduction. You will not escape this time."

"What?" Penelope blinked. Massive, ugly, rusted manacles—at least she prayed the red upon them was rust—were embedded into the stone. "Oh, God. No!"

Lady Violet reached into her pocket and withdrew a large, ancient key ring. "Oh, Miss Penelope, yes."

Penelope gulped. "How . . ."

"I have had plenty of time to explore. What with Matthew chasing after this bride and that." She laughed. "In truth, I had planned this for Lady Sherrice. But she disappeared."

"Lucky her," Penelope murmured, staring. She frowned. "But you said it wasn't until after Sherrice Norton disappeared . . ."

Lady Violet shrugged. "Very well, I lied to you. I did not know you were a candidate until then. Regardless of what that batty old Aunt Clare said."

"Batty! You call *her* batty?" Penelope couldn't help herself. That was the outside of enough. "Aunt Clare is not batty."

"While I am?" Lady Violet advanced with her sword.

"You must own that it is r-rather ridiculous to believe I would not be discovered."

"Why should you be?"

"My coachman—I mean, Uncle Theodore's coachman—awaits me outside. He can testify to the fact that this is where I came. In fact, he should be waiting for me still."

Lady Violet laughed. "He is not your coachman, so *if* he still waits for you, I will simply make some agreeable arrangement with him. Just like I intend to do with Matthew once he understands you are vanished for good. I had returned here with the intention of seducing him upon his own return. But then you appeared—with the same intentions, no doubt."

"No!" Penelope gasped in complete astonishment. "I would never . . ."

"Oh, very well, Miss Prude, you were coming here merely to bring him to heel and accept his renewed proposal. I know. You are keeping yourself for the marriage bed like a proper lady does."

"Of course!" Penelope's eyes widened.

Lady Violet giggled, evidently reading Penelope's thoughts once more. "As I said, a girl can do much more when she is not watched. And many men enjoy secrets as much as I do." That frightful smirk appeared. "Though this one will be my best secret yet. You arrived here at the ideal time. I could not have planned it better."

"You truly wouldn't have me die down here, would you?"

Lady Violet's eyes glittered with rage. The answer was clearly in the affirmative. Then she shrugged. "I do not know. I haven't had time to think. You just fell into my lap, as it were. I only know that Lord Severs shall be wed to me before you ever see the light of day."

Penelope swallowed. If Matthew were taken from her she wasn't sure it was important to see the light of day again. She shook herself. What a missish thought. With life, there was always hope.

Lady Violet pursed her lips. "And then . . . well, I shall have to think upon it. Perhaps I shall . . ."

Penelope groaned. "I know, send me to America or Australia."

"I hadn't thought of that. What a very good notion. I like America. It is so uninhibited." She frowned. "No, America would be too good for you. I'll send you to India or something. I will have to consider." She heaved a sigh. "Bloody hell. It is too much trouble to think about right now. Letting you die down here would be the simplest thing."

Penelope froze. Not only because her situation was plummeting into the most mortifying and morbid of circumstances, but because a strange greenish-amber glow flared behind Lady Violet. It appeared to be advancing upon them from the stairs. Penelope gulped. "D-do you believe in ghosts, Lady Violet?"

"No." Lady Violet cast her a look of condescension. "And you shall not distract me by pretending you see something behind me. I am not so gullible."

Penelope's eyes widened in shock as Aunt Clare traipsed into the dungeon, a shuttered lantern held high, its dimmed light brushing the confines of the doorway around her. Smiling, she waved in greeting and then touched her fingers to her lips. Sir Percy stalked beside her, his tail high and snapping. "I do not know, Lady Violet. I do think I see a ghost."

"Of some unfortunate sod who died down here, perhaps?" Lady Violet was ungracious enough to snicker. "How Gothic. Now, back to the wall."

Penelope watched with interest as Aunt Clare looked around and then tiptoed over to set the lantern down, its muted light putting a glow on a mound of swords nearby. It explained where Lady Violet had found her particular sword.

And that was where Aunt Clare was clearly going to find hers. As that dear lady reached for one, Penelope set up a wail, determined to cover any possible noise. "Oh no! Please, no, Lady Violet. Have mercy! Don't do this!"

"Weakling," Lady Violet spat.

Aunt Clare had chosen a rather nice-looking saber. Perhaps that dark crust wasn't rust on it, but so much the better. Holding it up, she winked at Penelope. She then emitted a strange, unearthly wail. "Oh, Violet!"

Lady Violet froze, her eyes widening.

Penelope smiled sweetly. "I told you there was a ghost!"

"Impossible!" Lady Violet swung about with blade in hand.

"No, it's just batty Aunt Clare, dear." Clare held her sword high. *"En garde?* Isn't that what we say?"

"No!" Lady Violet charged at Aunt Clare, swinging her sword. Sir Percy yowled and sprang. She slashed down. Sir Percy bared his outrage and jumped to the side. A battle-scarred veteran, he resorted to experienced tactics that had, in the past, always stood him in good stead. Ears back, he dove beneath Lady Violet's skirts, leaving her with the conundrum of striking at him without stabbing herself.

"Have at it!" Aunt Clare, announcing her fierce challenge, proceeded to weave and dance back and forth, her saber held out like a banner.

Penelope did not wait for the final engagement. She darted over and snatched up her own choice of swords while Violet Stapleton was bedeviled by a clawing demon beneath her skirts all the while being struck dizzy by a circling Aunt Clare.

She tiptoed up behind Lady Violet and placed the sword to the center of her back. Knowing from experience how quelling it could be, she spoke with confidence. "Drop your sword, Lady Violet! And do not think I won't run you through. I love Aunt Clare."

"Batty though I am." Aunt Clare smiled with obvious pride.

"Ouch! Ouch!" Lady Violet dropped her sword. Penelope could not be positive the speedy surrender was due to her command. It could also be due to the bellicose Sir Percy remaining in hidden combat.

"Percy, dear one. You may leave Violet alone. Why not see if there are any mice hereabout? There should be some huge, juicy ones. At least, they are in the books."

Sir Percy yowled once. So did Lady Violet. The cat pelted out from underneath her skirts.

"I hope it is only mice he discovers," Penelope murmured.

"So do I, dear." Aunt Clare treaded over and picked up the dungeon keys. She jangled them.

Penelope laughed. "Aunt Clare, surely you do not intend to lock Lady Violet to the wall?"

"I certainly do, dear," Aunt Clare said it with a gravity that her twinkling eyes belied.

"What?" Lady Violet gasped. "You cannot!"

"Yes, dear, I can and without too much guilt, I confess. After all, it was you who suggested it. You thought it a proper place for dear Penelope. Why should I think it unfit for you? Besides, dear, you have shown yourself to be very untrustworthy. I doubt either Penelope or I will permit you to try and . . . ply your whiles upon Matthew."

"She is right, Lady Violet." Penelope narrowed her gaze. "Now move toward the wall."

One thing must be said for Lady Violet Stapleton: she but nodded her head and walked over to the wall. Aunt Clare clamped the manacles upon her. "There. Now do be a good girl. It shall not be for very long.

At least, I hope it isn't. It will only be as long as it takes for Penelope to forgive Matthew."

"I do already," Penelope said with fervency.

"I expected so." Aunt Clare nodded to Lady Violet. "I shall leave Percy with you, so you are not lonely."

"No," Lady Violet said. "I detest cats."

"I know, dear. And they do not like you any better." Aunt Clare hurried to pick up Lady Violet's sword. "That was your undoing, my child."

"What?" Lady Violet asked.

"Yes." Aunt Clare dusted her hands off. "That and your propensity to smoke. They were the signs that lead me to sneak into the house by the secret passage . . ."

"There is a secret passage?" Lady Violet asked.

"Yes. That is what *we* found while hunting for Cecily," Aunt Clare offered with just a hint of boasting. "I employed it because I did not wish for you to know that I was present. However, just as poor Penelope, er . . . fell into your lap . . . you, too, were quite easy to discover. Needless to say, when I arrived to see you carrying a sword about, I knew that the signs were correct. Though I do wonder why you were wishing to hide the sword downstairs."

Lady Violet lifted her chin. "I could not very well keep it in my room, could I? With Mother, nothing is private. She is always pawing through my belongings."

"With good reason," Penelope murmured without thought.

Lady Violet glared at her. Aunt Clare nodded. "That is why you pass your cigars off to other ladies."

"How did you know that, Aunt Clare?" Penelope asked with interest.

"Matthew tore off after you, dear, because of the clues left behind by your uncle. Which from what I overheard was a wise decision. However, he had left under the assumption that the smoke within the room came from Theodore's cigar. Which it could not be, for he smokes the same that dear Bendford smokes. It comes from a little shop on Ludgate Hill. The owner is a dark-skinned Indian and he wears a turban and he has the most peculiar of cats. An Abyssinian, I believe he said it was. It looked like the Egyptian cats you see at the museum. It was so regal. Until it met Sir Percy, that is. Now, what was his name? Rameses. That was it. What a wonderful name for a cat. I offered to bring Alexander the Great to meet him. Alex is the most regal of my kitties. But he would not like it, I fear. He does not like Bendford's cheroots. He chews them to pieces. He certainly would not like an entire shop of them. However, I recognized the smell of that blend quite readily. Indeed, there is nothing like turning one's head on the pillow at night only to turn it into a furry face that reeks of tobacco. But, tonight the smell in the room was of a tobacco blend I could not recognize." Aunt Clare stopped in apparent rumination.

"Why did you think it would be mine?" Lady Violet asked the question before Penelope could.

Aunt Clare turned her mild blue eyes back to her. "Why, who else could it be, dear? I know that one of those cigars was discovered in Lady Sherrice's possession, but her mother was so overwrought that I did not think it a proper time to say anything to the contrary. I may be a widgeon, but I would be completely addlepated if I did not realize that Lady Sherrice told the truth when she said it was not hers. After living with Bendford for my entire life, a lady knows never to mix cigars with perfume of any sort. It is fatal to the taste."

"Oh, very well," Lady Violet said testily. "So you knew it wasn't Sherrice's. But it still does not explain why you thought they were mine."

"That was simple," Aunt Clare said. "One could not overlook the fact that the kitties disliked you, dear."

"Those stupid cats!" Lady Violet's face twisted with rage. "Never say that is why you knew it was me!"

"I think you should take it as a compliment, dear, if it is your wish to be an untrustworthy and dangerous female. For though my kitties disliked you, they also sat a far distance from you. They were clearly considering you with caution. You saw how they frolicked with all the other girls?"

"Frolicked!"

"But with you . . . why, I have never seen them behave in that fashion before. It was then that I had the passing thought. I wondered just who was the friend who had given Lady Sherrice the cigar. No doubt she understood who you were like my kitties did and did not choose to blow the . . . er, gaff upon you."

"So you knew I smoked and you knew the 'kitties' did not like me. It still . . ." Lady Violet clanked her manacles in frustration. "It still does not make any sense why you came after me tonight."

"Oh, but it does," Aunt Clare said. "You might not have known it, but I had also had a *foreboding* about dear Penelope."

"God. Why?" Lady Violet howled, her tortured voice echoing in the dungeon. "Why could such a batty old lady do this to me?"

"Penelope has suffered many dangerous things for the sake of her love," Aunt Clare said, her tone reproving. "But none of them made me feel as if it were my foreboding coming to pass. Tonight, however, I knew that my foreboding was about to happen. And all the signs pointed to you."

"They did not!" Lady Violet stamped her foot and shook her chains. "It makes no sense. No one would have known. No one!"

"Oh, you dear, poor child." Aunt Clare's eyes teared. "Do not take it so to heart. Logic is not everything. If you are naughty you must know that it will always be discovered sooner or later."

* * *

"Penelope!" Matthew shouted out her name with joy as he spied her standing upon the hall's doorstep with a lantern held high. Aunt Clare stood beside her. He should be surprised at that, but he wasn't. He only cared that Penelope awaited him.

"Matthew!" Penelope called back in return.

Matthew didn't even bring his horse to a final halt before dismounting. Neither did Penelope give him one second more as she flung herself into his arms. He kissed her swiftly. "Thank God you are safe."

"Yes. I am safe. And free! So very free." Penelope gazed up at him, her green eyes sparkling. "Will you elope with me, Matthew?"

Her words jolted Matthew. Then he grimaced, torn between enchantment and disappointment. "Confound it, Penn. That was to be my line."

An impish smile crossed her lips. "So I have heard."

Matthew peered over to Aunt Clare, who had remained a distance away, holding the lantern and ineffectively pretending not to be listening. Percy sat next to her, offering a non-interested regard. "Hello, Aunt Clare. So you tattled on me."

"Hello, dear." Aunt Clare waved one hand. "But no, it wasn't I who told Penelope about you."

"That doesn't matter." Penelope gripped a portion of his cape and tugged. "Please, answer me. Will you run away with me tonight?"

Matthew grinned. "Gladly, sweet Penn."

"Good." Penelope sighed with clear relief.

Matthew drew her tight against him, saying sternly, "But only if you know it is because I love you, and *only* because I love you."

"I know that now." A flush rose to Penelope's cheeks. "Since Uncle Theodore was going to send me to America because of it, I cannot doubt it one whit."

"Yes. I met him upon the roadside. I wanted to kill

him, but he vowed you had dealt with him sufficiently."
Matthew shook his head. "I am sorry, Penn. I bungled
it again."

"What do you mean?"

"My intentions were to be a dashing pirate and carry
you off in the dead of night. But first I lost you, and
then you saved yourself from Uncle Theodore."

"No, Matthew, I was glad that I managed him myself.
I have learned many things tonight. And one of them
is that I do not need you to be dashing. Nor do I need
you to save me from villains."

"You don't?" The thought unsettled Matthew. He
wanted to be the pirate of her dreams.

"No." Penelope's voice lowered and her eyes shone
brighter than any star above. " I only need you to love
me."

Matthew caught his breath. "Then that is what I
shall do, sweetheart."

"Thank you, gallant sir." Penelope gazed at him with
a look that shot heat through him. Then her look
turned considering. "In truth, I feel that . . . well, it
was important that I did my fair share of combat for
the evening. Indeed, I feel like I have finally . . . come
up to snuff."

"What do you mean?" Matthew stared at her in astonishment. "You have always been up to snuff."

"No, I haven't." Her eyes turned grave. " I-I wasn't
making a push for love in these past years. I was merely
sitting at home and waiting my life away. This Penelope
didn't weave worth a groat. I didn't even make a decent tablecloth out of it all."

"Of which I am forever thankful," Matthew said
quickly. "For if you hadn't been waiting for me, you
would now be married to some other man."

"No." Penelope's gaze darkened. "I knew I loved
you, but instead of doing something about it, I rather
spent all my days denying it. If Aunt Clare had not
been determined to find your true love for you . . ."

"I know." Matthew shook his head. "But then you could also say that if I had not proposed to Lady Julia, which caused Aunt Clare to abduct me, and if she hadn't taken the time to listen to me in my drunken ramblings . . ."

"Or if she had permitted you to marry Lady Julia. Or if . . ." Penelope laughed. "Faith, it is a tangle. For the truth is that if Uncle Theodore had not lied about your father, and you had . . ."

"Excuse me, children," Aunt Clare called and hurried up to them. "I wasn't eavesdropping, at least not very much. However, I feel it important to tell you that if you start attempting to trace the steps of your fate . . . why, you shall be at it all night. I know, for I often do so. I have never found any conclusions from it, other than I always wake up exhausted and more confused than common in the morning. But I assure you, Penelope, I love you *now* for who you are. And I love Matthew for the man he is *now*. There is no telling who you would be if everything had been different. Or who he would be. Or how your love would be. Or . . ." She threw up her hands. "Oh dear, now you have set me off as well. But truly, dears, I think it is important to remain focused upon the important issue. You should proceed with haste to Gretna Green."

"Why?" Matthew tensed. "Is it your *foreboding*?"

"No, dear, that was cleared up this very evening. However," she added and visibly cringed, "I do not care to wait to see if I experience another one."

Penelope laughed. "I quite agree with her, Matthew. I have waited long enough—even one more second seems too long."

"Besides," Aunt Clare sighed, "I am burnt to the socket with trying to determine just who else might appear to stop you two from wedding. Lady Violet was clearly a dark horse. There might be others."

"Lady Violet?" Matthew frowned.

"I shall explain later," Penelope said. "Once we are

safely away from here. Or perhaps once I have your ring safely upon my finger. Only know that I actively fought for your love tonight."

"Indeed?" Matthew asked, only slightly interested. He was too involved with the realization that Penelope was soon to be his.

"Indeed. I am prepared to be as heroic as you from now onward."

"I thought you just said you did not need me to be dashing anymore." Matthew lifted a brow. "I assumed you meant we could settle down and raise a parcel of young sword-wielding pirates and little pistol-swinging Penelopes."

"That is precisely what I meant." Penelope nodded. "It sounds like a delightful adventure to me."

"Famous." Aunt Clare nodded. "Now, please do go, children. Let us not wait for someone else to put a spoke in your wheel."

Matthew sobered. "Like your father, Penn. What of him?"

"Father cannot separate us." Confidence flashed in Penelope's eyes. "Aunt Clare and I have already considered it. You and I are going to Gretna to become wed. Father might be as practical as Sir Morris and will accept us once the deed is done. But if he does not, you and I are going to travel until Aunt Clare writes that Father has accepted our marriage. Absence is known to make the heart grow fonder. He must know that he will not see me until he accepts the marriage and hands over that infamous strongbox."

"What if he never does?"

She shrugged. "Then after seeing the world, we shall settle down as paupers."

Matthew's love almost overwhelmed him at that moment. Penelope would throw her lot in with him, regardless of the shaky future. She would even forgo her fortune because of it. Somehow, he would ensure that she never suffered from marrying him. "That won't happen. I vow it. You'll not be a pauper."

Penelope nodded. "I know it."

"Indeed not," Aunt Clare said. "Your father is a very fractious man, Penelope, but he will come about, I am sure. We will hit upon the right scheme. But do go now."

"Faith, but you are fast to send us on our way." Matthew started to laugh, and then found himself choking on it. "Blast. I wasn't thinking. You must come with us, Aunt Clare."

"I cannot, dear," Aunt Clare said. "I must remain here and take care of the matter of Penelope's father. As well as a certain other matter."

"Penelope we cannot go." Matthew clenched his teeth even as his stomach knotted. The scandal of a runaway marriage he might survive, but Penelope was to be his wife and he would not wish to dishonor her before their wedding. "Not without a chaperone."

Penelope's eyes widened. "Oh dear. You are right. I-I had not considered."

"But children . . ." Aunt Clare blinked in confusion. "You . . . well, you should make your escape when you can."

"You do not understand, Aunt Clare," Matthew gritted. "We . . . we are not able to behave ourselves when left unchaperoned."

Aunt Clare beamed. "I know."

"You know?" Penelope gasped. "But you said you thought we had no . . . no fire between us."

"Yes." Aunt Clare smiled with pride. "That was Lucas Montieth's notion. He told me that you two must think I meant you for someone else and then I was to leave you two alone to discover for yourself that . . ."

"Why the bas . . . er, devil." Matthew grinned. "I shall return the favor, I assure you. But for now . . ."

"No, Matthew, I shall not wait." Penelope shook her head and stepped back from him. Her look was first determined and obstinate. Then a look of sheer excitement crossed her features. "Indeed, you will have to catch me."

"What?" Matthew frowned.

"I just realized it. I have the coach and I have Uncle Theodore's coachman still. I think it only fitting that he tools the vehicle that carries me to Gretna Green."

"And you shall take mine, Matthew." Aunt Clare clapped her hands. "Meeker can drive you. Though the trunk I brought for Penelope must be put into her coach first."

Matthew stared at them. "Are you two ladies hoaxing me?"

"No, most certainly not. I am in earnest." Penelope blew him a kiss. "Good-bye, my love. I shall beat you to flinders and be awaiting you in Gretna Green."

"Do you wish to lay money upon that?" Matthew laughed, catching onto the notion with spirit.

Penelope's brows lifted. Then she smiled. "Why, I do wish to lay money on it. In fact . . . I will bet my entire fortune upon it. If I win . . . I shall keep it as you suggested."

"Penn, you vixen!"

"Well? There is nothing like a good race-and-bet to help keep us focused upon reaching Gretna without seeing each other." She smiled all the more. "Besides, it will be apparent to the world—and even to you, my overly honorable Lord—that you are not marrying me for my money. However, if you can win it, fair and square . . ."

"Ha! You already have the makings of a Severs," Matthew teased. "You are punting on tick. Jacob may never come about and will hold your money indefinitely. I shall clearly win and be left holding your voucher for life."

Penelope laughed. "Oh dear, then I would be beholden to you, wouldn't I? That will never do."

"Oh yes, it will." Torn with laughter, Matthew managed to shout regardless. "Meeker! Where are you?"

"Jeremiah!" Penelope called. "I have a commission for you."

"Gracious," Aunt Clare murmured as the two dashed away. "Who shall I place my bet upon, Percy?"

Sir Percy did not answer.

"Percy?" Aunt Clare looked down. Percy had decided to sprawl upon the steps and indulge in a catnap. She laughed. "Indeed, you are quite right. What does it matter? We have been successful once more. Matthew and Penelope are together as they should be. I do adore it when true love wins."

Thirteen

"Anvil Priest at the Finish Line "

Out of all the astonishing stories to reach this paper, this surely must be one of the best. The Earl of R. had been reported to have entered into a race with the hitherto un-known heiress, Miss P. L. The finish line of expectation was to be a certain blacksmith shop in Gretna Green. There the Anvil Priest was commissioned to await them, first to determine the winner of the race, second to wed them.

He was there as were many onlookers from the district, the story of the race having gained attention from every toll keeper and coaching house en route. No doubt those residing along the infamous North Road have espied many fleeing couples upon said course, but none before who had taken separate coaches with the intent upon racing each other to the anvil. Neither the earl nor the intrepid heiress was known to stop for sleep, but only for refreshments and new cattle.

You may ask why this haste? According to our sources, what hung in the balance was of no small matter. It is reported that Miss L.'s fortune, quite sizable, was to be the pot. If the heiress won, she was to keep her fortune within her name and control, whereas if the Earl of R. won, he would, as is far more customary, take control of it.

The reader must surely find this fort amusant. It is no secret in the ton that the earl has been in need of a

*rich wife to repair the S. family fortunes. In that respect,
however, it was his younger brother, Andrew S. who beat
the earl to the mark. It is to be mourned at White's that
no opportunity was given to lay bets in the infamous
books. The odds of such an onslaught of matrimony
within the House of R., and prosperous marriages at
that, should surely have gone on record for posterity. Only
days before this Gretna Prix du Mariage, Andrew S.
had wed one Miss C. M., daughter and heiress to the
shipping magnate, Sir H. M., at the very same blacksmith shop.*

*The announcement of this union can be found upon
the last page of this journal. The on-dit has it that Sir
H. M. wished to announce his daughter's successful
marriage to a noble house. He has also reported the news
of great import that his shipping venture, which had
been thought sunk, was instead proven to have been successful and is, in fact, well docked. His fortune, to quote
him, is "as stout as ever it was." The news was greatly
received at the exchange and has been duly recorded in
the Morning Advertiser.*

*This good fortune for the second son may very well be
a good thing. For your journalist is saddened to report
the earl did not successfully beat Miss P. L., though she
did not beat him, either. As too often happens in love,
and the races, it was shown to be a tie at the finish line,
the Anvil Priest testifying to this as did the locals.*

*While neither was successful at winning the race, the
Earl of R. and Miss P. L. were successful in being wed.
It is reported they have since disappeared from the district; their whereabouts at this time is found to be unknown.*

*It certainly leaves in question just what will happen
to Miss L.'s fortune. Rumor has it that her father, Sir
J. L., holds this fortune in trust for her and without his
consent, she may very well be penniless. One can only
surmise, since the two chose to flee to the border, that Sir
J. L. is not in agreement with the union. In which case,*

the Earl of R.'s marriage to Miss L. is quite a pip. Furthermore, it may well be his brother's marriage to Miss C. M. which will repair the noble estate of S. Surely, this is an event that should have had the opportunity to incite action within the books of Brook's, White's, and Boodle's. Then the occasion to make or break many more fortunes would have been gratuitously provided.

"Heavens!" Penelope looked up from the article that she had read aloud to Matthew. She sat upon a blanket next to a gurgling stream. "I had no notion. I realized we created a stir here in Scotland, but that it has come to the attention of the London papers is quite unexpected."

Matthew studied her with grave eyes. "Does it upset you?"

"No. Nothing can upset me at this moment." Penelope smiled at her husband. She had known Matthew as a good man. She had known him as a friend. She had known him as the man she loved. She flushed. None of it compared to knowing Matthew as her lover and her mate. Indeed, it quite took her breath away.

"I am pleased to know that, my lady," Matthew laughed, though his blue eyes darkened. "It shall be a scandal for some time to come, I fear."

"Good." Penelope nodded. "I worried that I might be too . . . too commonplace for your family."

"Commonplace?" Matthew stared at her, astonishment stamping his features. Then the wickedest smile crossed his face. "No, madame wife, you are anything but commonplace." He sat up from his relaxed position and leaned over to kiss her warmly upon the lips. "For all my raking about before, I have never known such a passionate woman as you."

"Thank you." Penelope blushed deeply. "Though I do think you are flattering me overmuch. You need not serve up Spanish coin."

"No, it is true." He studied her, and his voice turned

musing. "Unless it is because we are a perfect match. For I have never felt as passionate with any other woman before, either."

"I believe that is it." Penelope found she was losing herself in his eyes. She cleared her throat and forced her gaze away. She still held a sealed letter that had accompanied the article. "But before you dare distract me, we should open Aunt Clare's letter."

"Very well." Sighing, Matthew sat back. "Let us hear her news. For my part, if Aunt Clare tells us to remain lost to the world, I will be glad of it."

"It is rather wonderful, isn't it?" Penelope smiled dreamily as she broke the seal and opened the parchment.

My Dear Penelope and Matthew,
  I wished for you to read the papers first. They have made all the difference and I can now write that your father has accepted your marriage. In truth, it was your Uncle Theodore and Sir Morris who hit upon this scheme . . .

Penelope stopped and looked at Matthew. "Uncle Theodore?"

Matthew frowned. "Read on . . ."

Penelope lowered her gaze back to the page.

  . . . and an excellent scheme it was. Your father took strong offense to the thought that Sir Morris would receive all the credit for pulling the Severs family out of the river tick, so to speak. Following that, when Theodore mentioned how your future children would be proud of their Grandfather Morris, and think their Grandfather Lancer a nip-farthing of the first order, why, your father made a complete turnabout. Indeed, he has vowed to write his own announcement to the paper in regard to the greatness of your fortune and how it will be the one to save the House of Raleigh. He also feels quite proud that he can inform those "encroaching mushrooms" that

your money is older than that of Sir Morris and you are, indeed, genteel compared to that of some "jumped-up caper merchants." Therefore, dear children, you are free to return home anytime that you desire.

"And if we do not desire?" Matthew asked. Penelope stifled her chuckle and continued.

That being nicely settled, I am sure you will wish to hear of your Uncle Theodore's reform.

"Now that I don't! Unless it was on a rack," Matthew interrupted.

He did not wait for anyone to tell your Aunt Susan. He said he might scrape by better if it were he to confess his sins. Your Aunt Susan did respond justly to the news. Indeed, I was not privy to the actual meeting, but your Uncle Theodore acquired some unexplained bruises and sore muscles upon his person, some of which have not allowed him to sit for the past week. Indeed, the servants have been whispering about the conditions of the fire irons within their chamber. He has spoken of making restitution to your funds, dear Penelope, but Aunt Susan holds the purse strings and she has not "passed over the dibs" as of yet.

Your uncle and aunt remain at your home for the nonce, for your aunt feels she dare not desert your father's side in his lone estate. I do believe that may be another reason he has decided to accept your marriage. Your Uncle Theodore told Jacob that he'd best accept your marriage, else he warned that he would never be shot of your Aunt Susan. He also advised Jacob to start casting about for a comely nurse to attend him, for you wouldn't be at his beck and call any longer.

"Hmm, I might forgive the man if he can effect that with your father." Matthew grinned. "He has the right of it, Penn. I want you at *my* beck and call, not your father's. He had your attentions far longer than he should have, in my opinion."

"You shall find no disagreement from me. I far prefer to give you my full attentions as well." Penelope cast him a saucy smile. "I most assuredly enjoy your form of payment in return."

"Do you now?" Matthew offered a growl and then pounced on her, kissing her firmly.

"Tsk." She laughed and pushed him back. "There is more to the letter."

"Who cares?" Matthew wagged his brows. "We may finish it later."

"No, we shall finish it now." Penelope schooled her attention back to the page even though her lips twitched, both in amusement and pleasure at Matthew's kiss.

I am sure you are concerned about Lady Violet.

"She's off the beam on that one," Matthew murmured, his eyes flaring. It was fortunate that he had been as far away as Scotland when Penelope had told him the tale. His rage had been a fearsome thing. Leaving Violet Stapleton in Aunt Clare's hands had been a far wiser decision than she had first thought. Though perhaps she could be more merciful to the girl because she was now married to Matthew and aware of what Lady Violet lost. Knowing how wonderful it was to be his wife, she could not fault any woman for having tried to win him, by fair or foul means.

Penelope shook her head and continued to read the letter.

We had a very long talk, I assure you. Once she realized that Matthew was lost to her forever, she seemed to regain her reason. I tried to console her the best I could as I have never lost a true love and, in fact, still await mine. We then discussed any other aspirations she might harbor to which she could instead bend her heart upon.

"I own that they were quite shocking to me. I am far too conventional, I fear. However, since she declares she will never love another man as she has Severs, and I must own that marriage might not be the proper choice for her . . .

"Ha. Aunt Clare has finally met a person whom she will not attempt to find a match for!" Matthew observed. "That is something."

I let her persuade me to her cause.

"Oh Lord, what cause?"

And truly, dears, it would be a shame to let her talents go to waste. She has determined that she wishes to be an actress upon the stage.

Penelope gasped and looked up to Matthew. "Gracious!"

I do believe the less restricted lifestyle of the actress would suit her. Also, she would no longer be forced to enact the one role of demure miss, but would have an inordinate variety of characters available to her. I own, I thought it an excellent notion. I was expecting that her parents might object, but I was firm with Violet in that regard. I could not in all good conscience release Violet to anyone's unsuspecting care. I stood firm with her and together we told her parents. Honesty is so very important, especially to one's family.

I am sorry to say that Lady Stapleton's reaction was far stronger than we could have expected. She flew into quite a pelter and declared she would send Violet to a nunnery before she would permit her to drag one of the finest names in all of England through the mud in such

*a manner. I believe she referenced the name of "Violet"
rather than that of "Stapleton." She repeatedly spoke of
Violet's namesake, her finest mare. This animal, she assured me, unlike Violet, had been a noble creature.*

*"I felt dreadful and, in truth, feared somewhat for
Violet's well-being when the family departed here as the
first Violet had been peremptorily put down for unfitting
behavior. This aside, I simply cannot imagine the nunnery as a good place for a girl of Violet's energies. However, I should have trusted in Violet herself. She
apparently stole the family silver and booked a passage
to the colonies. The dear child posted me a letter before
she set sail. She actually thanked me for my efforts and
she promised that within a year she would be sending
me news that Violet Stapleton had made it good upon
the stage. Though what kind of theater there is in that
wild land, I do not know.*

"I cannot believe it." Penelope dropped the page
to her lap.

"I can." Matthew's lips twitched. "When Aunt Clare
sifts through your dreams and aspirations, she manages
to uncover the most amazing things." He leaned over
and offered her a gentle, lingering kiss. "Only look
what she did for me."

"Indeed. *Now* you may say that, but you were frightfully unkind to her in the beginning."

"I was insane then." Matthew shook his head. "I
hope not as insane as Lady Violet, grant you, but I was
a fool."

Penelope sighed and wrapped her arms about him.
"I was no better. We owe Aunt Clare a great debt."

"So we do." Matthew swiftly enveloped her in a
warming embrace. "And we shall repay her, to be sure.
Now I know why the other fellows assist her in her
matchmaking ruses. She was right about it—once you
find true love, you feel that you ought to help others
to do the same."

"Wouldn't it be famous if we could find Aunt Clare her own true love?"

Matthew stared at her. He barked a laugh. "Gad's, Penn. That would be quite an undertaking, wouldn't you say?"

"I imagine it would be." She smiled. "But it is still something to ponder upon."

Matthew's gaze darkened. "Madame, have I told you that I love you?"

"Yes, I believe you have." Penelope's heart leapt as it always did when he spoke those words. "But I would like to hear you tell me so again . . ." She kissed him. "And again . . ." This time she permitted him to draw her down to the blanket. ". . . And again."

Matthew's eyes sparkled. "I assume I now have your permission to distract you?"

"Oh, yes." Matthew's lips covered hers and Penelope closed her eyes in bliss. As far as she was concerned, Aunt Clare's letter was quite finished, and surely, this was the perfect ending to it.

More Zebra Regency Romances

Put a Little Romance in Your Life With
Shannon Drake

DO YOU HAVE THE
HOHL COLLECTION?